# THE
# WAITING
# ROOM

# ALSO BY EMILY BLEEKER

*Wreckage*

*When I'm Gone*

*Working Fire*

# THE WAITING ROOM

A NOVEL

# EMILY BLEEKER

LAKE UNION
PUBLISHING

Published by Lake Union Publishing, Seattle

www.apub.com

Amazon, the Amazon logo, and Lake Union Publishing are trademarks of Amazon.com, Inc., or its affiliates.

ISBN-13: 9781503900882 (hardcover)
ISBN-10: 1503900886 (hardcover)
ISBN-13: 9781503901421 (paperback)
ISBN-10: 1503901424 (paperback)

Cover design by Shasti O'Leary Soudant

Printed in the United States of America

First edition

*To my parents—One day I hope
my children will know that I love them
as unconditionally as you love me.*

# CHAPTER 1

"Nick, the baby is crying again." Veronica half turned over in her bed and slapped to the left, trying to wake her husband. "Nick," she called again, this time a little louder.

The room was dark, and colder than usual for November in North Carolina. Half-awake, she sat up and checked the alarm clock on her side of the bed, her e-book reader falling to the floor with a thump. 12:23 a.m. Her eyes burned, and the invisible arms of sleep pulled her back toward the bed. She patted his spot just in case her eyes deceived her. The bed was cold and empty. Where the hell was he?

Veronica closed her eyes tightly and then opened them again, one, two times, trying to clear the cloud of sleepiness, feeling as if she were on sleeping pills. Even though they had an agreement that Nick would take the night shift and Veronica the day shift, she wasn't just going to sit there while Sophie screamed her head off.

But wait. The baby wasn't crying anymore.

The haze finally clear, Veronica hefted the covers off her legs. The floor was uncarpeted and cool against her bare feet, and goose bumps ran up her exposed arms. Nick must've fallen asleep on the couch, watching TV. She'd gone to bed early, right after they had put Sophie down with a fresh diaper, a tight swaddle, and a pink Binky. As Veronica had changed into her pajamas, Nick had pulled on a sweatshirt and said he'd run to the store for some milk and gas drops for the baby and then join her in bed. Maybe he'd decided to watch the end of the baseball game.

"Nick," she whispered, this time trying to sound like a loving wife rather than the annoyed one who had been calling him with a nagging edge to her voice just moments before. She was lucky to have such a hands-on husband. Nick did it all—nighttime diaper changes, runs to the store for supplies, endless rocking when Sophie couldn't calm herself. She and Sophie were two lucky ladies, and Veronica knew it.

"Babe, you okay? I was getting worried." Veronica padded silently down the hall, wrapping her arms around her midsection to retain some heat. She passed the open door to her art studio and the nearly closed door to the hall bathroom. Sophie's door was open. Veronica peeked in. The rocking chair where Nick usually comforted Baby Sophie or fed her a bottle of expressed milk was empty. Shuffling her feet so she didn't wake the baby, Veronica crept up to the edge of the white crib and peered inside, hoping to get a glimpse of the sleeping infant. She was so beautiful when she slept—Cupid's bow lips, delicate eyelashes against her cheeks, the light dusting of blond hair always slightly out of place on the top of her head, as if she'd had a hard day at the office. The child was perfect, absolutely perfect. But tonight, Veronica didn't get to bask in the beauty of the tiny human she and Nick had created together, because the crib was empty.

An unfamiliar panic dropped into Veronica's stomach, heavy, as if she'd swallowed lead. With trembling fingers, she ran her hand over the mattress and soft, pink fitted sheet. It was cold, just like Nick's spot a few moments earlier. It should have been warm. She'd just heard her crying, right? The video monitor—did she even look at the monitor?

She'd envisioned becoming a mother as this instinctual nirvana where her hormones would whisper the answer to every parenting secret into her ear. It took one diaper change and trying to nurse without a lactation consultant nearby to prove that fantasy wrong. Mostly, being a new mother was filled with moments of confusion followed very quickly by moments of panic when, instead of whispering helpful hints, her hormones told her what a failure she was.

Veronica struggled to get her sleep-soaked brain to function at a normal speed, trying to stave off panic with reason. *God,* she thought, *maybe Sophie wasn't in her bed when she was crying. Maybe Nick took her downstairs so I could sleep. Or she wasn't crying at all, and it was all a dream. Maybe . . .*

"Nick, this isn't funny. Where are you?"

By now she'd forgotten about the goose bumps on her arms and nearly ran down the stairs into the family room, where a microfiber sectional faced a dark TV. She flicked on one of the switches at the bottom of the stairs, and the room was filled with light. But the illumination did little to calm the terror building inside Veronica—because just like her bed and the crib, the room was empty.

"Nick!" she yelled. "I'm not kidding. If you're here, you'd better tell me—now." Still no answer. The brown-and-pink diaper bag sat by the door to the garage, and a rack of sterilized bottles lined the side of the stainless-steel sink. It was all as she'd left it, just with no husband and no daughter in sight. No note on the counter or fridge. No sign of any life but her own heartbeat pounding loudly in her ears.

*The car.* The thought came to her as if it had been pinged into her brain with an antenna. He'd taken the baby on a drive in the car. That had to be it. Her pulse slowed as she noticed that Nick's shoes were missing from the rack by the door to the garage, where the mat was slightly askew.

The door opened with a loud squeak that Nick had been promising to fix for months, and the cool air from the fall night pinched at her cheeks. She didn't even need to turn on the light—Nick's car was gone. Relief replaced panic and annoyance replaced fear. They were on a steep learning curve with this parenting thing. No way Nick could've predicted how much taking the baby out for a midnight drive would freak out Veronica. He'd never known "Mom Veronica" before. They'd only been living as "Mom" and "Dad" for two weeks and four days.

Two weeks and four days since Veronica had found out that there really was no limit to the amount you can love a person. Two weeks and four days since she'd learned that Sophie's face was the most beautiful thing on the planet. Two weeks and four days since she'd known her life would never be the same again—and loved it.

Her phone dinged in the kitchen—Nick, finally.

Veronica swooped up the phone off the granite counter in one smooth movement and then held it up in front of her, already thinking of some way to tease him about his impromptu drive. Would she pretend to be angry or clueless? Would she act confused or frantic? What would make him laugh but also help him understand how scared she was?

She glanced at the message on the screen but had to look again. The text was from Nick, but it wasn't an "FYI, went for a drive with Sophie. Be back soon." It wasn't even a picture of a sleeping baby with a thumbs-up emoji under it. No. It was one phrase, two words: I'm sorry.

The fear that had just lifted settled back on her shoulders again as if it were seeking familiar company. She pressed her thumb against the home button, and the screen opened to the texting app. Gray bubbles bounced up and down on the screen. Nick was writing something.

"I'm sorry" what? Did he forget the gas drops? Did he spill the breast milk in the car? Did Sophie scream in her seat rather than fall asleep as planned?

The bubbles went away, and a soft whoosh left one more sentence, far shorter than she had expected after the protracted delivery.

It was my fault.

She dialed his number frantically.

"I'm sorry, but the person you've called has a voice mailbox that has not been set up yet. Please call back . . ."

What in the world? Why wasn't his usual message on the other end of that phone number? She hung up and touched his name on the screen again, waiting for a ring. Still nothing but an automatic click to the generic message.

She stared at the text screen. Left with few options, she typed in a few panicked messages.

What the HELL does "I'm sorry" mean?

Call me—now!

Where are you?

Why are you doing this?

Where. Is. Sophie????

No response. No more bouncing gray bubbles. No more pictures or emojis or texts. Nothing but those six words. "I'm sorry. It was my fault."

She'd get in the car and drive until she found Sophie and Nick and uncover what in the world was going on. But even as she threw on a cardigan, not even bothering to put on her nursing bra or pull back her disheveled hair or put on shoes other than the dingy slippers she kept in the side hall for winter, Veronica understood something she'd been trying to avoid. It was a creeping, disgusting feeling that she should've known as soon as she found the bed empty and cold, found Sophie gone, found the garage only half-full. As she dialed her mother's number and jumped into the front seat of her Prius, Veronica finally understood that feeling she'd been fighting.

Today was one of "those" days. Just like the day Sophie was born or the day Veronica's dad died or the day she signed her first contract as a professional artist. Today was another day that would change her life forever.

# CHAPTER 2

*Six months later*

The hallway was blah. That was the only way Veronica could describe it—blah. Even with four years in art school and ten as an illustrator, she didn't know of a technical term that could explain it better. White ceiling, off-colored waxed tiles, scuffed-up beige wallpaper—if the hallway were a person, it'd be plain Jane or someone trying to hide out in the witness protection program. The only things breaking up the monotony of the infuriatingly boring hall were wooden doors with forest-green placards to the left with numbers, odd on the left, even on the right.

Veronica's destination was all the way down by the fire escape.

*Of course,* she thought, bristling. She didn't want to be there, but she had to go to the top floor and trudge to the last door in this palace of beige and blah.

Okay, fine, maybe she did have a "bad attitude," as her mom liked to call it. But when Barbra DeCarlo picked up where she'd left off her last lecture on the varied yet very detailed list of her daughter's shortcomings, it was hard to just sit there and take it. Veronica could only bear it so long before she'd yell back, "I'm a grown-ass woman, for heaven's sake! I have a kid of my own. Stop treating me like a baby."

Even that made her feel like a petulant teen. However, this wasn't her first attempt to "fix" her mom's diagnosis of an "attitude problem." She'd worked on the issue on her own for six months, moving to a new town and throwing herself into her studio work. The stress of a move and the isolation of work only seemed to drag her down further.

But it didn't matter what her mother called it; Veronica knew none of her crazy compulsions or the dark days in bed were part of an attitude problem. No, she was seeing Ms. Lisa Masters, MA, LCPC, about the crippling postpartum depression that had ruled her life like a tyrant every day for the past six and a half months.

PPD was like one of those gargoyles at Notre Dame that creeped her out and fascinated her back when she'd studied abroad in Paris, grotesque and frightening figures jutting out of the towering beauty of the cathedral. The stone monstrosities seemed to be standing guard, threatening to descend, and her mind came up with a million reasons why the architects would introduce such fearsome creatures. While fellow art students gasped at the stained glass or the beautifully carved masonry, Veronica couldn't stop studying the gargoyles and their deeper purpose. To her great disappointment, they turned out to be functional rain gutters that saved the breathtaking cathedral masonry from water damage.

And here she was again—unable to see beyond the gargoyles. PPD possessed her like one of those hauntingly dark creatures, diverting any joy or hope or clarity, distracting Veronica from enjoying the beauty of her daughter and her life.

Today was a good day. Today she could get out of bed. Today she pumped milk without lingering on her failure when the bottles filled less and less each session. Today she sang to Baby Sophie from the threshold of her bedroom when she cried, instead of begging her mom to take her and then going for a run to escape Sophie's suffocating cries. Today she didn't feel like dying.

But not every day was like today, and it wasn't because of a bad attitude. The only thing that seemed to help these overwhelming feelings of failure that came along with her PPD was pouring herself into making sure everything was perfect for Sophie. That meant her nursery was beautifully decorated, she had the safest car seat, her clothes were washed in the gentlest baby detergent, and only cloth diapers touched her bottom.

Everything was "the best" for Sophie, all the way down to the homemade nontoxic diaper-rash cream for the occasional breakouts. For some reason, when Veronica could point to all the improvements she'd made in Sophie's life, they became a way to measure and then prove what a good mother she was, almost like a grade. Soon, she was counting everything—the number of ounces of breast milk she pumped at each session, the number of cloth diapers used every day, the number of hours Sophie slept, ate, and played.

Somewhere deep inside, Veronica could acknowledge that these feelings weren't even about her being a subpar mother. It was depression, chemical, hormonal, situational . . . all of the above. So when her mother threatened to move out and leave Veronica to be a single mother to Baby Sophie without any support if she didn't *finally* get help from a mental health professional, Veronica agreed to go to Lisa.

Veronica's hand rested on the cold nickel handle, and she took a deep breath, hoping she looked confident, dressed in her nearly fancy black slacks and casual-but-expensive-looking flowy silk blouse. She didn't mind telling a perfect stranger about the dark places her mind sometimes went when the crying wouldn't stop or when her breasts ached after a less-than-successful pumping session. But she did mind sounding like a failure while looking like one too.

The door was heavier than she'd expected, and it took an extra shove to force it open. She stumbled over the carpet, not ready for the transition from beige land to a room of warm colors and soft fabrics. It was as though she'd wandered into her auntie Ruth's sitting room, except instead of rock-hard butterscotch candies on the table, there were a variety of popular magazines, and instead of her now-dead aunt Ruth with her long gray hair and hippie shirt, there was a tallish, dark-haired man with his face buried deep in a magazine, safely hidden off in the back corner of the waiting room, and a heavyset woman with short brown hair, crying and sitting against the wall by the inner-office door. She reminded Veronica of the lunch lady who used to scold her for grabbing the brown chocolate-milk carton instead of the red whole-milk one.

Seeing the woman's tears was enough to make Veronica want to bolt out the door, but a young woman behind the divider waved her forward. The glass swooshed as it opened.

"I have an appointment at ten with Ms. Masters. My name is Veronica . . . ," Veronica whispered across the counter, but the receptionist stopped her.

"I've got you right here." She pointed at the flat screen in front of her; a placard on her desk read, "Carly Simpson." "Looks like you filled out all the paperwork online. Good for you." Carly beamed at her. Her straight white teeth and perfectly styled blond hair reminded Veronica of a younger version of herself. Before Nick. Before Sophie. Before this monster called depression took over her life. How she wished for the naïveté of that version of herself.

Veronica's phone buzzed against her thigh as a text came through. She forced a smile at the bubbly girl and maybe mumbled a brief thank-you before turning and searching for a seat. The crying woman was still sitting on a bench against the far wall, lost in her tears, and the politely anonymous man was still occupying the only semiprivate area in the room, but the couch was open. She took an incredibly indirect route to the empty seat while glancing at her phone to avoid eye contact with either of the waiting-room inhabitants.

Another text from her mother. Shocker.

PLEASE try to keep an open mind. And for heaven's sake, tell her about Nick.

Veronica somehow held back from rolling her eyes. Like she wouldn't mention the father of her child when talking to a therapist about her postpartum depression. Veronica already knew one of the first questions would be, "Where is Sophie's father?" It was one of the moments she dreaded most about this whole fiasco—telling a stranger about what happened to Nick. Veronica shoved the phone back into her pocket and stood behind the table filled with magazines.

The worn green leather couch sighed as she took her seat. The crying woman startled. Veronica briefly lifted her eyes off the collection of reading material on the coffee table, and for a tiny moment, the women's eyes caught. It didn't take a specialist to see the pain in the middle-aged woman's face: dark circles under her eyes from the sleepless nights grief brought, creases along the sides of her mouth only elongating her frown.

Veronica tried to reason why the stranger was lost in a mass of tears and half-repressed sobs, but as she considered the options—cancer, divorce, bankruptcy, addiction—she started to fight back tears of her own. There was so much pain in the world; she couldn't figure out why more people weren't weeping constantly.

"Hey there." The woman spoke with a soft Southern accent that matched most of the inhabitants of Sanford, North Carolina, but not the image Veronica had been developing of an out-of-work lunch lady. "I'm sorry. I'm a total mess. Today is one of the hard ones, you know?"

Veronica did know. Hard days were the ones when she couldn't stop the tears or, even worse, the anger from robbing her of any normal interactions with other humans, even her mother and her child. But she hadn't signed up for group therapy, and there was no way she was going to open up to a stranger unless the person had a jumbled collection of letters behind her name.

"I'm sorry," Veronica whispered, trying to copy the way everyone said it to her, with sympathy but also a deep desire not to get involved any more than necessary. She reassessed the magazines and picked one with a glossy photo of a politician on the front, hoping to mimic the man in the corner and escape any interactions but also dodge any "feel good" articles or columns on parenting.

"Nah, it's okay. Guess we all are here for a reason, right?"

Veronica pressed her lips together, unsure what to say and desperate to dive into the anonymity of her magazine. Just as the silence went from awkward to uncomfortable, the door next to the receptionist's window opened. A petite woman with dark hair and a warm complexion smiled as if they'd been friends since second grade. Lisa Masters looked just like her picture on psychology.com. There were five or six therapists in the practice, but from the profiles her mom had compiled, Lisa's was the only one that listed postpartum depression as a specialty.

"You must be Veronica. Are you ready?" Her smile was genuine, at least from what Veronica could decipher, and she was a pretty good judge of those kinds of things.

"Uh, yeah, I think so." With a little nod to the lunch-lady woman, Veronica stood, relieved to be out of the frying pan but feeling remarkably as though she'd jumped into the fire.

"You are welcome to take that with you," Lisa said, pointing to the unread magazine still clutched in Veronica's hand.

"Oh, no . . . no . . . I . . ." She tossed it onto the table, wiped her hands on her thighs, made sure her phone and keys were safe inside her pockets, and then straightened a strand of sloppily styled blond hair. "I'm ready."

"All right, follow me." Lisa waved and started to walk. They made small talk through the hall as Veronica followed her therapist to the door of her office.

Her therapist. Veronica cringed at the phrase. Then again, maybe help was on the other side of that door, or just as likely embarrassment or maybe even a complete waste of time. She straightened her shoulders and pictured Sophie smiling as she tried to put her toes into her mouth or laughing when Veronica stuck out her tongue. Sophie was worth it. Only time would tell what would happen in that room, but at least Veronica could prove she'd tried.

After the pleasantries—generic talk of Veronica's career and then the compliments that usually followed any discussion of Veronica's work illustrating the popular children's book series Mia's Travels—Lisa clasped her hands in front of her and sighed as if she were clearing the air. Veronica's temples pounded, and she picked at the skin around her thumbnail like she always did when anxiety overwhelmed her. She used to have beautifully manicured nails, but now they were so short they bled when she bit them.

Lisa was watching. Veronica slipped her hands under her legs to hide the evidence of her habit, the only outer symbol of her internal struggle. She'd sounded almost normal when they talked about her career, but that would all end very soon.

"So, Veronica, what brings you here today?"

She'd considered this moment, even practiced it out loud in the car on the way over.

"I have a little girl, six months old now. Her name is Sophie." Lisa smiled at her as though she'd already seen the baby. Veronica hesitated, shifted in her seat, and then continued. "I love her. No, I adore her, I really do, but I'm having a hard time with the transition into motherhood. I . . . I thought it would be different. I thought *I* would be different, I guess. I'm scared all the time, that I'll do something wrong or that I've already done something wrong."

"Hm, so I'm hearing you say that you have a lot of anxiety when it comes to parenting, is that right?"

Veronica balled her fists tighter, trying not to be annoyed. "It's more than some anxiety. When she cries, I shut down. I can't breathe. I can't think. I want to run away. That's why my mom had to move in. I can't . . ." A fat, unexpected tear left a dark blob on Veronica's pants when she blinked. "I can't pick up my daughter. I can't even touch her."

# CHAPTER 3

*Six weeks later*

Veronica took the keys out of the ignition and turned to grab the jumbled pile of mismatched cloth grocery bags from the back seat. After her weekly session with Lisa, she still had forty-five minutes to get home before Sophie would be up from her nap. She looped her hand through the twisted straps and turned to leave, but one pulled her back. The green-and-white library bag she'd gotten when she renewed her library card was hooked over the side of Sophie's empty car seat. Veronica yanked until it flew off.

She leaned back to examine the seat and assess the damage. It was the best seat money could buy. She'd had it on her registry, but no one had splurged for it at either her friend or her family baby shower. So when Nick's office gave them a gift card, they'd both agreed that safety was most important and used the whole amount on the fancy seat. But now the empty chair held an even heavier meaning. Lisa had sent Veronica home with an assignment—take Sophie on a drive, just the two of them. Even after six weeks of therapy, the idea still made Veronica's heart pound.

But she'd made progress in other ways, or at least that's what Lisa tried to remind her of at their most recent appointment. With the help of

Lisa's assignments, Veronica had sung a song to Sophie from the threshold of her room, posted a picture of Sophie on her private social media account, and stayed in the house during one of her colic attacks rather than going for a run. Just last week she skipped her middle-of-the-night alarm for pumping so she could get more sleep. Lisa called them "healthy choices," and Veronica was trying to make more and more of them. She flung the cluster of bags into a corralled shopping cart, wrapped her hands around the worn red handle, and then headed for the supermarket.

She'd save the car ride for next week because today she was going to get formula for the first time ever. Formula. It used to be a dirty word in her house. When Sophie was born, Veronica made Nick throw out all the sample containers from the hospital so she wouldn't be tempted to give up on breastfeeding. Turned out she didn't have to worry; the lactation consultant at the hospital called Veronica a natural. But that only lasted until Nick . . .

The automatic doors of the grocery store slid open, and a cool rush of AC beckoned her in. Even though she'd recently moved to Sanford, her old house was only a few miles away in the small town of Broadway. Sanford looked like a busy metropolis compared to Broadway, where your only option for milk or bread was from the Dollar General, where everything definitely cost more than a dollar. Now she had the luxury of an actual supermarket. The Piggly Wiggly was full of the familiar sounds of carts clanking and mumbled announcements over an ancient speaker, which helped calm the growing tension between Veronica's shoulder blades. There was some order to this madness—a list, a sale ad, a procedure for lines and checkout. It was nothing like motherhood, which surprisingly had very few predictable outcomes despite all her attempts at preparation.

Veronica shook her head. Lisa was trying to help her with this overwhelming load of guilt and panic that she couldn't seem to escape. If she could just get out from under it a little bit, maybe she could be the kind of mom she desperately wanted to be. The kind of mom she'd promised Sophie she'd be while she grew in her belly.

After grabbing supplies for this week's round of homemade baby food from the produce section, Veronica entered the baby aisle. The only way she was going to get through this challenge was to face it head-on. The longer she delayed, the easier it was to just ignore the idea completely.

Veronica located the can of formula she'd researched and decided was the best—organic with an iron supplement as well as DHA and ARA. Then, trying not to think about it too hard, she wrapped her fingers around the can and tossed it into her slowly filling cart. It was just powder; it contained nutrients and vitamins her daughter needed and Veronica's body was struggling to create, but as it settled in between the butternut squash and bag of avocados, some part of Veronica's self-admitted messed-up brain screamed the illogical word: failure.

No, a failure would be a mother who let her child go hungry, or at least that was what Lisa told her, and Veronica couldn't bear to see that hidden horror on her therapist's face again. She'd seen it a few times, the silent judgment that even a practiced therapist had a hard time covering. The first time was when she told Lisa that she hadn't touched her daughter since she was two weeks and four days old. She saw it then. She saw it again when she told her about the dark thoughts that entered her mind when Sophie's colic set in and the crying started. And again when she finally told her about the night that Nick went out in the car with the baby in the back seat and only Sophie came back home.

Veronica assessed the cart—diapers, rice cereal, veggies, the yogurt puffs Sophie liked. She might not be able to hold her daughter, but that didn't stop her from taking care of her. She filled her every need and made sure she was well provided for, and soon she'd be able to hold her in her arms again.

The back wheels of the cart skidded as she turned into the checkout lane. Usually she'd consider self-checkout, but that would take actual thinking, and her brain was nearing posttherapy shutdown. It was a new thing—it only started happening after her first visit to Lisa—but the mental and emotional exhaustion after a session was real, and Veronica sometimes wondered why she didn't plan her schedule better so she could come home and take a nap of her own before Sophie woke up.

Today she'd finish the laundry and get the squash steamed, mashed, and in an ice-cube tray to freeze for storage; she'd sterilize all the bottles from the day; pump at four o'clock, seven o'clock, ten o'clock, and once in the middle of the night just to keep up her supply; and finally bleach out the diaper pail. Barb always used to say that moms didn't get naps, and that saying "sleep when the baby sleeps" was just something people said to make pregnant women think they would sleep again.

Veronica shook her head and started to load the belt with her items. Napping didn't bring her comfort anyway, not with the nightmares filled with images of broken glass, bleached-out hospital hallways, people dressed in black and crying—always Sophie's cries filled Veronica's sleep, even when Sophie was playing contentedly with Veronica's mother in the other room. No, what she needed was a good, long run. When she was a teenager and wanted to get away from her mom's newest boyfriend, who was always inevitably screaming about something insignificant while her mom nearly killed herself trying to make him happy, she'd slip out the back door and go for a run. If she ran hard enough and long enough, the pain in her legs and lungs would erase the sound of a man degrading her mother and the even more sickening sight of her mother taking it as if she deserved it. Worked well with baby screams too.

"Looks like someone has a baby at home." Lost in thought, Veronica jumped at the deep voice behind her. Typically, if she kept to herself in public and looked completely frigid and disinterested in any type of human communication, people left her alone. But there were always the ones who wanted to tell you how much you'd miss these years as a parent right at the moment your five-month-old had an explosive diaper, or the friendly bystanders who noticed how tired you looked and made sure to tell you all about it.

She forced what she hoped looked like a smile and glanced behind her. A tall, handsome man in a jet-black business suit and blue tie stared back at her. Her heart jumped because she recognized him from Lisa's waiting room. He was in his midforties, at least, but was aging well, his hair only gray at the temples and the fine lines around his eyes making him look distinguished. No ring on his left hand, and his skin was a rich shade of not exactly tan, but not I-burn-after-five-minutes white either. To top it all off, he held nothing but a blue box of tampons. He must have recognized her from the therapists' office; they'd seen each other once a week for six weeks now. Why would he talk to her *here*? She took a breath, stood up straight, and tried to act normal.

"Looks like you're shopping for a special someone too." Veronica pointed at the box of feminine-hygiene products with the tube of toothpaste in her hand before putting it onto the moving black belt.

The man didn't even blush; he just tapped the box against his fingertips and smirked as though buying tampons at a grocery store was his favorite hobby.

"My daughter. She's thirteen. She texted me a crying face, an angry mask, and a drawing of a Hershey's bar. After I responded with a very clever 'Huh?' she told me *exactly* what she needed me to bring home. It wasn't even chocolate. Though I think I should toss some in for good measure, don't you?"

When Veronica put the plastic divider behind her groceries, the waiting-room man leaned across the array of baby products and produce and grabbed a bar of chocolate. He was close enough that she could pick up the masculine scent of his cologne, or maybe it was his deodorant. Either way, it reminded her of Nick and made her take another step down the aisle of the checkout counter.

"You must be a good dad," Veronica said without stopping to realize that she was now entering a full-on conversation with the man. Hopefully this wouldn't mean he'd start talking to her every week. She could take chats at the supermarket, but Gillian, the lunch-lady-esque waiting-room companion, already pushed her limits there. "Not a lot of guys would be okay with that kind of thing." After her parents' divorce, she'd only seen her own father for a week or two each summer until he moved to Alaska when she was fourteen and then dropped off the face of the earth completely until he passed a few years ago.

"Nah, times are changing. I'm sure your husband would do the same for your daughter." He pointed at the pink pacifiers traveling down the belt to the clerk checking her items.

Veronica's face flushed. She glanced down at her left hand; the platinum setting with a 2.3-karat diamond sitting heavily in the center stared back at her. Recently, Lisa asked her why she still wore her ring. Veronica explained that at first it was because she missed Nick, missed being married and the idea of a loving husband. But then she had to admit that there was a part of her that wanted to keep up appearances. She didn't want people to think she was a single mom who got knocked up and had a kid out of wedlock. Damn it. When she'd said it out loud in that session, it sounded really judgmental. God, even thinking through it now made her cringe.

In the past, she'd play along with the farce, pretend she had a loving husband waiting at home for her, pretend she could pick up her daughter and that she knew how to calm her cries. She twisted the ring around her finger with her thumb. She loved how it felt there, wished she never had to take it off, but there was also something different about today, about this man. He knew she had issues—no one went to a therapist for a source of social interaction—but he still talked to her as if she was a regular person. Then again, he must have some issues too, since he didn't seem to miss an appointment, but after chatting, he seemed so . . . normal. He made her feel as though it didn't matter that she couldn't hold her daughter and that she still fantasized about waking up to Nick by her side. As the checker asked if she wanted to use the bags in her cart, Veronica glanced back and told the truth for the first time in a very long time.

"Actually, I'm a widow."

# CHAPTER 4

Veronica could hear the crying through the front door. Worried when she drove up that too many open and shut doors would wake Sophie, she'd tried to get all the groceries in with just one trip from the car. Her arms were so weighed down with her shopping bags that both hands were tingly and heavy, like useless mannequin appendages. But apparently she was too late, and Sophie had woken early from her nap.

*Damn it.* Every time she left Lisa's office, Veronica was sure that she was cured. The whole way home she'd think about walking in, picking up her baby the same way any normal mother would, and just going on with life as if Nick were sitting in the other room. But then, like today, she'd hear the crying and her pulse would skyrocket, skin tingling as if she'd been smacked, and the permanent pit she already carried in her stomach grew deeper, like a bottomless abyss.

Today part of her wanted to turn around and get back in the car, pretend she'd been stuck in traffic or that lines at the store were unusually long. Her mom would probably know she was lying, but she also probably wouldn't care. Barbra DeCarlo was increasingly tired of her daughter's issues. For some reason she couldn't seem to grasp that depression wasn't something you just snapped out of.

Veronica juggled the groceries so she could pat her front pocket for her keys. The front door was always locked—always. Two women and a baby alone all the time—it made Veronica's already heightened anxiety reflex vibrate. Doors double locked. Windows firmly shut and bolted. Curtains drawn. Top-of-the-line security system installed. But sometimes the triple line of security backfired and she couldn't get into her own house. Her pocket was empty, keys probably still hanging in the ignition of the car. *Damn it.*

With a quick flip of her elbow, Veronica rang the doorbell of her two-story bungalow. There was an immediate shuffling behind the door, and after a few metallic clicks and the loud beep of the security system, the broad white door swung open and her mother stood behind it, eyes bleary and the imprint of a textile against her cheek. Ever since Veronica could remember, Barb had worn her hair the same way: short, bleached blond, and spiked slightly at the top. Now it was slanting slightly to one side, like the Leaning Tower of Pisa. Veronica tilted her head to add some balance. The cry was louder with the door open, and Barb's arms were empty.

"You take a little nap, Mom?" Veronica held out one of her numbed arms with a silent request for help. Barb rubbed at the side of her face and straightened the remnants of her lip liner from her complicated morning makeup routine. She always said, *You never know when the man with the big paycheck might end up on your doorstep, so you should always look your best.* She had a similar saying about cute paramedics after a heart attack and clean underwear in a car accident. How could her father ever have left such a sage?

"Yeah, just dropped off for a little snooze while you were gone. How'd it go?" Barb answered, taking the lighter bags with the crush-ables in it and shuffling toward the kitchen as if she didn't even hear the screaming in the background. It was true that when you had a baby with colic, you had to just get used to some level of crying, but the way her mother could tune it out drove Veronica insane.

"Fine, I guess, but how long has Sophie been screaming like that? Please tell me you didn't sleep through it, Ma. If you want me to go to therapy, you have to promise me that you'll take care of Sophie while I'm gone."

Half-awake, Barb rolled her eyes, annoyed.

"I dozed off for a bit, but she's in her swing now." Barb stood at the entrance of the kitchen, watching Veronica struggle with the bags, rubbing her hands together as if she were dying to snag a handle. "Here, let me help."

"I got it," Veronica said and shooed her off, not interested in having her mother so close to her while she was still annoyed. Barb took a step back and used her nervous hands to rub at the corners of her eyes, keeping her heavy mascara untouched, a little too groggy for a proper caregiver.

Veronica unloaded the heavy bags, her hands tingling as the blood flooded back in and painful pins and needles filled her extremities. Without a further thought to the groceries, she yanked open the refrigerator and assessed the bottles of expressed milk in the fridge. The four o'clock feeding was still sitting untouched on the shelf. "Damn it, Ma! No wonder she's screaming. Were you texting with Val again and got distracted?"

Her mom's longtime best friend had a daughter, Sommer, who was the same age as Veronica. Both Val and Barb initially hoped that the two girls could find a similar bond as the one their mothers shared, but personality, situation, and biology seemed to have different ideas. Sommer (with an *O*, she'd always tell substitute teachers and boys who asked for her phone number) was perfect and always had been. In high school she'd been tall, gorgeous, witty, a math wiz, and a cheerleader who could get any guy she wanted. As an adult, even a cursory glance at her Facebook page could tell you all you needed to know about Sommer's continued perfection with her handsome, adoring husband and three perfectly groomed children, two girls and one boy. Veronica would never live up to Sommer's or Val's equally high parenting standard.

"Val is a nurse and gives me parenting tips, so you should like that I text her. And I didn't forget anything, Ronnie," Barb shot back, a bit of real hurt in her clear blue eyes. "It's only"—she glanced at her wristwatch—"ten till four. You're early. I'm only halfway through the routine: music, diaper change, then turn on the swing while I get the bottle. I did it like you wanted."

Veronica shot daggers at her mother with her eyes and turned the kitchen faucet all the way up to its hottest setting. She plunged the bottle under the rushing waterfall of steaming tap water and sighed. Barb stood in a tense reverie, as if she were waiting for an explosion but at the same time didn't know how to manage when it came. Veronica hated feeling so unreasonable. This was her *child*; she should be able to have expectations for her care.

At moments like these, Veronica wished more than anything she could go into her daughter's room and scoop her up in her arms, lift her shirt, unlatch the hook on the top of her nursing bra, and just feed her child. It was infuriating that she had to depend on a third party. Part of her felt guilty about being so mad at her mom. She did a lot, way more than most grandmothers had to do, but it wasn't like Veronica didn't pay her what she'd pay a nanny or au pair. Not to mention Veronica gave her a place to live and free food and . . . Shit . . . Sometimes she took a step back from her life and really saw how messed up it was.

"I like Val and I love having a nurse on call, but, Ma, she's still crying." Veronica turned off the tap and then swirled the bottle, turning it upside down to test the temperature. Barb yanked it from her hand, her cheeks flushed a deep red like they used to when Veronica was a teen and got the car back an hour later than curfew.

"Today you say change the routine. Last week you said to never deviate. I don't know what you want, Ronnie. If you want things 'just right,' then maybe you should go into that nursery and give it a shot yourself." Small but feisty, Barb shot out her proclamation and then stumbled backward over a filled bag of groceries, sending a can of formula rolling across the floor. Barb froze, the bottle slowly dripping after its time in the water. "You bought formula?" she asked, calming slowly.

Veronica cringed, wishing she'd hidden the formula till she was ready, or at least been able to put it away in the cupboard until she could figure out how to manage the transition. She knew her mother tried to keep her opinions to herself, but it rarely, if ever, happened. She crouched down to retrieve the yellow can.

"Yeah, Lisa suggested it. She said that Sophie might be crying from hunger because I'm getting less milk lately." She placed the full container on the counter and looked at her mother, defiant. "I'm not giving up breastfeeding, though. Just supplementing until she eats more solids."

"So you like her? Lisa, I mean," Barb asked, taking a step toward Veronica, who continued putting away groceries so she didn't have to look at her mother and see the hope in her eyes.

"Yeah, I like her. She's . . . helpful. I don't know." Veronica shut the cabinet door under the sink a little harder than necessary, making the bottles of cooking wine jingle against each other.

"Maybe . . ." Barb blinked a few times as though she had something in her eye and then took another step toward Veronica. "Maybe I can meet her soon. It might help if I knew what your treatment looked like, and maybe she'd have some questions for me." Barb placed the bottle on the counter, painted coral fingernails clacking against the countertop.

Veronica stared ahead of her, surprised by the question and that she didn't say no instinctually like she usually did when her mom tried too hard to manage her life. She didn't really want to let her mother into her therapy bubble just yet. The only reason she picked up the phone to call Lisa was because Barb had finally stepped back and let her daughter go through the list of grief counselors provided by Central Carolina

Hospital on her own. She didn't like the feeling of her mom breathing down her neck, but then again, the potential was there. If anyone could help Barb and Veronica resolve the long-standing push and pull of their mother-daughter relationship, Lisa could.

"I don't know, Ma." Veronica shrugged. "Maybe." Sophie's crying slowed in the background, only a small whine and then a little whimper as Barb reached out and touched Veronica's arm. When her mother touched her, Veronica always felt a little closer to Sophie. The hands that did what hers could not yet. But hopefully soon . . . soon.

With cautious movements, Barb slid her arm around her daughter's shoulders and then, when she didn't pull away, added another. It always surprised Veronica when she realized how small her mother was. Memories of her mother's arms were usually of her as the protective giant and Veronica as the frightened child. But today her mother felt like the fragile one, and though her knee-jerk reaction was irritation at her mother's over-the-top response, when Barb's shoulders shook and she pressed her face into Veronica's neck, her hot tears and breath touching Veronica's skin reminded her that her mother had the same love for Veronica as Veronica had for Sophie.

It wasn't easy. In fact, it was nearly as hard as putting that formula in the cart and then letting the checker put it in a bag so she could take it home, but Veronica put her arms around her mother, the woman who seemed to find fault in her every time she turned around.

At first Veronica's arms floated there, hovering around the crying woman who had raised her nearly singlehandedly. But then, as though they were responding to some instinct from far in her past, they tightened, and her fingers rested in the soft side she used to put her face into when she was embarrassed and clutched the loose material limply hanging there.

"I said *maybe*," Veronica reiterated, detaching herself from her mother's embrace, forcing the moment to a swift conclusion. Letting in any emotion made it hard to hold all the other ones at bay. Distance was better. "And the formula isn't that big a deal."

Barb wiped at her eyes and stepped back to the end of the counter. "I'm proud of you for trying, sweetheart."

Instantly the irritation was back. Veronica stopped herself from rolling her eyes and then sighed. She *was* trying. Every day she woke up and went through the motions of life, she was trying harder than she'd ever tried. Anyway, she knew the only reason Barb was so excited about formula was because she wanted her daughter drugged up, and the excuse of nursing was the only thing holding her mother's passive-aggressive nature from rearing its nasty head.

She wanted to snap at her mother and tell her she could see what she was doing, but today she paused before the bitter words on her tongue burst out when she had a thought. How would she want Sophie to talk to her when she was grown? She cleared her throat and opened the cabinet above the sink before responding.

"Thanks, Ma," she said calmly, wondering why it felt like she was lying to her mother about her gratitude.

Barb held her gaze for a moment longer and then grabbed the bottle again. "I'll take this in to the nursery, then."

"Yeah. I mean, if she fell asleep in the swing, don't worry about waking her. Just point the camera at the swing so I can watch her." Veronica resumed unloading the groceries, this time starting to clear out the brown cloth grocery bag.

Barb took one last look at her daughter that Veronica pretended not to notice. But then, when her mom turned to leave, Veronica paused, the jar of artichoke hearts in her hand halfway to the cupboard in front of her.

"Please," Veronica added, carefully placing the jar in its spot on the shelf, avoiding any glances at her mother. "I meant to say please."

"I know you did, dear." Veronica could hear the smile in her mother's voice, and as Barb went off to the nursery, Veronica allowed the corners of her mouth to turn up a little as well. Maybe therapy was worth it. Today she had bought formula, told a stranger about losing Nick, not run away when the baby was crying, and hugged her mom and felt empathy for her. So it wasn't a magic pill, but maybe there was something to getting help after all. One day it wouldn't be strangers and formula—it would be holding her daughter in her arms.

# CHAPTER 5

"So you told the man from the waiting room about Nick? The whole story?"

Veronica nodded and picked at the fraying seam in the armrest of the overstuffed chair. There were two chairs side by side and then one across the narrow room. The first time she'd walked into Lisa's office, Lisa had offered her any chair. After Veronica had settled into the one closest to the back wall, Lisa had sat and said, "Congratulations—that will most likely be your chair for every visit we have together." She had explained that people were creatures of habit. Once they picked a chair, it usually was theirs for life.

"I mean, we were at the grocery store, and I told him I was a widow, which seemed to make him feel bad for me or something at first—and that made me mad because I should know better by now, you know?" Lisa nodded at her as though she did know. "It kinda made me want to show him I was okay and that I didn't need his sympathy. So I blurted it all out. I told him how I went to sleep early because Nick was supposed to take the night shift with Sophie. I told him about searching the house for them and then the weird texts. I told him about the phone call and going to the morgue. God, I even told him about Sophie's surgery and how I wasn't allowed to pick her up for a month and that by the time it was okay, I couldn't bring myself to do it."

Tears welled up in her eyes, and Veronica grabbed for a tissue from the box on a little carved table to her left. She was always surprised at how pretty the office was and at the whirring sound machine in the hallway that almost sounded like waves. At first it made her chuckle in her wry, sarcastic way, like the counselors were trying too hard. But now she found it comforting, like she was visiting an oasis from life each week when she walked in the door.

"Wow, Veronica, I love that you felt like you could open up, but you do know that you don't have to tell anyone your story that you don't want to, right? It is your story to tell, and no one has the *right* to know it."

"I know, but at first I thought he was looking at me like he didn't believe me, like I'd lie about my husband dying just to get rid of a guy hitting on me." The outrage swelled inside her again, but it wasn't his questioning look. It was how that look changed when tears filled her eyes. Then he'd looked at her, really looked at her after she'd said she was a widow, as though he could read her sorrow in the lines around her eyes or the fall of her hair. It was unnerving.

"Maybe what upset you wasn't that you perceived that he didn't believe you, but more that he showed interest in you. He did give you his business card, right? What do you think about that?"

Veronica remembered the card; she'd put it in the small wallet attached to her phone case. She kept a couple of random bills there and an emergency credit card in case she ever lost her wallet. Now she had his card, safe and hidden from her mother's prying eyes and safe from her guilty conscience. She ran her thumb over the diamond ring she still kept on her left-hand ring finger. It felt so right there, so comforting. Between a diaper bag for a purse, a ring, and a less-than-cheerful attitude, she had a nearly impenetrable fortress when it came to men. It felt good. It felt safe.

"I'm just not ready to date yet. I can't even think about it. I should have a husband and a baby. We should be commiserating about how hard it is to get going in the morning after being up all night. I should be taking a video of Sophie crawling across the floor and texting it to Nick. I should have his unending love and support and be able to give it back in return. But I don't. And when that desire to love and support bubbles up inside me—I can't imagine giving that to anyone else but him."

Veronica stared at her ring. It glittered just as brilliantly as the day Nick had gone down on one knee in the middle of the Guggenheim and yelled, *"Will you marry me!"* garnering them more than one dirty look. How could a ring last longer than a human being? How did it go from being a symbol of their future to a symbol of their love to a symbol of all she had lost? "I know he's gone, but . . . I can't seem to refocus that love onto anyone else. Not my mom, not Sophie, and definitely not the random man at the supermarket."

"This is the time in our session that I remind you there are medications that could help you, Veronica. Zoloft is completely compatible with breastfeeding and prescribed all the time for PPD. I have a psychiatrist that I refer my patients to regularly. I promise you'll like him." She flipped through her organizer and fished out a crisp, off-white business card. "Dr. Larkin. He's great."

Lisa held the card out toward Veronica, crossing the divide that usually acted as an invisible barrier between them. Veronica stared at it, sure that if she touched it, she'd break out in hives like when she ran through the patch of poison ivy in the third grade.

"No, thanks," she said, putting up her hands, not even willing to look at the card much less hold it in her hands. It wasn't that she had anything against medication; she'd seen it help her college roommate when she was overcome with the crushing anxiety that came with OCD and perfectionism and a full freshman course load. And at one point a few months after Nick died, her editor confided that she'd taken antidepressants after her son was born and that after therapy and time, she tapered off the meds and was doing well now. Medication was fine, good, lifesaving even, but Veronica wasn't ready for that just yet.

"I'm going to ask you every week, you know that, right?" Lisa said, as she had every week for almost two months.

"Yeah, I know."

"One of these days, you are going to take that card," Lisa said as she tucked the card back into its slot and closed her zippered binder.

A bubble of stubbornness inflated inside Veronica at Lisa's confident tone. It was the same feeling she got when her mother told her she needed to start dating or that she put the toilet paper on the wrong way. If she was going to take medication or stop nursing or go to a psychiatrist, then it would be her decision. Not her mother's and not even Lisa's.

"We'll see." She resettled herself in her seat and thought of a way to change the subject. "So I let my mom feed Sophie a bottle of formula last night."

Veronica studied her therapist's face carefully to see if she would respond. Would it be joy or relief or—the most feared mask, the one she imagined on the faces of those around her nearly constantly—judgment. But Lisa's face was almost always calm. She hid behind a kind void that was safe but also infuriatingly blank, only letting brief moments of shock break through when Veronica surprised her with a new symptom like how she was starting to wake from her nightmares in different locations than where she'd fallen asleep. The other day she awoke from the dream about the night of the accident, screaming and sitting in the front seat of her car in the garage. Lisa's horrified concern was easy to see then, and Veronica hadn't even told her that the car was running.

"Oh, well, that is news. How do you feel about that?" Lisa leaned forward, polished silver pen clutched in her hand. Hands were notoriously difficult to draw, but there was something beautiful about Lisa's hands, her long fingers and short, polished nails, that made Veronica dream of drawing them. Or maybe thinking about how she'd draw Lisa's hands kept her from thinking about the panic she'd felt when her mom walked away with the bottle full of formula and came back with it empty. It was like when the hot bartender at the pub they used to frequent in New York had a huge crush on Nick. Anytime Veronica left his side, she'd be there pushing up her boobs, touching his arm, and laughing as if Nick were a professional comic. Even though he looked more like a trapped animal than a man flirting with a curvy bartender, she couldn't help the touch of jealousy and rejection she'd always feel as she walked back from the bathroom. This felt similar.

"It was harder than I thought it would be. I feel like I'm giving up the only way I've been able to take care of my baby. Someone else's arms comfort her. Someone else's voice soothes her. Someone else's hands dress her and change her, but it was *my* milk that kept her alive and helped her grow. But now . . . she doesn't even need that." Those twin emotions of rejection and jealousy started to build up inside Veronica, and the calming voice that used to keep her from losing it on Tasha the bartender wasn't speaking up today. Because unlike Nick, who had no interest in the flirty woman pursuing him, Sophie didn't even notice the difference between the formula and the breast milk. Both bottles filled her stomach and came back empty. "Let's be honest—she doesn't need *me* at all."

Veronica was growing upset. There were only three minutes left on the clock before her session was up, and she knew it. The plan was to tell Lisa about the formula right as they were walking out the door and make sure not to mention how hard it was to give away the only thing that made her feel like a mother. Veronica hated going over her time, and Lisa was very punctual, so it should've worked. But she had to go and open her big mouth. Now Lisa didn't seem to notice the clock or the time or anything else in the room but Veronica and how she was biting at the cuticles around the nub of her thumbnail. She tasted blood on her tongue, and instead of compelling her to stop, it made her bite a little harder, the coppery taste distracting her from the pain of failure.

She didn't mind physical pain; deep down she felt as though she should be punished, but since everyone wanted to be so infuriatingly forgiving toward her, she had to take the job on herself.

"Hey, hey, stop. Listen, that is why you're here, Veronica." Lisa pulled a few tissues out of the box to her left and passed them over, glancing at the blood gathering around Veronica's nail. "If you let me, I can help you. You don't have to feel like an outsider in Sophie's life anymore. You are *not* replaceable." The neutral void of Lisa's features filled with a sincere expression of concern. She shook the tissues at Veronica like a white flag. Her voice was soft and caring as Veronica tended to her self-inflicted injury. "These thoughts are worrisome to me. I know you said that you don't think about hurting yourself or Sophie anymore, but I need you to promise me something. Even if it is a brief flicker of a moment, even if just one idea or thought or plan slips into your conscious mind, you will call me, and if you can't get in touch with me, then tell me you'll call the suicide prevention lifeline." She shuffled through her binder again and brought up another card, this one with glossy red lettering, and held it out.

"I'm not having bad thoughts." Veronica snapped the card out of Lisa's fingertips, knowing it wasn't going to fly if she rejected this one. There was a rule about therapists and their confidentiality—it was only ironclad if they didn't think you were going to hurt yourself or others. She wasn't planning on hurting anyone. Not anymore, anyway. She used to think it would be better if she and Sophie joined Nick in heaven, but when she once suggested the idea to her mother, logically, as if she were explaining why it was better to be an LLC than an S corp, Barb had threatened to call the police and try to get her committed. Veronica wasn't going to let that happen again.

She wasn't ready to tell Lisa about that yet, not when her therapist was already handing her suicide hotline numbers. Her sessions were completely safe and confidential; Veronica could control how much she told and what image she shared with Lisa, unless she broke one of those two tricky cardinal rules by appearing a threat to herself or others. Then all bets were off and the hospital was no longer just an option offered; it could be required, by force if necessary.

Lisa nodded, assessing her carefully with a reserved and practiced eye. "I know, I know. But it is important, Veronica. That promise means something."

"Fine, I promise." Veronica stood, ready to run out the door today instead of taking the slow stroll to the lobby like they usually did. Gillian was usually waiting for her there after seeing her therapist, Stacey. She'd pretend to read a magazine so they could "run into each other" and walk to the parking lot together. As far as she could tell, Mark, the suited mystery man from Piggly Wiggly, attended the single-parent support group at the end of the hall that Lisa was always trying to push her into. It was run by a social worker in the practice and sparsely attended, but Mark always seemed to be there. He hadn't been there this afternoon, which was puzzling yet also a relief, but who knew what his schedule was like.

There would be no strolling today. She just needed to get out and fast, making her wish she still had her running shoes on from her morning workout instead of the wedges that added two inches to her height but also made her feet sweat.

"I will call you, but I also promise you have nothing to worry about." She threw her diaper bag/purse over her shoulder. Lisa was left behind, stunned and still sitting in her overstuffed leather chair.

Usually Veronica would stop by the front desk and pay her copay before heading out to the lobby and attempting to evade the ever-friendly Gillian. But today she just kept walking. She'd pay next time. She rushed past the waving receptionist, past the surprisingly empty waiting room, and even past the elevators until she reached the stairs.

The urge to run grew inside her like it did when Sophie's screams echoed through the house. It was almost as if each footstep in the cavernous stairwell were like another one of Sophie's cries. But just as she couldn't ever really escape her own daughter, she couldn't escape her own feet either.

Rushing now, her heart pounding and sweat building at her hairline, Veronica ignored the way her angled shoes dug into her toes and pretended that she didn't look as insane as she felt. As soon as she broke through the windowed door, the heat from the June afternoon not helping her sweat issue, she beelined for the closest patch of grass she could find. Her footsteps were muffled by the soft earth and blades of grass, and she collapsed onto the manicured lawn.

The normal sounds of the outdoors were calming, and even the early summer sun felt like hot kisses across her skin. Her pulse slowed and her rapid breathing soon matched. These panic attacks were like a madness that came over her, crawling up her arms and down her spine. While in the middle of an episode, it was hard to perceive the beginning or conceptualize an end. All she could see was the choking, blinding panic of the moment. But the fog was dissipating, and the control of her faculties was returning bit by bit.

Unfortunately, she also knew that even when the panic left and her mind cleared, the hollow ache of sadness from losing Nick would never completely leave—ever. It was her constant companion and in a twisted way reminded her that if she hadn't loved him so deeply, then it wouldn't hurt this badly. Sometimes she was proud of that pain.

With her wits finally about her, Veronica straightened her shoulders and stood, stumbling as she reached her full height. She leaned over to grab her bag and tried to stealthily glance around the parking lot for anyone who might have seen her lose it on the back lawn of the medical clinic. The only thing worse than being crazy was having other people *see* that you were crazy.

There were three cars besides hers in the parking lot. With pursed lips and closed eyes, she took a deep breath and then another and then another, until her lungs felt nearly as big as balloons and the kink between her shoulder blades unwound into a loose coil instead of a spring ready to pop. She opened her eyes; sanity was restored.

Veronica walked deftly from the grass back to the sidewalk, forcing herself to ignore the clap of her shoes against the pavement. She clutched the door handle on her Prius; the keyless entry popped open the lock as the superheated metal nearly burned her palm. She knew she should flinch back, but she didn't; she let the burn settle in and spread from her palm to her fingertips, hoping the pain from the heat would take away some of the other pains in her life.

Just as she was about to pull on the handle and give up on the self-flagellation, a flash across the parking lot caught her eye. It looked like a car driving up and the sun reflecting off its glass, but as she counted the cars again—blue Civic, red Accord, silver minivan—there were no additions. Just the same three sleeping cars. Maybe she'd imagined it.

But then another flash, this one while she was looking up. The back lot was shaped in an upside-down L that surrounded the building. All three cars and her own were parked with headlights facing the glass hall of the back corridor. With so much glass, it was hard to tell where the flash was coming from. Squinting, she examined the bushes at the long top of the L and then the transparent walls of the building. Nothing. Veronica shook her head. It was just the stress; it had to be.

"Veronica!" A woman's voice calling her name made Veronica jump and let go of the door handle. Over her shoulder, Gillian came tromping down the sidewalk leading from the offices. Her short, crisp hair stood frozen in the breeze, only shifting slightly like reeds surrounding the marsh by her house. "Veronica," she huffed again, her pace slowing now that Veronica's escape was not imminent.

"Gillian." Even Veronica could hear the annoyed edge to her voice, but Gillian never seemed to catch on. Turned out she wasn't a lunch lady, but a cashier at the area's only Walmart—nearly divorced and mourning her only son who died of cancer a few years earlier. That was the bit that got Veronica to take down the electric force field around her razor-wire-topped fence—Gillian's son.

To lose your only child when you were already alone—the thought made the aching in Veronica's midsection grow. If she lost Sophie . . . every time the thought started to develop in her mind, she pushed it away. The idea of losing her without holding her again made Veronica want to hide in her house forever. Maybe that was why she was nice to Gillian—to prove to herself that she was different. It couldn't happen in her family.

"Hey! I got out from talking to Stacey a little later than usual, and you were gone." Gillian stopped on the curb, her slightly shrunken purple T-shirt hung crooked over her enlarged belly. There was a small hole by the collar where an embroidered flower was pulling away from the seam and a faded pattern around the sleeve that made Veronica think it was supposed to be her dressy shirt.

Gillian's face was mottled, stark white in odd spots but bright red in others, sweat gathering around her hairline and dripping in large trails down the side of her face. Running from the back of the building to Veronica's car had left her as out of breath as Veronica on a twenty-miler. Veronica clinched her fists and tried to focus on the sharp cut of her nails against her tender, burned palm.

*Stop being a bitch,* she scolded herself firmly.

"Sorry, my mom is out running errands with Sophie, so I thought I'd go home and clean while the house was empty." She searched her mind for the right kind of thing to say next. If Gillian had her way, they'd sit and rehash their sessions every week and talk through all the most sensitive pain points. She'd come to see that Gillian worked through pain by vomiting it all out in words, but Veronica was stingy with her grief. It was like if she talked about it too much, it would go away, and then she'd lose Nick forever. That mixed with the embarrassment of losing control in front of someone like Gillian, who was in no way equipped to help her, made Veronica sure that she'd rather keep her tears to herself.

"It's okay. How was your session?" she asked and smiled at Veronica, a broad, needy smile. The woman reminded her of a large golden retriever all excited for a walk.

"Short," Veronica answered briefly, and then smiled back, tight-lipped.

Gillian dropped her hands and smile at the same time, taking a hint for perhaps the first time in her life. "Oh, okay, well, you should get going. I'm sorry I bugged you. I know it's busy being a working mom." She chuckled and pointed at herself. "Been there, done that."

And there it was—the reason Veronica couldn't ever look herself in the eye after being mean or cold to Gillian. They were almost nothing alike, from the sex of their only child to their age as mothers to the circumstances leading to their lonely lives, but it was still there—this cord of similitude that linked Veronica to Gillian and made her want to be kind. It took so little to make the lonely woman happy, like giving the golden retriever a dry bone from a box of treats.

"I have a second or two. Did you want to tell me about your session?" It was difficult to make those words come out, but once she saw the excited shuffle of Gillian's small feet, clad in the most reasonable walking shoes ever created by man, the dullness inside Veronica wavered for a moment.

"Eh, not enough time for all of that. It was a rough one today." The red in her face suddenly blanched white like she'd been hit by a giant gust of cooling wind. "It's Christopher's birthday. He would've been twenty-one today."

"Oh," Veronica said simply. "I'm so sorry, Gillian." Sometimes it was the only thing you could say.

Gillian twisted her fingers together, but after blinking a few times, she looked up, eyes a little teary but with strength and resolve that Veronica was always jealous of.

"Yeah, I knew you'd get it. But I'm trying not to sink down into the muck again. So hard to do, right?"

Veronica nodded, jaw clenched to keep from saying too much.

"Well, this Friday Stacey thought I should go out to a nice place and have a drink for Christopher, you know, because he'd be twenty-one."

Veronica hesitated. It was her turn to say something, but she thought Gillian wasn't finished. The other woman's lips twisted to one side, and the red splotches came back to her cheeks, a few showing up on her arms like a trail of stepping stones. It was getting late, and though the immediate panic had left, the posttherapy exhaustion was setting in, and all Veronica wanted was to find the magic words to get out of this conversation.

"That sounds nice . . . ," she finally responded.

At the same time, Gillian blurted out, "Would you like to come?"

The question hit Veronica in a hot wave, as though she'd opened the door to her superheated car. She hadn't gone out since Sophie was born and definitely hadn't had any alcohol. It was hard enough to get a steady milk supply while pumping exclusively; she didn't want to have to waste a session to the infamous "pump and dump" required after drinking.

But now there was formula, and Sophie was older, and the look of need and loneliness in Gillian's eyes was strangely touching, as if she were looking into the eyes of a woman she could become one day if bad luck or tragedy hit her world again.

"Uh, let me talk to my mom but, um"—she bounced her head back and forth, considering how hard it would be to cancel later—"sure."

Gillian's nearly-washed-away eyebrows shot up, sweat gathering in the wrinkles on her forehead. She started to bounce again, and Veronica couldn't tell if her excitement was annoying or humbling. It made her feel something, and that in and of itself was strange.

"Oh, you just made my day," Gillian said, and leaned forward as though she wanted to give her a hug, but stopped when Veronica took a shuffled step backward, the idea of an odd woman touching her when she couldn't touch her daughter striking an imbalance in her mind.

Instead, Gillian held out her phone as if it were an offering. "Can I text you later?"

"Um, sure." Veronica flipped through her phone and got to the contacts page, and they exchanged. It was funny how her own phone felt like home but someone else's felt foreign even if it was the same exact model. But Gillian's was not. It was not only many years behind in technology, but also looked as if it had been dropped twenty times and possibly run over by a semi. The side of the screen was cracked, the back scratched with deep gashes, and the attempt at a screen protector was peeling at the corners. The phone was a lot like Gillian: it had been through hell, and you could tell just by looking at it. Veronica scolded herself again for being so damned shallow and then quickly typed in her name, first only, and phone number, knowing she'd regret it later.

"Hey, your phone is ringing." Gillian held it out and rolled her eyes toward the sky in a clear effort not to look at the caller ID.

The women swapped phones again; this time Veronica nearly dropped both in the exchange. The caller ID read: "Central Carolina Home Security."

"What the hell," she whispered under her breath, bringing the phone closer to her face, squinting, sure she was reading it wrong.

"What? Everything okay?" Gillian asked, growing anxious.

Veronica didn't have the mental energy to respond or even care what the purple-and-red blur in front of her was saying. Sometimes the alarm got tripped if her mother forgot to turn it off when she got home from a walk with Sophie or when Veronica ran the vacuum into the wall by the front door with too much force. But she'd never gotten this call. The alarm had always been disarmed with the special code: Sophie's birthdate.

There had been too many rings. If she didn't pick up soon, then it would go to voice mail. With a quivering finger, she pushed the "Talk" button.

"H-hello?" she stuttered out.

"Hello, Mrs. Shelton. This is Dennis from Central Carolina Home Securities. I'm just calling to make sure everything is okay in your residence."

"Um." She cleared her throat. "I'm not home. Maybe my mother forgot the code when she got home with my daughter. I can text and remind her." Veronica sighed. They'd had to up the entry-delay time twice already in an effort to avoid these kinds of calls.

"Okay. Would you like me to hold? You know, just in case?" Dennis asked with a total lack of urgency that calmed Veronica rather than irritated her.

"Sure," Veronica responded quickly before she pulled the phone away from her ear and typed a quick message to her mom, explaining the situation and reminding her of the code. When the gray dots popped up immediately, the bubble of fear that had been slowly inflating inside Veronica started to empty. Her message appeared immediately.

Still at the store. I already set the alarm and of course I remember the code.

I'm not senile—yet.

Why? Are you okay?

Veronica stared at the screen for a second, not sure what any of it meant. Her mind reeling and her hand shaking, she put the phone back up to her ear, the anxiety bubble that had started to deflate ballooning again instantly.

"Uh . . . It's not my mom," she whispered, her mouth dry and heart pounding.

"Okay, Mrs. Shelton, no need to panic. The alarm was triggered first on your back door. No code was entered . . . Wait . . . Do you have a dog?"

"No . . . What are you talking about?" she blurted, leaning against her car, foot tapping to a nervous rhythm. This was not what she needed today.

"Well, it wasn't just the rear door that I see lit up. The sensor in your back bedroom was also tripped, just before the internal alarm sounded. It says here it was the fourth bedroom. Sometimes if a dog gets overanxious, they mess with the motion sensor and . . ." He paused as though he could read Veronica's confusion and annoyance in her silence. "Listen, we have to make this call before we can contact local authorities. Do you have the safe word, or do you want me to contact the police, Mrs. Shelton?"

Then it all came together in one magnificent whoosh.

The back bedroom.

Upstairs.

*Oh my God.* Veronica pressed the phone against her face. The trembling in her fingers spread to her arms and shoulders, making her voice wobble in her near scream. "Call the police. Now. *Now!*"

That was Sophie's room.

# CHAPTER 6

A single squad car was waiting outside Veronica's house when she finally pulled into the driveway fifteen minutes after hanging up from her call. No lights and no one in the back seat of the vehicle. It should've been comforting to see the police car in front of her house, to know that someone was there to search her home and protect her and her family, but it also brought back memories from the day of the accident. The packed emergency-room hallways, the taste of vomit in her mouth, the flickering lights of the morgue, the shoes sticking out from under a sheet. No, she couldn't let herself remember that moment; she'd been running from it ever since. That day it had been a somber police officer who drove her home when she was too distraught to do it herself. It brought back those swirling, nasty words that had sent her world crashing down. "Drunk driver . . . accident . . . so sorry . . . not everyone made it . . ."

Veronica tapped her foot and swallowed a few times after putting the car in park. This time would be different. This time it really was just a horrible misunderstanding. This time she wouldn't lose someone. Before she could open the car door, a shadow passed by the passenger side and there was a loud knock on the window. Veronica let out a half-stifled scream.

"Are you okay?"

It was Gillian. Veronica wanted to actually scream this time. Half-stooped, the well-meaning but impossible-to-escape woman squinted in through the closed window.

"God, did you follow me here?" Veronica asked, a sense of outrage barely controlled. The idea of this random woman from her therapist's office now knowing her home address seemed . . . unwise. Unsafe. They were both in therapy for a reason, but what if Gillian's reason was that she was an ax murder with a propensity to single white females she met in public places?

"No, I mean, yes. I mean . . . you seemed so upset, and I was worried about you, so I thought I'd make sure you made it home okay."

Veronica got out of the car, ignoring Gillian for a moment and cringing against the loud wailing coming from the house alarm. She scanned the front of the bungalow, the door, windows, front porch. Nothing seemed to be out of place besides the incessant scream of the alarm.

Crazy Gillian or no crazy Gillian, she needed to find out what was going on and if her house was secure. Her mother had answered on the first ring when Veronica called on the way over, which gave her some comfort. She was still out shopping, and Sophie was safely in her car seat. Sophie was having a hard time falling asleep, so they went for a drive. She told her mom to stay out until she talked to the police and got a handle on the situation. At least they weren't home. Veronica would be breaking down the front door and running headfirst into danger if they were.

An officer in full uniform came around the corner of the house from the backyard. He had his hands on his belt and was scanning the upper windows. He didn't look fierce or even like he was following a big lead, more like he was confused. The officer's mouth was turned down on one side, and his eyes shifted over every inch of the exterior of the house. Veronica bristled. This was not what she'd imagined would happen if her high-tech, top-of-the-line system was triggered. In her mind, she'd seen men in SWAT uniforms storming the house and then tear gas rolling out of the broken-down front door. Goodness, if there *had* been foul play, then a casual stroll around her house wasn't going to help catch someone inside it.

"I'm okay. You can go now," Veronica said to Gillian, walking away from the car. She took long strides toward the officer, wishing she looked more professional than the white tank top and khaki shorts she'd thrown on that morning when the news said it might edge into the nineties by noon. The young officer didn't even seem to notice her approach. If she'd been an intruder, he'd be on the wrong side of the exchange.

"Hey!" she called out, thinking it was smart to announce her presence, since he didn't seem to be at the top of his game. The officer's head whipped to the side, and he looked her over from head to toe, his hand on his gun. She put up her hands slightly and shouted over the alarm, "This is my house."

He flashed a glance at Gillian, still trailing behind Veronica but puffing with each step, and then back at Veronica. His hand dropped from his weapon, and he patted the air in front of him.

He said something as though a siren louder than a jet plane weren't blaring through the neighborhood. She could barely make out any of the sentence.

"What?" Veronica shouted, stepping closer.

"Your ID," he yelled this time. "I just need your ID."

"Oh, damn it," she cursed, mad at herself for not thinking of that necessity. "Hold on! My purse is in my car."

"Sounds good," the officer replied, returning to his very cursory examination of the exterior of the house.

As Veronica turned around to head back to the car, she slammed into Gillian. She was breathing heavily, and some of the sweat from her arms rubbed off on Veronica's skin. She had that eager-to-please puppy look on her face again.

"I'll get it!" She turned immediately, not waiting for permission, and rushed back to the Prius. Veronica stiffened but faced the officer and smiled as though Gillian was her BFF and had every right to grab her wallet from the car.

He took his eyes off the house for a moment and placed his hands back on his belt, this time keeping them off the gun. As they waited the officer continued to survey the house, the sun beat down on Veronica's back, and the sweat between her shoulder blades made her skin sticky. The wandering officer, in his stiff black uniform, seemed to be suffering even more, though he was trying hard not to show it. Sweat poured down the sides of his face and neck and then soaked into his collar, and his forehead flushed red all the way up to his receding hairline. Veronica knew that if she felt as though she were in an oven, then he must feel as if he were in the fiery furnace itself.

There used to be a pair of oak trees in the front yard when she moved in back in February, but the wood was diseased and rotted, and the home inspector had suggested they be cut down before it spread to the rest of the oaks in the backyard. She had only recently gotten around to the chore and couldn't believe how the light in her house changed when the trees were gone. Instead of the soft, quiet shade of the oak trees blanketing the house in a comforting coolness all hours of the day, the front of the house was warm in the winter, hot in the spring, and stifling in the summer, no matter how high the air was turned up or how thick the blackout curtains were. She'd yet to spend a fall there, but no doubt there would be some uncomfortable temperature issues when the time came. She shuffled her feet and wiped at her own forehead. What she wouldn't give for a little shade right now.

"I got it!" Gillian half ran, half stumbled across the dried-out grass, nearly crashing when she reached the cement walkway that stood between the women and the officer.

Veronica tugged the bag out of Gillian's outstretched hands and quickly found the small bifold wallet that held her credit cards and a few loose dollars folded behind the clear window that displayed her driver's license.

"Sorry," she shouted, "I thought I just needed to give a code word or something. Here's the ID."

The officer examined her driver's license carefully, checked something briefly on a notebook he pulled from his chest pocket, and then held the card out to her again.

"That's just for the alarm company, ma'am." He jotted a few illegible things on the pad and put it back in his pocket, seemingly satisfied. "All of the doors and windows seem secure. No evidence of a break-in. I can go inside and look around if you like, just to be sure."

"Yes, I mean, yes, please, if you wouldn't mind. But the alarm isn't just from one of the external doors or windows. There is an internal door to my daughter's bedroom . . . ," Veronica responded, her words colliding with his. She stopped short when the officer gave her a raised eyebrow. She cleared her throat. "Uh . . . I mean, yes, please, if you wouldn't mind, Officer . . . I'm sorry, I didn't get your name."

"Burdick, miss." The young officer with dark hair and a medium build looked at her with a little more softness now that he knew she was the frightened homeowner and not a criminal. "I'd be happy to take a look around."

"Um, okay, thank you, Officer Burdick," Veronica added, desperately trying to regain some form of politeness. Between the way she'd spoken to and thought of Gillian to her annoyed demeanor with the officer, she was getting worried that she really was as unlikable as she feared.

Veronica removed her house key from her purse and headed toward the front steps, with Officer Burdick close behind. This time Gillian didn't follow. She stood alone on the front lawn, her blue Civic parked in the street. She seemed to be waiting for an invitation.

Veronica cringed internally. She didn't want to invite this strange, needy woman into her life any more than she'd already forced herself in.

If this was "pre-Lisa," Veronica would've turned off any feelings about Gillian and focused on the alarm, the officer, and the house, but after getting asked thoughtful questions continually in session, she'd started to ask some thoughtful ones of herself. It was becoming an annoying and enlightening habit.

Like, why did she continue to push away kindness? Maybe she didn't feel like she deserved it, because she was such a horrible mother? Probably it was because she was worried that if someone got to know her, they'd find out how bad she was, how her mind was full of sad thoughts nearly all the time.

But Gillian, standing on the lawn with a hopeful twitch in her cheek, might be safe. Veronica looked her over again, remembering the frayed shirt. Her hair was soaked through with sweat and looked as though she'd taken a shower, but she wasn't scowling. She didn't even look annoyed. Drenched and red, she was smiling. Veronica handed the keys over to Officer Burdick and half whispered, half shouted the code for the alarm into his ear. Then she met Gillian on the lawn.

"Um, he's going to make sure it's safe. Do you want to sit in the car? We can put on the air." Veronica swallowed hard, her heart beating as if she were asking out a boy on a date or something.

"Yeah," Gillian said, her smile broadening, "that'd be great."

# CHAPTER 7

When they reached the car, the two women sat down in unison. Veronica pressed the power button twice, turning on the middle console. She flicked on the AC, and it went from stifling inside the car to pleasant almost instantly. Once comfortable, she kept her eyes trained on the front door, wondering if the officer had called for backup or was facing the unknown inside her house alone.

"That feels amazing," Gillian said, leaning forward, her eyes closed to the cool blast of air pumping out of the vents. Her comment diverted Veronica's attention.

"Yeah, it gets cool fast."

"I've never been in a Prius. Christopher always wanted one. He used to consider himself quite the environmentalist."

A mournful burning grew between Veronica's shoulder blades at the mention of Gillian's dead son. Whenever people spoke of the dead so easily, she wanted to hold her breath to get rid of the burning that made her wonder why she couldn't talk about the losses in her time on earth.

"I don't know." She attempted to sound interested in Gillian's life. "I've always wondered if having AC in a car that was supposed to help save the environment was an oxymoron."

Gillian laughed, which made Veronica feel accomplished in some way. Her little internal therapist was giving her a big thumbs-up for finding ways to relate to someone outside herself.

"I know what you mean. When Christopher was in junior high, I went with him on a field trip to this nature center. This hippyish director got on the bus when we got there, and he lectured all fifty school kids on the dangers of air-conditioning. He told the kids, 'Put your windows down—now, that is nature's air-conditioning!' Christopher wouldn't let me run the air for that whole summer." Gillian laughed as if they had just been on that bus five hours ago. "He liked to think of himself as a little conservationist back then too."

"Well, wish I could say I got the Prius because I'm that noble. It was 20 percent to save the environment and more like 80 percent to save on gas money. Your son probably would think I'm just a hypocrite."

"Nah, I'm sure he'd give you a free pass. You are saving his mama from heatstroke." She talked about him so fluidly, as if he were at home, waiting for her to make dinner and pull cookies out of the oven. Veronica couldn't even say "Nick."

Impressed envy swelled inside her. She took her eyes off the front door and only half noticed that the alarm had finally turned off, and she stared at the side of the almost stranger's face, wondering how Gillian could do something so strong when she seemed so weak.

"I live to serve," Veronica said, attempting a joke, and Gillian snorted a little laugh, adjusting her neckline so the air could get better access to her skin. A thin gold chain was glued to her flesh with sweat, and a large locket about the size of a silver dollar hung low on her chest. "Is that a picture of Christopher?" It was strange to say his name, knowing he was gone.

A sweet half smile pulled up the corner of the woman's mouth. It seemed to be a mouth that had liked to smile at some time in her life. The creases that cascaded up her cheeks were well defined and made Veronica's stomach fill with a hollow ache. Her own cheeks were smooth and unpracticed when it came to smiling. It had been so long since she'd felt a real smile on her face, an eternity since her cheeks ached from overuse and laughter. That locket held a picture of Gillian's son, but the smile said that, for her, it held the last remnants of him as well. Her fingertips fiddled with the latch.

"Sure is. Wanna see?" But before she could get the metal circle open, a loud tap on the windshield made Veronica let out a loud "Eep" and Gillian drop the locket back into place and shout, "Oh my *heavens*!"

The officer stood outside the Prius, arms crossed as though he'd been waiting. Veronica had no idea how she got so distracted that she'd almost forgotten about the reason she was sitting in her driveway with a woman from her therapist's office. With a sharp shake of her head, she popped the car door open, already talking before she was at full height.

"So what did you find? Were we robbed? Was it the baby's room? Should I get a hotel? Is it safe?"

"Ms. Shelton, everything is secure, but let's go for a walk through the house to see if anything is out of place." He gestured for Veronica to follow him.

Gillian's shuffled steps followed closely behind as the officer picked up his pace, maybe tired of being in the sun in his stiff black uniform.

The front door was ajar.

"So was it like this?"

"No, ma'am. All doors and windows were secure," he said politely but also with enough of an edge to remind Veronica that he'd already told her that information. "I just need to know if anything is missing."

Veronica walked inside and scanned the room, but nothing was out of place; it was neat and tidy just like her mother always kept it. Before her mom moved in, there were piles of randomness all over the house. In her grief, Veronica couldn't seem to manage anything but breathing and keeping things as close to perfection as possible for Sophie. Now she'd gotten used to the neat interior and found comfort in the structure of it.

There were smiling pictures of Sophie and Nick on the mantel of the fireplace, the few that they had of them together from the first weeks of her life. They were still in the same expertly dusted spot as this morning. The runner down the middle of the large mahogany dining room table still sat in a flawless blue line. The carpet that traced a path from the front door to the kitchen across the polished hardwood floors was in the right position, vacuum lines from her mother's morning chores undisturbed.

The kitchen, family room, and breakfast nook all sat untouched. Other than a bottle-drying rack and a high chair in the corner of the kitchen, no traces of babies or childhood existed. It bothered Veronica sometimes. A little toy on the floor or used burp rag across the armrest of the couch occasionally might be nice.

"Your house is beautiful," Gillian whispered as though she were walking through a cathedral.

Veronica had almost forgotten she was still tagging along. Almost everything the mourning mother said made Veronica sad. Her house was tidy and well taken care of, but it was no palace. The wonder on Gillian's face drew an image of what her home must be like; if Veronica had her charcoal, she could sketch it easily. She'd smudge every edge until it felt like the room was closing in on a solitary form, crying into her hands on a twin bed, framed pictures on the walls, all pictures of the same face but changing slightly through age.

"Thanks," Veronica managed to mutter to Gillian as she scanned the room one last time. It all seemed incredibly normal. She pointed toward the stairs. "Did you look up there?"

Officer Burdick gave her that stare again that said, "I know how to do my job."

"Okay, okay . . ." Veronica put one foot on the stairs but stopped. "I know you already looked, but maybe you should go up first . . . you know . . . just in case."

"Yes, ma'am." Officer Burdick didn't betray his annoyance if he felt any. He walked briskly upstairs to the bedrooms, his hand on his gun, which made Veronica nervous and relieved at the same time.

The first room was Sophie's, a beautiful soft pink with cream and light-blue accents. The room felt like snuggling into a banana split covered in whipped cream. This time of the day, the sun hit the front of the house, leaving the rear cool and shaded by the giant oaks in the backyard. The crib was neatly made, comforter hanging off the edge of the railing as decoration with little bluebirds embroidered on it. The lifesaving swing that kept Sophie calm during those long nights of colic sat across from the crib, and the tidy wicker changing table with all necessary supplies stacked in neat piles sat in the corner.

Mostly, Veronica loved the aesthetic of the nursery. She created it out of what must've been an office for the previous owners. Her mother had watched tiny, recovering Baby Sophie in the first weeks after Nick's death, throughout the hasty move, and after Sophie's homecoming while Veronica painted the walls and filled the room with all her hopes and dreams of what a perfect life she'd give that little girl.

It had taken years of trying and months of medication before the positive test came back, but it finally did, and her world had changed. The warmth of that room had nothing to do with temperature; it was about the love she still had for Nick and Sophie. She swore bits of that love were trapped under the paint and between the wainscoting and the wall. It seeped out and surrounded whoever stepped inside it.

But as soon as Sophie had moved into her cozy, impeccably designed room, Veronica never entered it again. She stood just outside its threshold so often she swore there was an imprint where her socked feet would rub as she watched Sophie's crib and wished she could hold her one more time.

Nothing hinted at the sensor and invisible tripwire across the threshold of Sophie's room. She'd gotten the device installed in the nursery almost on a whim. When the technician suggested it as an extra precaution for the future, her mind had flashed to obvious worries that could plague her life as a single mother, like if Sophie learned how to climb out of her crib and suddenly wandered off during nap time. Until those days of dangerous mischief, the alarm sat dormant, only armed by default when the whole house alarm was turned on.

Alarm or no alarm, she hadn't stepped inside the room in months. But Veronica still knew every detail of the room's content, and once again nothing was out of place. Except—the carpet just inside the nursery door—the corner was flipped up.

"I think someone was here." She stepped back from the open door and bumped into Gillian, who was craning her neck to see inside. "Don't go in there. Maybe there are fingerprints."

Officer Burdick cocked his head and took a step forward in front of the two women and then stepped over the wooden threshold as though it wasn't even difficult. Veronica held her breath, wondering if he could feel what she used to in that room. But if he did, he didn't let on. Burdick scanned the room slowly, turning in a circle, stopping after a few quarter turns.

"What is that?" He pointed at the bookshelf in the rear corner of the room, next to the window. Besides some decorative knickknacks and a book or two from the baby shower, there was a white-and-black glassy lens pointed across the room.

"Oh, it's the baby-monitor camera. I have it set up so my mom and I can watch Sophie from other parts of the house or if I'm on a business trip or something."

"Does that thing record?"

"Oh . . . oh!" Veronica gasped. "I'm so stupid. Of course. They are stored online. I can get them on my phone, but I usually watch on my computer monitor. It's so much easier to see clearly. I can review them every night if I want to. Damn it—why didn't I think of this earlier? Come on." She waved to both Gillian and the officer. "We can watch in my studio."

# CHAPTER 8

The door to her studio was always closed with her mom living here, and usually no one was allowed inside. When Veronica pushed open the heavy door, papers fluttered, hanging from the wall with tacks and tape, some filled with color, some completely painted black, some with childlike paintings of flowers and rainbows but others filled with dark, scary faces like the gargoyles she used to be so obsessed with. Her workspaces were always a mess, but since her loss and moving to the house on Mayfair Lane, the walls and floors and tabletops of this one room had become blanketed in artwork. It was like the creative chaos of her mind, layered and unexpected and always moving, like the way each step Veronica made set a shimmer of movement through the pages.

"Excuse the mess," she said halfheartedly. No part of her was embarrassed by her chaos. Wasn't that the beauty of art—taking the chaos of a blot of paint or a streak of chalk and turning it into something more? One day she had found her mother in here, rifling through papers and taking pictures off the wall as though she had any right to say what had value and what didn't. That was the problem with her relationship with her mom. She always thought she knew better than Veronica until Veronica had no choices left to make but her mother's choices. When she was younger, there were big fights and days of passive-aggressive silence, but now she skipped the fight and just installed a lock. In fact, she had learned to shut her mom out of any part of her life she attempted to push her way into before Veronica was ready.

"The mess? This is amazin', hon." Gillian was lost in a daze. She traced the lines of each piece as if she wanted to know exactly what the images had to say to her. It reminded Veronica of how she felt the first time she went to the Louvre, the echoing halls holding paintings that had been touched and created by her idols. Somehow Gillian seemed to feel that same emotion inside Veronica's studio.

Shuffling papers into a few makeshift stacks on her desk, Veronica retrieved her closed laptop and placed it on top of the pages in front of her. Officer Burdick also seemed taken aback by the ten-by-twelve workspace. While Veronica's computer powered on, he stopped by the easel where she did her watercolors. There one of her work projects sat, untouched for days. The proofs had been due a month ago. Missing her deadline was hard at first, but every day that went by, her shame was deadened by necessity. How could she work on anything but herself and her family right now?

"Wait, I recognize these. This is Mia's Travels." He said the title of the series with a smile as though he suddenly remembered they were friends. "Wait, are you *the* Veronica Shelton? You write the Mia books?"

Veronica blushed. People rarely remembered her name.

"I'm the illustrator, not the author," she said dismissively. The computer chimed on, and she toggled through the open tabs, looking for the right file.

"My daughter loves these books!" He wasn't just smiling now; he was all-out grinning and grasping at his pocket for the notebook he'd been writing notes in. "I didn't know you moved to Sanford. She will never believe me."

As Officer Burdick chattered on about his six-year-old daughter, Gloria, and her love of the main character of the book, Mia, a little Latina girl with a pet dog that only spoke Spanish, Veronica maximized the camera monitoring program, and Sophie's room came into focus.

The storage icon in the corner was flashing a glowing two over the outline of a cardboard box. She hadn't reviewed and deleted yesterday's files yet, but both would need to download from the server before she could view. Even with her high-speed internet, it would take a few minutes. She didn't always watch the video files back at the end of the day. Usually it was the live feed through her computer. The real reason for the camera wasn't to catch an intruder but so Veronica could feel connected to Sophie through the screen.

"I really shouldn't ask, but can I take a picture of this? Is this the new book?"

The painting on the easel was just the landscape of the fictional world the characters lived in, half real world with cars and streets and half fantasy with magic trees that could transport the characters to other countries and, in later editions, different times in a blink of an eye.

"For Gloria?" she asked, glad she remembered his daughter's name. He grinned hearing her name come out of Veronica's mouth. It was strange feeling as though his whole opinion of her had changed in the two minutes since he had found out what she did for a living. "As long as you don't post it on social media, take any pictures you like. There are more new ones in that portfolio." She pointed at the large rectangular art portfolio leaning against the wall next to the easel and checking the slowly loading status bar.

"Just for Gloria, I swear. I don't even have a Facebook page," Officer Burdick said, smiling as he pulled his phone out of a back pocket and clicked a quick picture of the half-finished painting in front of him first. Then he started to flip through the collection of paintings in an open black portfolio on the floor to the right. He went through them slowly, one stiff page at a time, pausing to take a picture occasionally. She should care about the possibility of the images being leaked, but the officer was more cooperative now than he had been all afternoon, and anyway, she liked the way he smiled when he talked about his daughter.

Gillian didn't seem distracted by the mention of Veronica's renown and instead studied some of the older charcoal and chalk pictures on the walls. It was funny how each creation could spark feelings in the person viewing it, but it brought the artist back to the moment she made each stroke, and sometimes, if she tried very hard, she could remember how she felt as the brush or chalk touched the page. It was almost like time travel.

The computer dinged, and every head in the room whipped over to look at the computer, reminding them why they were really there.

"I found it," Veronica called. Officer Burdick gently closed the portfolio and put his phone away reluctantly, as though he could've looked at the wordless pages of a children's picture book for the rest of the day. The officer stood by Veronica's side, leaning over slightly to get a better look at the screen. Gillian didn't even try to get behind the desk. She stayed in her spot, arms crossed in front of her, watching their faces as though she could see the video just by witnessing their reactions.

The recordings always started at midnight, but Veronica quickly clicked to the very end of the file so they could work backward instead. Using the rewind button, she backed through the afternoon thirty seconds at a time. The camera was focused on the crib, and the only time there was a flicker of movement from the doorway was when Officer Burdick stepped inside and located the camera. Other than that, even their own visit was marked with no more than a few shadows flitting over the crib's mattress and a murmur of conversation from the hall.

"Oh, it has sound?" he asked, straining to hear.

"Yeah, you need it on?"

"Couldn't hurt. Why don't you rewind to the last time you know someone was in the house and see what we can find."

"Well, I got the call at 3:55 p.m. So I'll go back to that time and see what's going on." Veronica dragged the bar backward, making the numbers flash, reducing before her eyes, nothing changing in the room but a flutter of a curtain when the air turned on for a cycle. She stopped the rapid decline when something dark flashed across the screen, but it ended up being a fly that had decided to rest on the lens of the camera. Officer Burdick shifted, and it felt as if she was losing any extended patience she'd gotten from her status as his daughter's favorite illustrator.

When the numbers on the screen matched the time the call from the alarm system had come through, Veronica slowed and then stopped. With one very short nail, she tapped at the volume button and let the recording play and leaned in till she was worried her breath would cloud up the computer screen.

The grainy gray image made her think of Sophie. How many hours had Veronica spent watching that crib through that screen through that camera? Today the room was empty and silent and still.

With Burdick leaning over behind her, his body heat arched across the thin barrier between his stomach and her back, and that gross, sticky feeling she'd been trying to escape while outside in the sun came back instantly. Thankfully, Gillian had settled in the overused armchair Nick had stolen from his frat house, giving Veronica more space than if both visitors had been staring and breathing and expecting. Gillian looked at home there, and when she was silent, she really was a chameleon that could melt into any scenery, patient from what must have been endless years of waiting for someone else to go first.

The security footage played at the slow, methodic speed of time passing. At first Veronica held her breath, sure she'd see something or someone, but once the alarm went off and blared in the background, she knew that they'd missed their chance to catch whatever set it off. There was no shadow or crash or really anything during those fifteen minutes before the alarm or even in the minutes after the siren whirred in a deafening cycle. Nothing but that fly and the emptiness of Sophie's room.

"Eh." Officer Burdick made an unsure sound and stood up.

"Come on, we only looked once," Veronica pushed, starting to panic. What if they were wrong? What if someone *had* been there and now the officer would leave and she'd be alone in a house with an old woman and a baby? She messed with the control bar and skipped back again, twenty minutes this time. "Maybe I could rewind it and go through in double time or . . . or get out the headphones and see if we could hear more?"

"I don't think there's anything here." He shrugged and rolled his shoulders, stretching after leaning for so long.

Veronica pushed "Play" and let the video play back at double speed, ignoring his comments. The fly sped from the side of the room, the curtains fluttered faster as if the fan in the air conditioner had been turned up to full blast, but still nothing out of place.

"Ms. Shelton, it's probably best to finish our walk-through and then let you ladies get on with your day."

Veronica ignored the officer and returned to her watching spot, poised over the keyboard.

"I'll bet you it was that damn fly. Anything can trigger those sensors if it gets hit just right," Officer Burdick offered, this time with sympathy in his voice, as if he were talking to a child who wondered how Santa got into her house when they had no chimney.

The tense energy of worry and curiosity had sucked out of the room, and Veronica started to feel the uncomfortable prickle of embarrassment with the unfamiliar eyes of the officer and Gillian looking at her as though she were crazy for thinking a fly was someone in her daughter's room. The gray screen kept flashing ahead on fast-forward, leaving Veronica half-hypnotized and half-desperate. Something. She had to find something. They couldn't go away yet. Not till she was sure . . .

A flash of light on the screen caught her eye.

"There!" Veronica slammed the space bar on her computer, pausing the image. With careful precision, she dragged the toggle back just a fraction of an inch, rewinding a matter of seconds, removed the double-speed feature, and pressed "Play." It was brief, so brief you could miss it if you blinked, but it was there, she was sure of it—a bright flash like a glass reflecting the sun. "See, right there."

Officer Burdick had made it halfway to the hall. He turned slowly on the balls of his feet, the leather of his boots squeaking against the paint-spotted ceramic floors. He didn't want to look—Veronica didn't need to be a people pleaser to read that look on his face—but he was going to appease her. She was probably the closest thing to a celebrity he'd ever seen.

"Here, sit down. I'll show you. It's there. I promise!" Veronica stood swiftly and pointed to the chair. When he settled in, she quickly rewound one last time and pressed "Play."

The image staring back at them was the same as it had been for the past twenty minutes, but off to the right side of the screen, coming from where the door would be, a brief but bright flash of light. Her hand darted out and stopped the video again.

"See! In the hallway. Someone was there. I'm sure of it." She placed both palms on the paper-covered desk, staring at the side of Officer Burdick's face. He turned the swivel chair slowly until he faced her, frowning.

"I'm sorry, Ms. Shelton. I think it is time for me to go. If you notice anything unusual, give me a call." He fished a crisp white card out from behind his overused notebook and held it out to her between two fingers. "Obviously, if it's an emergency, you should call 911."

He stood and brushed past Veronica with an air of finality and authority that seemed official. But she wasn't having it.

"What do you mean *if* I notice anything? I just showed you *something*. That flash of light on the screen. Someone was there." She pointed an accusatory finger at the computer. "You can't just walk away. You've gotta—dust for prints or something."

The officer shrugged, put the card back in his pocket, and then kept walking. Veronica followed him out of the room, the papers lining the walls lifting, reaching out as if they wanted to touch her, their angry whispers following her into the hallway. He didn't stop. Instead he bypassed Sophie's room and headed down the stairs, his boots shaking the pictures on the walls. Small and light on her feet, Veronica followed him, nearly slipping on the polished wood at the bottom of the stairs.

"I'll call your supervisor. I'll bring in the video. You . . . you're gonna be in big trouble if you don't help me . . ."

Officer Burdick stopped by the door and turned to face Veronica. She nearly slammed into his chest, the momentum that had carried her down the stairs still driving her on full-steam ahead.

"I'm sorry, ma'am, I didn't see anything in the video. Not the first time, not the second time, and definitely not the last time you went through it." He retrieved his business card and held it out again, shaking it this time. "Take it. You can email me those video files if it makes you feel better. You can even copy it to my supervisor. His name is Captain Dan Carpenter. I'm sorry I couldn't be of more help, Ms. Shelton. I really am a big fan."

She started to protest again, but Burdick's eyes had a soft, pitying quality that made the fire inside Veronica dim to a low simmer. He wasn't going to do anything. Even if she emailed the captain—they'd probably all laugh at the quirky artistic lady and make fun of her in the break room. She took the card.

"Thanks," she said generically. "And tell Gloria I said hello," she added, hoping that this whole story wouldn't end up on Twitter somewhere. He put his hand on the doorknob.

"Will do. She's gonna be so excited to know you live in our town. She's gonna be Mia for Halloween this year, you know."

A warmth spread through Veronica's chest that felt something like pride. Sometimes, working in her studio alone, she forgot that actual children loved Mia and thought of her as a real person.

"Please bring her by for trick-or-treating. I'd love it."

"Yeah, I think she'd like that. Thanks." Officer Burdick opened the door, and a moist rush of hot air washed over her and filled the still coolness of the foyer. He took one step out the door and then turned around so quickly Veronica took a step back out of shock. "Hey, quick question. I know I probably shouldn't ask, since you weren't even supposed to show me those illustrations, but—Is there a new character in this next book? I mean, I didn't see Mia in any of the paintings, just that other little girl."

Her forehead rippled, and she looked at the officer out of the corner of her eye. "Other girl? I'm not sure what you're talking about. Those are all paintings for Mia's Travels. Same characters as always. They're unfinished, though, so maybe that's why they feel a little different." She wanted to add that they were due a month ago and she had at least a month's work left, but she kept that anxiety-raising detail to herself.

"Oh, yup, that's probably it." He nodded and pointed at Veronica as if he'd just figured it all out. "You probably didn't color her hair yet, 'cause all I saw was that little blond girl. Guess I'll have to wait till the book comes out, eh?" He gave her shoulder a friendly tap and then wished her a good afternoon one last time before heading down the front steps.

*Little blond girl?* Veronica shook her head as she shut the front door and locked it, first on the doorknob, then the dead bolt. She was starting to wonder if Officer Burdick was even fit for duty. He must be messing with her, a quick revenge for "wasting" his time with this extended call. Preoccupied with the strange comment, she typed in the code to rearm the alarm system and headed back upstairs, suddenly wondering why Gillian hadn't followed them down.

With slight but swift steps, she rushed up the staircase, passed Sophie's room without a second glance, and then returned to the sanctuary of her studio. Gillian was still there but not sitting on Nick's old chair anymore. No, now she sat on the floor, legs crossed in what had to be an uncomfortable pretzel, her purple shirt gathering up at her sides, making it look more like a tent or a blanket than a wearable garment. All around her were full-color paintings on stiff cotton sheets. She seemed lost in the magical world on those pages.

"Thanks for your concern, Gillian, but I'm going to call my mom and tell her the coast is clear. I think it's time to make dinner and pump for Sophie and . . ."

Gillian lifted her gaze from the page in her hand to meet Veronica's stare. "You have a real talent, you know that, right? I mean, I wish I could do anything in my life half as well as you draw."

"Everyone has something they do well." She brushed the compliment aside, adding silently, *Like you could probably hug your baby or change his diaper.*

"No, no, this is special. Everyone has small talents. This is something . . . spectacular."

"Oh, Gillian," she sighed, not sure how to communicate with someone so eager to be kind but also so slow to pick up social cues.

Veronica stooped down, her runner's knee crackling, and started to gather papers. They were out of order; she could tell that right away, even without looking closely. The page numbers were added later, but she used a coding system that kept them in order and gave an official date and signature on each original. She tapped them gently with the palm of her hand and then held out the pile to Gillian so she could place the last page on the top.

"Thank you, but these are for my job, so I would feel better if we put them away for now," Veronica said, determined to be patient with at least one person in her life. Gillian, her sweat fully dry and face cool, was returning to what must be her normal, pale coloring. She carefully placed the painting on the top of the pile.

"I'm sorry, did I overstep?" Gillian got up on her knees with a grunt after two pushes off the floor. "I sometimes do that. I'm working on it. It used to drive Carl, my ex, crazy. 'Quit while you're ahead,' he'd always say." She gave an odd chuckle as if the asshole statement from her ex were actually funny. "I'm not just saying it, though . . . I really do like your artwork, especially those. I'm going to have to look up your books at the library." She grasped the edge of the desk and pulled herself to her feet.

"I'm glad you liked them, but these are unfinished." Veronica finally looked down at the pages in her hands. Each stroke brought back a memory from the past six months that she had pushed and struggled through while creating these pieces.

Well, maybe she didn't remember every stroke. In the middle of the happy woodland scene, with Paco the trusty dog sitting silently and staring at what should be her master, she saw it. Not Mia, the bright, brown-eyed eight-year-old with long dark hair and a russet skin tone that Veronica had perfected after mixing and layering paints for weeks with her first book. Instead in the middle of those fantasy woods stood a small blond girl, perfectly painted and shaded, her back to the reader, hair and skirt trailing behind her, one sparkly boot lifted as if she were running.

"What the hell?" she whispered to herself and held the picture up as though more light might remove the confused panic from her chest. "Who touched my painting?"

Gillian started to say something in the background about never meaning to hurt the pictures and just wanting to see them closer because Veronica had let Officer Burdick look at them . . . but her desperate explanations trailed off in the background as Veronica took the top page off the pile and placed it in the back of the stack, revealing the next scene, a nighttime road in Paris, lined with yellow streetlights and the Eiffel Tower peeking out in the distance.

Once again, the scene was right, the dog was right, even the empty space where the words would one day go was right, but running down the road with her back to Veronica was the little blond girl, caught in a game of tag or late for her bus. The image frightened Veronica, and she wanted to make the girl stop before she fell down or got hurt.

Any sound from the room sucked out and the papers on the walls and Gillian's near-panicked presence faded away. For only half a second, there was a flash of a memory. Her favorite rounded sable paintbrush in her hand, dipping into a mixture of yellow and brown with a touch of white to get the honey color just right. When it touched the page, the cotton fibers drank in the watery colors like the desert sand when it rained. She shook her head. That wasn't *this* picture and this little girl. That memory was from when she'd been commissioned by one of her old college friends to paint a portrait of her niece for a Christmas gift. Wasn't it?

Veronica's pulse raced even harder than when she thought there was an intruder in her house. She pulled the Paris portrait off the top of her pile and let it fall to the ground. If she didn't paint it, then who did? On the next page, the setting carefully constructed and painstakingly painted, blurred, and all she could see was the girl, the one the officer had been talking about.

"What in the world?" she whispered, a high-pitched whine in her ears causing her to wobble on her feet and reach for the desk to steady herself. Confused, scared, and suddenly weak at the knees, she let the pages slip from her fingertips and cascade to the floor in a fanlike pattern. Each page was beautifully painted, visually accurate, and appealing, but they had something else in common.

On every page there was a little girl running for her life.

# CHAPTER 9

Veronica flipped her hair back, the blow dryer sending the nearly dry strands across her face as though she were on a photo shoot. After her Friday fifteen-miler, she'd spent an extra ten minutes in the shower, buffing and shaving all the neglected areas that might show in the dress she'd laid out for the night. It was a simple maroon shift dress made of a T-shirt material that was comfortable but wouldn't be too out of place in Marco's, the nicest restaurant in town and the only bar on the west side of the city that wasn't a dive.

When her mother came home with Sophie safely in her car seat after the alarm fiasco, Veronica had decided to at least bring up the idea of going out with the waiting-room lady, especially since Gillian had sworn that she'd never tell a soul about the strange figure in all of Veronica's paintings. The rest of the week was spent secretly painting over the little girl in her illustrations. It was going to take some time to get them all taken care of, but even more daunting than the work was figuring out a way to ignore the insanity of not remembering painting the child to begin with.

There was a part of her that said she'd tell Lisa about it, but deep down she knew she never would, because just like waking up in the car with it running or the dreams of her wandering through an endless maze of hospital hallways, screaming, all of this made her look crazy.

Her last appointment with Lisa had ended with an emotional break-down. Next appointment she had to go in with some sort of explanation for escaping that sounded strong and not as weak as she felt. And all this drama was not the way. When she was trying to convince her mom that therapy was useless, she'd come upon a study that said 80 percent of people in therapy lie to their therapist, little white lies to make themselves look better. At the time, Veronica thought it was ridiculous to lie to the one person who was paid not to judge you, but now she got it. She wanted Lisa to like her and be proud of her, and more than anything, she wanted her therapist to think she was normal.

And tonight "normal" was what Veronica was going for. Her shoulder-length bob was easy to style, and after a few turns with the round, metal brush in the heat of the dryer, she was almost ready. A light coat of foundation, the broad swipe of shimmering eyeshadow, a quick dash of eyeliner and mascara, and she was ready.

The dress slipped on in a wave, smooth and comforting against her moisturized skin. She stood in front of the full-length mirror in her bedroom, which hung on the back of her bathroom door, and the woman who looked back at her was almost pretty. No, to be fair, she *was* pretty. The last time she wore this dress, Nick had put his hands around her waist and let the palms of his hands trace the swell of her hips. He had kissed her neck and whispered, "You are so beautiful." Back then she believed it.

Tonight she didn't feel beautiful, but she could believe that the petite blond woman in the mirror was pretty, and once she added a long silver necklace and pair of nude heels, she almost felt guilty at how amazingly new she felt. It was a lot like when she'd bought the formula: she knew she had to do it, she knew it would make Lisa and her mother proud, she knew anyone looking in from the outside would say it was "healthy" and "good," but deep down it still felt like a betrayal. The only way she was going to get out of the house today was to keep moving and try not to think about it.

On her way downstairs, she stopped and listened at Sophie's closed door, afraid to open it and ruin her chances of leaving the house tonight. The whoosh of her sound machine penetrated the wood, and Veronica put her hand against one of the panels and closed her eyes. Would she ever touch her baby again, carry her in her arms, kiss her flushed cheeks while she cried? She imagined walking into the nursery and running her hand over Sophie's wispy baby hair, dreamed of how it would tickle her palm and comfort her sleeping baby.

Veronica's eyes opened slowly as an idea sank in—maybe that was the answer. On Tuesday, she'd talk to Lisa about attempting to touch Sophie while she was sleeping. It was the first time in a long time that she had some sort of plan for making progress with Sophie. Until this point she'd focused on the few things she felt comfortable doing for her, like providing milk and buying supplies and watching to make sure she was safe while she was sleeping, but today she had a goal for actual interaction with her baby, and it wasn't her mom's idea or even Lisa's; it was Veronica's.

She'd keep the thought to herself for now; in fact, she'd probably wait a while to tell her mom, even if she was successful. The less pressure the better. Besides, Barb could live off the high of getting her daughter to leave the house after 6:00 p.m. for at least a month. That would give Veronica plenty of time to test out "Project Sleeping Baby."

Veronica pushed off the door silently and held on to the railing as she descended the stairs, still finding the raised shoes awkward after months of gym shoes and slip-ons. The clack of her heels against the wood floor brought her mother out of the kitchen. In her pj's already— a pair of cutoff sweatpants and a shrunken tank top—Barb put a hand over her mouth and made a choking sound.

"Oh, sweetie, you are so beautiful." Tears gathered in her mother's eyes, and Veronica tried to push away the flash of enjoyment at having her mom be proud of her for once.

"Oh, I don't know about that," she said, wishing she'd worn flats or a little less lip gloss. She didn't want to look as though she was trying too hard. Even if it was taking all her energy to hold it together, she didn't want anyone to pick up on that. When her mom sniffed and wiped away a tear from the corner of her eye, Veronica had to turn away, getting embarrassed. If she didn't leave soon, she might lose her nerve.

"I have an extra bottle in the fridge so you don't have to touch the ones for tomorrow, but if you need more . . ." She paused, remembering what Lisa said about taking a deep breath if she felt panic starting to build inside her. "You can always use the formula if you feel like you need to." She distracted herself by collecting her phone and the tinted ChapStick on the counter and tossing them into a small handbag she'd kept stored in the hall closet for far too long.

Her mother tried not to smile in the background, as if she were going to pretend this was just a normal night out on the town and she was the babysitter. But Veronica knew her too well. Barb was holding back tears again, just like when Veronica had brought home the formula.

"I'm not going to stay out too late, but don't worry about waiting up for me." She tossed the thin strap on her shoulder and dared another look at her mother, who was leaning against the counter. She had no more tears but was still unable to remove the silly grin from her face.

"You stay out as late as you want. I'll hold down the fort."

"It's only one drink, Mom, and I don't think Gillian is exactly the party-animal type. I'll be back before midnight, I'm sure."

She nodded silently, raising her eyebrows. "You do know how to call an Uber, right?"

"Ma!" Veronica snagged her keys off the counter and tried to keep her own growing smile hidden. "How do you even know what an Uber *is*?"

"How out of touch do you think I am?" Barb waved at her daughter. "I'll call *you* an Uber if you can't figure it out."

"I got it! I got it!" Veronica said, enjoying the temporary playfulness. She turned the brass knob on the door that led to the garage and stopped before shoving it open. "I love you, Mom," she shouted over her shoulder, and then walked out toward her car, swinging the door closed behind her before she could hear an answer.

As she drove through streetlight-lined roads, enjoying the whoosh of her tires on asphalt, she let herself take account of all the feelings swirling around inside her. Usually she ignored them, or better yet numbed them with her work, or occasionally a sleeping pill on the list on her pediatrician's website of safe medications while breastfeeding, but today she felt them, and it was terrifying but also exhilarating.

Between her plan to hold her daughter again and the improving relationship with her mom, there was something new, a little flame in her chest right under her breastbone that must be what hope felt like. Hope was one thing she'd been bereft of for far longer than she wanted to admit, but today there was a crack of light in the darkness, and she was heading toward it.

When she pulled up to Dave's Ale House, the small front lot was full. An arrow pointed to a lot across the busy Highway 42, with a sign underneath: "Additional Parking." Veronica clutched the steering wheel and dug her freshly painted burgundy nails into the soft leather.

She'd been riding on a burst of determination mixed with adrenaline, but even this small obstacle made her hesitate. It would take less than fifteen minutes to get home, ignore her mother's stares, and brush past Sophie's room without any foolish thoughts of beating back the panic and fear that went along with holding her; she could strip out of the soft dress, leave it in a pile on the floor along with all her aspirations for change, pop a sleeping pill, and climb into bed. A white Lexus pulled in behind Veronica, the bright headlights reflecting off her rearview mirror right into her eyes.

"The lot is full," she muttered to herself and the other driver at the same time, still frozen in a moment of anxiety. She'd hesitated for what must've been too long for the luxury car behind her; the driver backed his vehicle up and then drove past Veronica with a squeal. The driver was a man in a business suit, but beyond that she couldn't make out many details in the dark after being blinded by his headlights, though she imagined a look of disdain on his face as he pulled under the canopy in front of the restaurant. A man in a black shirt came out from behind a podium pressed against the brick facade surrounding the entrance. Valet parking.

Veronica had never done valet alone, but after watching the ease with which the suited man left his keys in the car and went inside with only a word or two exchanged and a casual wave with two fingers, she craved the convenience of not having to think or walk across dark streets or remember where she had parked when it was time to go home. With a gentle push of the gas pedal, she urged the car up the slight incline to the front door and tried to mimic the man in the suit.

She stood carefully as she exited the car, her dress shimmying down her thighs to lie smooth against her legs and her silver necklace hanging down to just above her belly button. With a quick hand through her hair, she snatched her clutch from the console between the two front seats and headed for the valet stand. After retrieving her ticket, she was free. It must be what parents feel like when they drop their kids off for the first day of school after a long summer.

Veronica's phone dinged in her purse as she walked through the heavy wood-and-glass doors. The restaurant was far nicer on the inside than she'd expected for an "ale house," which, to Veronica, sounded more like a bar. The room was dim with yellow-tinted lights along the side walls and an oblong light fixture with amber-colored crystals around it, adding to the warm tones. Down two short steps was a large bar in the same shape as the light fixture above it, with lines of bottles under the counter all the way around. Large, softly lit wooden tables surrounded the bar in an unpredictable pattern, all full of prettily dressed people eating beautifully plated food and drinking all kinds of fancy concoctions from elegant glassware.

If she painted the scene, she'd use oil paints to get the colors right and add the textures of the scene. It'd be a warm palette, with a few cool splashes where the light hit the bottles under the bar and if she included the woman in the blue dress and the man with the green tie. The irony of the warm colors was how cold the room was, the air on at full blast, bringing up goose bumps on Veronica's arms. A hostess dressed in a black tailored dress with no sleeves approached her quickly, a polite patience to her voice.

"Hello, table for . . . ?" She glanced around as though she was looking for a husband or friend to pop out from behind one of the tall wooden pillars behind Veronica. *No husband,* the little voice inside her mind whispered.

"I'm meeting a friend," Veronica offered quickly, scanning the room for Gillian but not having any luck at locating her spiky hair or modest wardrobe. "I can just wait at the bar."

"That sounds great. If you want to let me know what he looks like, I can send him your way when he gets here."

That spot in her chest cramped like it always did when she saw a couple walking hand in hand down the street or a family playing together at the park. It had gotten to the point that just seeing a man wearing a wedding band sent the ache of loneliness spreading through her like the liquefied aluminum one of the guys in her sculpting class used for his final project. It filled every space of any object he poured it into, settled into the cracks and crevices, and then hardened into mysterious and unique pieces of art. She wondered what the sculpture of her wounded soul would look like.

"I'm not meeting a man; I'm meeting a woman." Veronica paused when the hostess quirked up one eyebrow. "No, I mean, I'm not on a date at all. Just a friend. Her name is Gillian. Short brown hair, late fifties . . ." *Sad eyes, air of desperation* . . . Veronica shook her head. All other identifying features she could think of were not exactly kind.

"Well, I'll keep an eye out."

"Okay, thank you," Veronica said, and then turned and walked down the two short stairs toward the long wooden counter she'd been eyeing earlier. Trying to look confident, as if she was used to sitting at a bar alone, she picked out a seat in the middle of the mostly empty counter with a clear view of the door. Her phone buzzed again in her purse, and as soon as she'd settled into the most casual position possible on the high stool, she finally pulled it out. The message was from Gillian: Running a bit late. Waterproof mascara is a bitch. See you in ten.

Ten minutes alone at a bar. That feeling came rushing back in, the one that told her to run away. If she hadn't just relinquished her car to some stranger outside the front door, she'd be climbing in, speeding home, and calling it a night already.

*What do you do sitting at a bar for ten minutes?* She'd never been one to lose herself in her phone, and the internet held very few attractions now that she saw the dirty underbelly of all those smiling family pictures on Facebook. She rarely posted on her profile anymore now that her pictures or posts didn't match the shiny, beautiful standards of all the other mothers and family members she followed. No one wanted to hear about how hard it was to get out of bed or how she was seeing a therapist to help her learn how to be a real mom again.

In fact, one night when she'd gotten yet another one of those reminder posts from Facebook that showed Nick standing next to her with his hand on her swollen pregnant belly, she'd deleted all her pictures from her profile but two. Now all that remained was a cover photo with Nick and Sophie in the hospital right after twelve hours of labor resulted in a perfect eight-pound human. And then her most current picture of Sophie eating solids for the first time, green mush spread over her face like clown makeup, as her profile picture. Veronica slipped her phone back into her bag and took another look around the ale house.

The room was enthralling enough for a few more minutes of observing, and if she could get her hands on a pen, like maybe the one behind the bartender's ear, then she could start sketching the way the amber slats of hanging glass overlapped and tapped against one another when the bartender rushed underneath, but only when he rushed, like when she sat down and he offered her a drink. But not when he moved slowly, like when he poured her a gin and tonic and slid it across the lacquered wooden surface of the bar. The move made her feel as if she were in the Wild West, and she was halfway tempted to lift the glass, chug it in one gulp, and say "Yee-haw!" or something as she choked it down. Instead, she sipped it and nodded politely and went back to watching the glass and plotting a way to ask for the bartender's pen.

"What's so interesting up there?" a deep voice from Veronica's left asked, making her jump, heartrate skyrocketing. It was the Lexus man, or at least she thought it was. Lots of men were wearing nice suits in the restaurant, but this suited man was familiar, from the way he tucked his tie into his buttoned suit coat to the way his face crinkled on one side when he smiled at her. She stiffened when she realized it was Mark from the therapists' waiting room. How could she run into him again? It was a small town, but not *that* small. God, was he following her? She tried to ignore the paranoid thought and focus on his question.

"Oh, the glass." She pointed up and took a sip of her drink through a cocktail straw, pretending she didn't notice who he was. Her drink was stronger than she'd expected, and she gave a little glare at the bartender, who must've thought she needed to loosen up.

Mark followed her gaze and ran a quick glance over the light fixture, but Veronica was acutely aware that his eye line returned to her face almost immediately.

"You don't remember me, do you?" he asked, leaning in. His voice was lower now and with a slight husk to it. Veronica hadn't taken the time to look directly at the man, but now she stared at him. There was more stubble on his chin tonight and a dreamy look in his blue eyes that had not been there under the fluorescent lights of the supermarket or in the dim corners of the clinic. This wasn't stalking; this was flirting. She blinked and fought a smile.

"Do you mean that I should remember you from when you passed me in the parking lot with your fancy car?" she asked, knowing she was flirting back and flinching at the realization. She tried to let the nice clothes, makeup, new attitude, and strong drink numb that nagging voice that felt disloyal.

"Oh shit, was that *you*? God, I'm sorry. I didn't mean to be rude; my tail was just hanging out in the street and it's a company car."

"Must be a nice company to give out such a nice car."

"I don't know; I've always wanted a hatchback Prius if I'm being honest." He put his elbow on the counter and gave her a playful smile.

"Hilarious," she said and rolled her eyes, trying not to be creeped out that he'd noticed her car and taking another sip of her drink. "Don't scoff at my choice of vehicle. It's not all environmental, you know. I also save tons on gas."

"Ah yes, that's right, Ms. Thrifty. I knew I saw a coupon book in your purse before."

"Yes, this drink right here was only thirty-five cents. Double-coupon day." She held it up and took another drink, the sting of alcohol lessening with every sip, along with the choke of her anxiety.

"There's something different about you today." He cocked his head and studied her, chin resting in his hand as though he wanted to know what had changed and why.

"Well, I *am* dressed a little nicer than the last few times we met."

"No, there's something else. Something new . . ."

Veronica took another sip, this time bypassing the straw and drinking directly from the glass, draining the last bit of fluid from the clustered ice cubes filling the base of the cup.

"How about another?" he asked, noticing her struggle to get any more alcohol out of her glass.

"I shouldn't. That was my first drink since . . ." She let the sentence trail off. At least he knew the truth already; that made it easier. Maybe that's why it was so easy to joke with him, to be her old self. He knew, and she didn't have to hide the fact that she was half a whole, that she had a little girl she couldn't hold and no husband waiting at home for her. He knew she went to a therapist, and she knew the same about him. In many ways, she was safe with him. "I'm still nursing, and I have to skip a feeding when I drink."

Mark shrugged. "If you're going to have to pump and dump anyway, then why not indulge, am I right?"

She snorted, surprised. "You know the lingo?"

"It hasn't been *that* long since my daughter was a baby. Her mom nursed her for almost eighteen months. Sometimes I thought she'd be ten before we got her weaned."

Even with the new attitude and slight intoxication, it still stung to hear about a mom who was so successful with nursing that she couldn't get her baby to stop. She took a breath and pushed down the feeling of shame.

"Well, I don't usually talk nursing with dads, but I'm glad you understand. And I guess I'll take one more." She held up one finger, feeling sure she'd regret this decision later. Mark gestured for the bartender, and Veronica got brave. "In case you don't remember, I'm Veronica."

"Oh, I remember. I'm Mark DeVenuto, in case you didn't read my card. Nice to meet you—again." They shook hands, more like fingertips squeezing fingertips, and then let go, and Veronica let him take over ordering their drinks and then watched them being prepared. She knew he was really interested in her; it was an old instinct from the days of going out dancing with her friends in New York. The way he couldn't take his eyes off her for more than a second and the way his mouth was more than willing to smile when she told a joke. It was a relic of a feeling; it felt uncomfortable but also familiar, like when her favorite pair of shorts were inevitably a size too small after a winter of treadmill runs, and if it weren't for the help of her cocktail, she'd likely be too full of guilt to continue the conversation. But it did feel a little good, and the worries hit her subconscious and slid down like rain on a windshield.

When the last lime was spritzed into the drink, Veronica took the glass gladly, this time taking a long drag from the slender black straw before putting it down.

"So tell me about yourself, Veronica," he said in the vacancy her silence left. He said her name as though he'd been waiting anxiously for the opportunity.

"You know a lot. Like, way more than most people." She tried to make a joke out of it, but it was true. He knew secrets only her therapist, mother, and a few trusted individuals knew. What else could she possibly share with him?

"Okay, okay, let's not go into all the deep stuff again. How about this—How was your week?"

She laughed loudly enough that the bartender turned around, stunned. Veronica quickly stared into her full glass. "This is not the week to ask that question."

"Yeah?" he asked, leaning in till she could smell him like she had when he reached across her in the supermarket. "Well, let's start with that tidbit. Sounds—exciting."

"Yeah." She nodded, sipping on her drink. "My alarm was tripped this week, and the police had to search my house. It was crazy. I think those alarms are meant to make the burglar go deaf as a punishment for breaking and entering."

Mark's forehead creased, and he lowered his voice in concern. "Wow, so, are you okay? Did you lose anything?"

She shook her head, still annoyed that not only had Officer Burdick not seemed interested in her case or the video on her computer, but neither had his supervisor.

"Nah, I don't think so, but it was still creepy. The alarm was from Sophie's room, so I don't know. I'm still a little on edge. This helps tons, though," she said, holding up her glass to Mark in a mock toast.

"I guess alcohol does have its upsides," he agreed, his laugh sounding fake and the concern returning to his features. "Have you thought about increasing your security level? Do you have motion sensors or cameras?"

She took another sip and coughed a little after swallowing it down too fast.

"I really have a pretty basic plan for now, but maybe it is time for an upgrade." She felt brave enough to look at Mark now. "What in the world would someone want from my house? I mean, I'm not fancy or anything. Anyway, I don't get it. And the police could hardly care, so maybe I'm overreacting. I tend to do that."

He shook his head and pushed his glass away from him, still half-full. "This sounds more severe than that. Listen, I have a friend in the security business. If you ever want someone who will take you seriously with this stuff, why don't you give me a call?"

Veronica was tired of talking about herself and feeling unsettled at the weight of Mark's concern. Why did he seem to care so much about her and her life? She wasn't sure if it was flattering or disturbing. She knew almost nothing about him.

"I'll keep that in mind," she said, and then added, "So what do you do in that suit, Mark? You seem to know a lot about home security. You an undercover cop or something?" Veronica's head spun a little, and a calm warmth came over her, as if she'd just had hot cocoa after playing in the snow. She'd looked at his card before, but now a comforting fog filled her mind.

"Uh, no." Mark coughed and rolled his eyes. "Nothing quite so exciting. I'm the VP at MDB Bank. The suit and car are just for show; I'm not really that big a deal."

"Sure, sure, sure." She tried to sound playful.

"No, really. I feel like I'm coming off as some kind of huge ego-maniac. Bravado and vehicles aside, I'd really like to get to know you better." He put both elbows on the counter and held his glass at the apex where his hands met and then looked at her through the window his arms created. "That lady is always talking to you in the waiting room, so I can't seem to get a word in, but I've wanted to talk again since we ran into each other in the supermarket. I can't believe my luck finding you here."

Despite the drink she'd been sipping on, Veronica's mouth went dry. Mark was handsome, and it wasn't just the suit. His dark hair was still combed into a perfect part even after a day of work and running his hands through it at least five times since he sat down. And those hands were strong. They reminded her of Nick's, only a little larger. Actually, that was Mark, like Nick but a little larger. He was taller, and his suit filled out more in the chest than it would've for slender Nick, but he had a smile that made you think you were the most interesting person he'd ever met and eyes that held a depth she wanted to uncover.

He was interesting to look at in a lot of ways, and the proportions of his body made her think of drawing models of different body types in college. During figure drawing she'd learned to mute the part of her brain that looked at a body as something to be attracted to, but tonight, with the soft hum of alcohol in her veins and clouding her mind, she couldn't stop wondering what it would feel like to touch his hand. Would it be warm or cold from where the drink pressed against it?

Veronica looked away from Mark's pressing deep-blue eyes and swallowed against her dry tongue, scrunching her eyelids together. This was not like her. She couldn't look at another man, not seven months after Nick died and maybe not ever again. She ran her thumb over the back of her ring finger on her left hand. She took in a sharp breath. It was missing. Where was it? Maybe she forgot to put it back on after her shower? She'd never forgotten—never. Why did she forget today?

"I'm sorry, Mark, I might be making assumptions, but . . . I'm not ready yet. In my heart, I'm still married. I know it sounds crazy, but I can't help it." A lump was forming in her throat. She'd forgotten her ring. What kind of wife was she? The tears gathered in her eyes, but she tried to blink them back, terrified by the idea of crying in front of this man. But instead of pushing her further for a date or even continuing their flirtatious banter, he sat back on his stool and put his drink down.

"Veronica," he said in a deep and warm tone, "I think it's beautiful that you love so deeply and loyally. Your Nick was a lucky guy. My ex couldn't even remember she was married before our divorce much less after. You must've been a good wife." He said it as though he'd just made the discovery.

"I don't know about that," she said, wishing it were true but knowing she could've been a better wife in a lot of ways. She'd been average at best, and there had been some explosive arguments over the years. Just because she loved her husband and missed him didn't make her perfect, but why did she need to share any of that with him? Veronica opened her mouth to say . . . something that made sense. It was easier shutting everyone out; this being-nice thing sucked.

"I . . . ," she started, but the stool to her right wobbled, and a small soft hand was on her back.

"I'm so sorry I was late." Gillian. Finally. Veronica smiled with relief, and it must've shown, because Gillian immediately glanced at Mark and sized him up with her eyes, starting when she seemed to recognize him. At first Veronica thought Gillian was going to make a comment, but instead she refocused on her friend. "I have a reservation. Let's get to our table and get you some food."

Veronica nodded at Gillian and then turned to get her drink and say goodbye to Mark, but he was already walking away. On the counter there was a white card; this one was upside down with a personal message written on the back. Veronica palmed it, not wanting Gillian to know she'd been mildly flirting when she played the role of mourning widow so often. Mark disappeared into the crowded dining room, and Veronica couldn't seem to locate him as she followed Gillian and the hostess to their table.

How was she supposed to feel about their discussion and about the part of herself she hadn't connected with in so long? Should she feel guilty . . . or relieved that she could even find the woman part of her again, the part that flirted and found men attractive? Surely in bed later she'd regret it—the drinks, the smiles, the laughter. But right now, she said yes when offered a glass of wine and no when asked if she wanted dinner, already feeling a little nauseated. She smiled as Gillian talked about Christopher, nodded when she talked about her divorce, and, most of all, pretended that she wasn't secretly dying to read the message on the back of Mark's business card through it all.

# CHAPTER 10

*Don't hesitate to call. —Mark*

Veronica looked at the card again and then flipped it over to the familiar front. She hadn't looked at it very closely the first time he gave it to her at the supermarket, didn't even care about the bank logo at the top or his last name, but tonight she took in every detail. She'd been shy after Gillian's loud realizations about Mark, but soon found that the alcohol and the relief at having someone to talk to trumped embarrassment.

"Are you going to call him?" Gillian glanced at her from the driver seat of her 2003 Civic, stepping on the brake in several short jerks till they stopped at a red light. There was a piece of tape over the indoor light switch, keeping it in the off position, and all the slats on the air vent in front of Veronica were broken off, leaving a gaping hole shooting out lukewarm air. If she wasn't feeling nauseated before, after drinking more than she had in nearly eighteen months, she was now.

"Call him? No. No way." She covered her mouth, wishing that she'd at least eaten something before drinking two gin and tonics and two glasses of wine. Her head was spinning, and the thrilling comfort of the early effect of the alcohol was starting to turn into an angry visitor who had stayed too long. The world blurred around her, and she focused on all the wrong things, like how the crack in the door handle pinched her palm when she closed the car door and the length of the red light that she swore was half as long last time she went down Main Street.

"I've always thought he was handsome in the waiting room, but tonight he was really charming, don't you think?" Gillian smiled, the one glass of wine she'd had with her dinner merely having a calming effect. Apparently, it wasn't just Christopher's twenty-first birthday they were celebrating; Gillian's divorce was also very recently official. It was more than Veronica had signed on for. She'd said drinks and bristled at the idea of having a full-blown dinner with the woman she had nothing in common with. Plus, dinner meant she had to stay. Drinks meant she could walk out the door at any moment. She watched Gillian eat as Veronica nibbled on bread, but as she loosened up and they came to talk about Christopher's birthday and memories of his too-short life, there was some comfort in finding out that it was normal to kind of wither when you lost part of your soul.

Gillian was better at mourning. She said it was because she'd had more time to get used to the process, Christopher having passed from cancer two years earlier at eighteen, but Veronica still sat back in awe at the way Gillian could talk about her lost child without breaking down into fits of "life isn't fair" and "why me." Gillian didn't even feel bad for herself about her jerk of an ex and the drawn-out divorce she'd just been dragged through. Drunk Veronica suddenly hated sober Veronica for not being kinder to this flawed but strong woman. She slapped the door handle and flinched back from the pinch of plastic again.

"You shouldn't be so nice to me," she slurred. "I'm a bitch."

Gillian turned the wheel hand over hand into Veronica's driveway and put the manual stick shift into park.

"Oh, sweetie, you aren't a bitch."

"You said 'bitch.'" Veronica laughed. Gillian's sweet Southern drawl sounded out of place when wrapped around that word.

"Yeah, yeah. Tease me all you want, but you aren't a bad person, Veronica." She shifted her body so it turned sideways in the seat. "Carl worked in Tramway when Christopher was little, before he started working road construction. Anyway, he was one of the animal control officers that took a skunk out of someone's attic or whatever. One day he had a call about a coyote with an injured leg limping around this really up-class golf course, so he went out to trap it and bring it in to see the vet at the wildlife preserve. When he got there, it had a piece of barbed wire wrapped around one of its back legs and hip. Every step he took, it dug in deeper, and it kept getting caught on tree trunks and shrubs, just tearing the little thing to shreds.

"One of the groundskeepers had been trying to trap the creature all by himself and had it cornered between two buildings and the chain-link fence by the pool. Carl said the creature was bleeding and frantic and snapped at anything that even came close to touching it. The groundskeeper kept staying stuff like, 'We just wanna help you,' and other stuff, but of course the wild animal had no idea what he was talking about.

"After checking out the situation, Carl went back to the van to get some supplies he knew he'd need to trap the thing alive, but while he was gone, he heard this horrible scream. Carl ran back and found the groundskeeper lying on the ground, the coyote on top of him, jaws around his neck. Carl had to shoot it. The groundskeeper almost died on the scene, severed his jugular, eventually lost his arm from an infection.

"When Carl got home, he sat Christopher down and gave him a very serious talk about how an injured animal is the most dangerous kind—even the gentlest of creatures will bite or scratch when injured and trapped. He told him that it takes a trained professional with the right tools to get it right. That coyote would be alive and the groundskeeper would still have an arm if he had just waited for help."

It was hard for Veronica to keep up with all the pieces of the story, but the image of a seething coyote, bleeding and wrapped in barbed wire, was vivid and for some reason almost too familiar. She ran her hand over her face and through her thin shoulder-length bob, the nausea making her want to escape almost as much as the story did.

"How does any of that make me not a bitch? You deserve a better friend than me. I can't be a friend to anyone right now. I can't even hold my own baby, Gillian. I can't help you."

"Help me?" Gillian chuckled softly, her soft midsection rising and falling with the laugh. "Sweetie, I'm the one helping *you*. You are the injured coyote. You are hurt, lovie. Of course you are snapping and snarling and tripping around aimlessly. You are trapped in barbed wire, and it hurts worse the more you try to get out of it, and you try to bite any hand that tries to help you."

Veronica hesitated, her clouded mind halfway getting the metaphor but also not liking it, wanting to get out, wanting to lie in her own bed and go to sleep and forget the hard parts of that night and maybe even forget the way Mark's smile made her feel and how nice it was to have Gillian as a friend.

"Well, if I'm the coyote, then you are the groundskeeper. You don't know *how* to help me; that's Lisa's job, and if you aren't careful, I might hurt you. I bite. I maim. I ruin everything good in my life."

Veronica snatched her purse off the floor of the car and yanked at the door handle with no luck, popped the lock, and tried again, desperate to be free of the rush of warm air in her face, the sad duct tape she was tempted to yank off the switch, and the sympathetic smile on Gillian's helpful face.

"Veronica, I'm sorry. I didn't mean to . . ."

Veronica slammed the car door hard behind her and stumbled on the driveway. The hot summer night didn't bring any relief to the bile rising in her throat. The house seemed miles away, and each wobbly step on her heels made Veronica feel as though she were going to fall off a fifty-foot cliff. With very little effort, she slipped out of the nude heels and stepped into the cool grass of her front yard. Everything seemed easier as she tiptoed through the lawn and then dashed up the rough wooden steps to the rubberized welcome mat. There were only four things in her clutch purse: a tube of tinted ChapStick, a wad of cash, her phone, and her keys. Gillian had gotten Veronica's car from the valet and moved it into the parking lot of the strip mall next door with promises to help her retrieve it in the morning. That seemed like a really good idea, since Veronica was in no position to drive or walk or even open her front door.

With some extended effort, she worked the dead bolt and broke the seal to her front door, the alarm beeping and starting the two-minute countdown to put in the code before alarms went off. Gillian's headlights shone through the front windows, leaving wavy shadows through the foyer and formal sitting room.

*Damn it—she waited till I got inside to leave,* she thought, skipping annoyance at Gillian's unending kindness and diving right into frustrated fury. Gillian really thought *she* was going to find the special magical way to help Veronica? Nah, no one could help her. No one. She closed the front door quickly, hoping Gillian finally got the message and would leave her alone.

The house was dark and quiet. Her mom must've gone to bed hours ago. There was one "welcome home" light left on in the kitchen like her mother used to do when she was a teen and would go out to a party with friends. She loved that light as a kid; it let her know that even though her mom was asleep, she was waiting for her to come home. Tears built up in Veronica's eyes. She'd been a bitch to her mom too. Worst daughter ever. Used her like a slave, yelled at her for doing everything wrong, blaming her for her father leaving, not even trying to get help. Why did her mom even want her to come home? She should've left the light off and bolted the front door.

Veronica dropped the clutch on the side table in the front room and missed. It fell to the floor with a loud clack, her smartphone still inside. Another fail.

"What an idiot," she told herself, holding the wall for support as she headed into the kitchen. Pulling harder than she meant to, Veronica opened the cabinets under the sink and grabbed the half-full bottle of cooking wine there. She'd felt stronger before, when she was drinking with Mark, talking to Gillian. She just needed another drink, get rid of the nausea; get rid of the guilt and the pain. The bottle clanked when she set it down on the counter.

"Shhhh," she whispered. If she wasn't careful, she'd wake up Sophie, and then her mother would wake up and see how stupid drunk her grown daughter was.

Sophie.

Veronica untwisted the cap on the bottle and took a long swig, not even tasting the thick fluid as it rushed down her throat. She broke the suction, liquid spraying out from the corners of her mouth, which she wiped away in a sloppy swipe.

Yes, Sophie. She was asleep upstairs just like when Veronica had left. She could try now. She could try to touch her or at least pull up her blanket or smooth her hair. Something.

Veronica reapplied the lid to the wine bottle the best she could and then turned off the light in the kitchen and made her way in the darkness to the stairs. There were thirteen wooden stairs with a carpet runner up the middle; she'd counted all thirteen every day, both ways, for five months. At the top was Sophie's room. She placed her foot in the middle of the runner on the first step, counting and planning.

One. Two. She'd open the door. Three. Four. She'd walk into Sophie's room and force her heart to not pound with anticipation. Five. Six. Seven. She'd walk over to Sophie's crib and look inside. Eight. Nine. Ten. She'd place her hand on Sophie's back and feel her breathing through her little cotton onesie. Veronica paused; the top of the stairs was so close. She could dash up them in one giant leap if she really wanted to, but if she was being honest, she felt a little too tipsy for any kind of superhero gimmicks. Her head was already spinning nearly as much as her stomach was churning. She had to do it now; it was her only hope. She held her breath, tensed the muscles in her legs, and lurched forward. Eleven. Twelve. Thirteen.

On the landing at the top of the stairs, Veronica turned and faced Sophie's door. It was time. Tonight she'd hold her daughter. Tonight she'd make Nick proud. Tonight would be the start of the rest of her life.

# CHAPTER 11

The sun played against Veronica's closed eyelids, a reddish-orange light breaking through the darkness of her oblivion. She'd been asleep, but she was sitting up, her arms folded across her chest and shoulders chilled by the air-conditioned room. Even through the barrier of skin, the light hurt her eyes and made her head pound between her eyebrows as if a nail were driving deeper into her forehead with each waking moment. She went to rub her eyes with her hands, but a soft blanket met her face instead. It smelled of Sophie's special laundry detergent and felt like the well-worn flannel shirts Veronica's father had abandoned when he moved out and that she used to wear on cold days in Massachusetts.

The chair swayed beneath her, and Veronica suddenly realized where she was—Sophie's room. She was sitting in the rocker usually reserved for her mother during feedings. With a quick squint, she tried to make out whether Sophie was awake or not but couldn't keep her eyes open long with the morning sun pouring in through a rebellious opening in the middle of Sophie's blackout curtains. There were no little cries or whimpers, not even the shuffle of a baby rolling around or soft sigh of wispy breaths. Either she was asleep or her mother had already gotten her for the day.

Shielding her eyes as effectively as possible, Veronica scooched to the edge of the rocking chair, away from the burning slat of light, and opened her eyes. As she'd suspected, Sophie's bed was empty. The sheet was crisp and pink despite it being laundry day, and Sophie's special blanket lay on the floor at Veronica's feet. She leaned over to pick it up.

It was comforting between her fingers, and she placed it in the crib where Sophie would normally be sleeping, with little to no anxiety. She was in her daughter's *room* right now. She barely remembered it, but she crossed that threshold and sat in the rocking chair that she had avoided for so many months.

Had she touched Sophie last night like she'd been planning? The evening went fuzzy after she got home, and besides a slow ascent to the second floor and grand plans for fixing all the hard parts of her life in one drunken moment, she couldn't seem to make out what had happened once she got to the top of the stairs. Obviously, it had been something good, very good. Just the thought of crossing the threshold into Sophie's room was usually enough to bring on an anxiety attack and prompt her to go run for a million miles till the panic went away, but not today. Today she felt rested and calm, almost normal.

It was time to test this feeling out. Maybe between the therapy and the decisions about nursing and having a night out with a friend and, oh my God, had she been flirting with a man at the bar? A little, mischievous smile nibbled at the corner of Veronica's mouth. She wasn't proud of the flirting, but if it was a sign that she was starting to recover, she'd take it. Without a watch or her phone, she guessed it was early morning based on the sun's position and the feeling of the silent house. It was like her house could tell her the time of day just by the sounds it made when a breeze hit its siding or the mild temperature before the sun hit its full arc in the afternoon sky.

Today the feeling was early, six, seven at the latest. Sophie was usually still asleep till eight, always needing a full twelve hours, but maybe today she'd woken up early because of Veronica's late-night visit, or there was always the possibility of a growth spurt changing the course of her nighttime endurance. Why hadn't her mother woken her, though?

That was the only question that still nagged at the edge of her pounding brain.

A chill went down her spine. This was too familiar. Empty crib. Quiet house. Missing baby.

She shook her head. That was seven months ago, that was in the Broadway house, that wasn't today. No one took Sophie out for a drive; there wasn't going to be a tragic phone call at the end of this search. She refocused. Usually Barb would go downstairs and make breakfast with the morning news programs blaring, but this morning when Veronica perched at the top of the stairs, it was silent down below. She'd set up a small Pack 'n Play in her mom's bedroom once Sophie got old enough to crawl. Sometimes Veronica was sure that her mother would put Sophie in it with a bottle while she got a few extra minutes of shuteye, but she didn't have a camera in her room, so she couldn't prove it. It wasn't Veronica's favorite thing, but she'd learned that there were times she had to give her mother her way, especially since Veronica wasn't able to do any of these important things for her own child.

Barb's bedroom was at the end of the hall, just after Veronica's studio and before the master suite. It had a private bathroom and shower; well, it used to share the bathroom with the art studio, but her mother had insisted that she have her own bathroom if she was going to be living there long-term, so they sealed up the door to the studio, and now it was so covered with drawings it was hard to even see it anymore.

She knocked lightly on her mother's door. "Ma," she whispered. "Ma!" she added with a little fervor, listening for any movement inside the door.

Nothing but a sleepy silence from inside the room. Using her lightest touch, Veronica turned the doorknob and opened the door with a slow, careful swing. The room smelled of her mother, in a good way, the way she smelled when she used to pull Veronica in for a snuggle when she was a little girl, or more recently when she stood by her in the kitchen while they made dinner. It was a smell that was more like a hug than a scent.

Barb lay on the far side of the queen bed that was arranged against the middle of the side wall. Sophie's playpen was obstructed from view by the bed and the mound of blankets that made up her mother. Barb's snores were soft and played like the constant hum of a sound machine.

Veronica was surprised by the gush of relief that filled her when she saw Barb sleeping so deeply. Maybe it was best if her second attempt at touching Sophie was without Barb's eyes watching her, eyes that would be filled with a hope she was always unable to hide. And inevitably, those same familiar eyes would be filled with sorrow if Veronica failed, as she had so many times in the past.

If this was real, if the anxiety was abating and Veronica was on the cusp of holding her daughter, soon she could pick her up and carry her to Barb. Veronica imagined her mother's shocked surprise if she came in to put Sophie in her swing after a nap, only to find her wrapped up in Veronica's arms, nursing.

She felt a touch of anxiety, raised heart rate, heat crawling up her neck, tightness in her shoulders and chest that very quietly whispered, "You don't *have* to try . . . You can wait . . ." But the symptoms were mild enough that she could use the breathing Lisa had suggested. Slow breath in counting to five. Another five count as she breathed out, staying as silent as possible to keep from waking her mom. It was time.

It only took a few noiseless steps to make it to the foot of the black wrought-iron bedframe. The taupe-colored playpen peeked over the top of the comforter, and Veronica felt the flutter of worry suddenly shift to anticipation. She was going to hold Sophie, and this time—she'd remember it. Veronica ran her palms over the rumpled skirt of her dress and patted at her hair like Sophie would have an opinion about her personal style and hygiene.

"Sophie," Veronica whispered. "Mommy is here, sweetie." She put her hands on the edge of the playpen and peered in, hoping for a smiling baby but also wondering if it would be better if she was asleep. Her nails dug into the soft canvas-like fabric, the padded bar pressing against her fingertips, and a short gasp burst out from her mouth. Seven-month-old Sophie wasn't asleep. She also wasn't gumming smiles from the bottom of the bed.

Sophie wasn't doing anything, because Sophie was gone.

# CHAPTER 12

"You've got to calm down a little, Ronnie. You're hysterical," Barb said for the twentieth time, head on her fists, robe loosely tied around her waist with a belt. She held out her hand for the phone Veronica was clutching with a death grip. "I'm calling Lisa. Is she the kind of therapist who can give you pills? Val thinks you need something to help you calm down."

Her mother's phone was upstairs. Veronica had taken it away when she wouldn't stop texting her nurse friend, Val, instead of doing something to help her. She kept saying that Val thought this had to be a misunderstanding, just like Barb did. That Veronica needed to calm down. She kept saying that if Veronica had been drunk last night and was able to go in Sophie's room, maybe Veronica was the one who moved her. Barb suggested she check the car seat in case she tried taking her for a drive or maybe the stroller on the back porch, but they were all empty. Veronica couldn't care less what Val thought anymore.

"Calm down? You've got to be shitting me. My baby is *missing*!" Veronica took her eyes off the front yard for a brief second to glare at her mother. She refocused on the phone she squeezed in her hand. Her mother remembered putting Sophie down for bed and turning on the baby monitor, but after that—nothing but sleep. She hadn't taken the baby into her room when she awoke in the morning, and there had been no midnight feeding. The night was apparently as blank and dark for Barb as it was for Veronica.

"I know. I know," Barb repeated, wringing her hands in front of her repeatedly, like she could rewind time if she just twisted hard enough. "It's going to be okay. It has to be okay."

"It's not going to be *okay*, Ma. You used to say that when your boyfriend Chuck would smack you around—and it was never okay. You are not a very good judge of okay." Reality clamped over her mouth like sweaty, fat hands. If it weren't for the thick blackout curtains she was gripping, she'd be on the floor of the living room.

"Hey, this is not my fault." She'd expected to hear some trace of tenderness in her mother's voice, but instead it sounded like anger. "I was trying to help . . . if you had gotten help sooner. If you would've tried even a *little* . . ." Barb rushed forward and put her hands on Veronica's shoulders from behind. "Look at me."

Her grip was heavy, painful, like blades straight into Veronica's bones. How could this happen again? Last time, she lost Nick and Sophie was saved only by her car seat. It was like the "powers that be" had decided to rebalance history, like Sophie should've gone to heaven with her daddy and now their little girl had wandered off in answer to death's call, leaving Veronica all alone. She had to call 911. She had to get help.

"My fault?" She shrugged her mom's fingers off her shoulders and spun around, almost getting tangled in the fabric of the curtains. "I can't talk to you when you're like this. I need to call the police."

Barb stumbled backward, her eyes wide and mouth open like she didn't know what to say. Veronica took an aggressive step forward, heat rising into her chest and flicking up to her cheeks, turning her vision blurry, like she was looking through flames.

"I'm sorry, Ronnie. Don't be mad at me," Barb whimpered. "You're right, this is my fault. I'll fix this. I'll call the police. You rest," she said, taking a few steps backward, heading for the stairs. Each word seemed like it'd been specially chosen, as if she were tiptoeing through a floor covered in razor blades.

"Damn it, Ma," Veronica shouted. "Can't you listen to me for once? If you want to help, go look for Sophie. I'm her mom, not you. I'm going to make the call." Despite the fire inside her, Veronica's voice was ice-cold. She lifted the phone in her hand and flipped open the phone app.

"Please don't be mad at me," her mother begged again, clasping her hands in front of her. It reminded Veronica of how toward the end of Barb's marriage to Veronica's father, Barb used to grovel at his feet, pleading for forgiveness in order to end a drunken tirade. Back then, though Veronica should've been upset with her father for being an abusive asshole, she was far more disturbed by the doormat her normally self-assured and strong-willed mother became when faced with the men in her life. Now that same gesture made Veronica cringe.

"I can't take care of you right now," Veronica slashed at the air. "Go call Val or wait in your room or something, but I can't carry you through this. I need to find Sophie."

Her mother's face crumpled, and she took a few more steps in Veronica's direction, the robe falling off her right shoulder, hair pressed into a flattened poof on one side like someone had blown off only half of the dandelion head.

Veronica couldn't watch her mother any longer. It brought up too many memories. Too many feelings. It made her want to run away, but she couldn't, because she had to find her daughter. She had to find Sophie, and there was no running away from that. She glanced down at the phone in her hand. Seeing the numbers 911 typed out in the cold, bricklike font made a sickening realization come over Veronica: This was not a mistake, and they weren't just going to find Sophie hiding in the hamper or crawling around in a neighbor's yard. She was a baby. If she was gone—someone took her.

With the fingers of one hand still wrapped in the stiff fabric of the formal sitting-room curtains and the other around the waiting phone, Veronica felt her knees buckle. She collapsed, hitting the ground with the full force of her weight. The impact reverberated through her bones and up into her jaw, where she bit into the soft sides of her tongue. It must've hurt, but she couldn't seem to feel it. Blood filled her mouth, and the hot, coppery liquid made her gag and dribbled out the side of her mouth.

"Oh, baby, you're bleeding." Barb rushed forward, arms open, like she was going to scoop up her adult daughter in her arms and make her boo-boo better with a cartoon-adorned Band-Aid. But she wasn't her mother's baby anymore, and Barb couldn't make any of Veronica's pains go away with words or adhesive bandages.

"Stop. Just go away, please," she begged, wiping at her mouth and flinching at Barb's open arms and the mascara-tinted streaks on her mother's face. That sight and the thought of Sophie in the arms of a stranger, hungry and scared, turned every thought and feeling into a growing fireball. Part of Veronica wanted to melt into her mother's embrace, ask for forgiveness, and truly believe everything really would be okay . . . but she wasn't that naive.

"Let me help you, Ronnie." Barb kept her slow advance, creeping closer and closer to Veronica, her voice filled with the panicked sound of pleading. Veronica needed her mother's groveling to stop so she could *think*, so she could call the police, so she didn't feel so terrible about who she was as a mother and daughter. "Let me help . . ."

"I told you to leave me alone!" Veronica shouted, and as her mother's hands touched her, the burning ball of fury that had gathered inside her, dense and blazing hot, raced down her arms to her palms, which landed with full force against her mother's chest. The sound was loud and hollow, like beating on a bass drum. Barb let out a loud "oof" and stumbled backward, this time her feet tangling in the sash of her bathrobe.

Veronica covered her face with her hands, the mascara still lingering on her eyelashes crunching against her fingertips. A sickening crack bled into her ears and another deep moan and then—nothing.

She'd heard that sound before, or one very like it, the night her father left. Veronica had been in bed when he came home from a night at the bar. The fighting started, and Veronica had waited, thirteen years old, with the covers pulled up to her nose, for the crescendo of her father's angry accusations and her mother's crying and begging. But that night the begging never came. Just a crack and a thump and a door slamming and an uncomfortable silence that was out of place in their home. Her mother woke her in the morning with a cut over her eyebrow and the news that her father had gone away. Veronica lay in bed, feeling the emptiness of her father's departure.

But now it wasn't the monster of her childhood that had hurt her mother; it was the monster inside Veronica. That was the thing about the demons inside: They were hard to see and even harder to escape. Just like when she was a child, Veronica pulled her comforter over her head. Her mother would come any second and whisper that everything was going to be all right just like she had when her father left. She had to.

Veronica sat in the same spot, having pulled the curtains around her in a protective skirt. They fell like waves of pale curls down her shoulders as she waited for her mother to pull her out of her hiding place, but she never came. She was a grown woman and not a child, so how could she sit there and wait? She had to help her mother. She had to find Sophie. Oh God, what would Nick think of her if he were watching right now?

The tears were there, hiding, in the deep recesses of her eyes. If she let them come, if she couldn't keep inside this sense of impending doom, then she would dissolve again. When she lost Nick she'd melted like salt in the rain, leaving nothing behind but a useless puddle. As Veronica's panted breaths made her head spin with lack of oxygen, rebellion surged inside her.

"You are pathetic," she whispered to herself. "You are a failure. You can't do anything right." She pressed the heels of her palms into her eyes till it felt like she was pushing her eyeballs back into her skull, completely disgusted at who she was. It was almost as though she were watching her pathetic display from the other side of a TV screen. Why didn't the character get up and try to fix at least *one* of her problems? "Get up, you idiot," she yelled at the screen. "Get the hell up and *do* something. *Do* something."

The rage she'd felt toward her mother intensified as she yelled at the frozen woman on the screen in her mind. It was a fury she wasn't used to letting herself feel. But she wasn't upset with her mother for being weak or wanting to solve all Veronica's problems, not really. This red-hot hatred was what she felt for herself.

There had to be a way to start over, do this right. There had to be a way to leave her hiding place in the curtains, to hold her mother's hand and find Sophie together. There had to be a way to not turn into a puddle. This time she would turn into something strong, something unstoppable. This time she would be a tsunami.

"Mom." Veronica took her hands off her eyes and batted at the fabric surrounding her, trying to get back out into the open. "Mom, I'm sorry. Are you okay?" She scrambled to her knees and finally broke out of the prison of stiff damask and billowy voile. "Mom?" Veronica called again.

The room was empty, and the house was quiet, no telltale footsteps or voices echoing down the stairs. It was eerily silent and reminded her of the night Nick had taken Sophie for that ride in his car. Just like that night, it was too quiet. Too still.

*Damn it, Mom,* Veronica thought, feeling a pang of betrayal and abandonment. *Why did you leave me too?*

Standing, she tried to breathe like Lisa had taught her and remember for Sophie's sake that her mother was right—she needed to remain calm. But she wasn't calm. Sophie was gone. Her mother was gone and probably injured, maybe even severely. And even though Veronica had told her to leave, she didn't think it would happen so quickly, so fully, so entirely. Now all she wanted was to make sure Barb was okay and to get the chance to beg forgiveness and ask her to stay.

The sun was coming in through the windows stronger now, illuminating the still-dim room. A slat of light from the partially opened curtains highlighted the overstuffed, high-back couches and reflected off the glass coffee table in the center of the formal sitting room. Time was slipping by. She shook her head and tried to refocus. She was alone, and that was terrifying and left her feeling empty, but her mother must've left of her own accord, which meant that she couldn't be hurt *that* badly, at least physically. Emotionally was another story, but Veronica would have to tend to those wounds after she got help finding Sophie. All this overthinking had to stop. No more hiding, no more worrying about moms or monsters. It was time to find her daughter. If she was going to be a tsunami, she needed to act now.

With the phone lying on the floor in front of her, Veronica leaned over to grab it and call 911. Even as she worked through all the steps to getting her phone open again. The 911 she'd typed earlier was still on the keypad, and taking another step out of the curtains, she hit the "Call" button.

"Hello, 911, what's your emergency?" a friendly voice asked on the other line.

"My daughter is missing," Veronica blurted. "She's seven months old. She was in her crib last night, and then this morning . . ." The words were a jumbled mess and didn't make sense even to Veronica. As the operator asked questions about where Veronica lived and Sophie's vital stats and offered empty reassurances, Veronica paced the living room, wondering if her mother had been right. She should've made the call. Maybe she'd come in and take the phone and Veronica could fade into the background, just like she had in Sophie's life.

When the line went quiet and Veronica was alone again, waiting for the officers that would soon be at her door with lights and guns and answers, her foot hit something wet, her toes sinking farther into the expensive Oriental rug, immersed in the wetness. Instinctively, she picked her foot up and yanked it back, and it fell into the slat of light that illuminated the whole scene grotesquely.

Blood. Her foot was covered in it.

She held back a gasp and wrapped her arms around her midsection, her stomach lurching. Was that her mother's blood? Veronica slapped her foot back down on the carpet and wiped as if she were trying to get dog poop from her shoe, but there was more there, a circle of blood on the carpet about the size of an orange, and a trail of crimson leading down the hardwood of the hallway.

"Ma?" Veronica shouted. "Ma? Where are you? You okay?" She ran to the foot of the stairs and called again. "Ma! You up there?" She dialed her mother's phone number and held the phone to her ear. The trill of her mother's ringtone sounded upstairs.

She dashed up the stairs, but as she rounded the top, the ringer went silent and the phone went to voicemail against her ear. Veronica skidded to a stop in front of her mother's bedroom door. The room was empty—no missing daughter, no blood trail, and no mother. She raced into the bathroom and Veronica's bedroom . . . but her mother was gone.

What the hell? Where was her mother? Why was there so much blood? Holding the phone to her chest, Veronica leaned against the doorjamb of her mother's room and let the panic roll over her. The police would be there soon, and they'd have questions, more than the operator had asked, and Veronica wouldn't have very many answers. There were really only three things she knew for sure right now. First, her baby was missing, second her mother was gone, third there was blood on her floor and a lot of it . . . What would they think?

She'd heard of triage, taking the man with a severed finger before the kid with a broken arm. Missing baby before missing old lady. She had to move fast.

Veronica pushed off of the wooden door frame and slipped the phone into her bra. With a quick shift of a couch and some baby wipes for the droplets of blood in the hall, she could hide it until her mom came home and the police started to search for the stranger who had taken Sophie and not focus on Veronica, the only one in her family left standing.

# CHAPTER 13

Veronica toggled the rewind tab again and pulled it backward, making the numbers on the screen flash by in reverse order. A uniformed officer watched the camera's video recording over her shoulder as the sound of flashes popping echoed throughout the house. They'd been there for two hours already.

She told them that Sophie was missing from her bed this morning, about leaving her mother to care for Sophie the night before. They had her run through every detail of her night and returning home and then waking in the morning to the empty crib. Then she tried to explain why her mother was missing in action. She told them about the fight and even about telling her mom to leave but left out the physical confrontation and the blood on the carpet. She'd considered making up a story but decided instead to be as honest as possible, while leaving out any details that might make the officers lose focus. Veronica was heartsick about her confrontation with her mother, but she wasn't going to let an argument get in the way of getting help for her child.

But it wasn't easy to keep the investigation on track. When they found her mother's car missing but her purse and phone by her bedside, she could feel the tone in the house shift. None of it looked very good, even without the blood spot just waiting to be discovered under the loveseat in the front room. Not to mention that the most recent recordings from Sophie's room were blank and no alarm, inside or outside, had been triggered that night.

Veronica tried to tell the investigators that she'd turned the camera's recording function to live feed when she'd been reviewing the recordings from the break-in so that the footage wasn't automatically overwritten. And then she spelled out the details of the alarm, explaining it wasn't set for the night, because Veronica was supposed to have put in the code when she got home from her night out. But after a while, no matter what she did or said, there was always a barely veiled tone of suspicion lacing every question.

There were only two people Veronica knew for sure had nothing to do with Sophie's disappearance and that was her mother and herself, and she could already tell that the police had both of them on the top of their suspects list.

At least they were finally taking pictures of Sophie's room and lifting fingerprints. Maybe they'd get lucky and find one that didn't match the samples they'd taken from Veronica and from her mother's room. In an effort to keep the focus on who took her child, Veronica was trying to show Officer Burdick the anomaly on the recording from Sophie's room on the day the alarm went off, since it was the only recent recording they had to investigate. As her frantic mind was tossing the pieces together the best it could, it kept landing on this moment in time as being significant.

"Here it is!" She hit pause and gestured for the officer to look over her shoulder. The black-and-white image of an empty nursery sat frozen in front of them. She set the speed to half time and then pressed play. At first there was nothing but the slow-motion flicker of the curtains nipping at the frame. But then it happened . . . a bright flicker of light off in the corner coming from the other side of the room where the door stood open just off screen. It was brief even in slow motion, but after rewatching what she'd thought was the sun playing off the mirror hanging in the crib, it started to look like something else—something familiar—a camera's flash.

"I still don't see anything," the officer muttered, and started to stand up.

No one was listening to her. No one seemed interested in the fact that an alarm had gone off in her baby's room just four days earlier. They wanted to know if she'd seen Sophie in the crib last night; where her mother was; when she moved to town; where they could find a copy of Nick's death certificate, Sophie's birth certificate, hospital records; and other totally useless information. And of course they also wanted to know why there were open bottles of alcohol on the counter. She'd tossed them a box of documents she'd collected over the year and then convinced Officer Burdick to follow her to the computer, which they'd probably take into evidence soon enough, but she didn't trust them to look at the videos closely enough without her being there to help. He'd been on babysitting duty ever since the rest of the house got turned upside down.

"Right here," she said as she jabbed at the screen with her stubby nail. With a quick rewind and play, she showed the same scene again in half speed. At exactly 3:54 p.m., a flicker of light spread across the screen and then receded just as quickly. "A flash, like from a camera. Someone was taking pictures in my baby's room."

Officer Burdick squinted and leaned in closer. Veronica's confidence swelled. She finally had his attention. She toggled the bar back one more time and pressed play, this time reducing the speed another quarter. The film quality wasn't strong enough to show much detail in slow-mo, but the flash came through nice and clear.

"Well," he said, clearing his throat and standing up to full height, hands on his hips. "There was some light there, but I'm not sure . . ."

He looked at Veronica and then at the door to the office. "Let me go see if we can get someone with more experience to look at that file."

Finally. They were going to listen to her.

Veronica rewound the film three more times, once taking it one frame at a time. It was a camera's flash; she was sure of it. She shifted in the chair, the faux leather speckled in paint stuck to her nearly bare thighs sticking out of the dress she still wore from the night before. She probably looked like a huge mess, but she didn't care. Where was Sophie? Was she hungry? Who took her? Did they have diapers or bottles or blankets? Did they care if she was crying? Was she already dead?

Her brain spun in a thousand directions to consider every person she'd ever encountered as a possible kidnapper—like the babysitter she'd interviewed a few weeks ago or the cable guy who'd installed a receiver in her mother's room two months ago. Both knew the layout of her house. Both knew the age and sex of her baby. Both made comments about her daughter that seemed innocent and friendly at the time but maybe were a spark of something more. Something dangerous.

She would give anything to take back the past seven months of dysfunction and hold her baby right now, comfort her cries, nurse her, pat her back till she burped. "Please, God," she closed her eyes to the screen and the frozen flash and prayed, not sure whom she was even praying to, "Please let me see her again. Let me have another chance. Please."

Two officers entered the room, one tall, slender man with a buzzed haircut and one official-looking woman in a tailored uniform, bulletproof vest, and low ponytail at the nape of her neck. Her hand rested on her gun. Behind them was Officer Burdick. Veronica took them in, glancing at their faces for a clue as to whether she really was getting help. But the hard set of the female officer's jaw and the nervous shuffle of the tall officer's feet set a lump of cold coal in her stomach. They hadn't come to see the video.

"Mrs. Shelton, can you come with us?" The stern female officer yanked her head toward the door.

Two hours earlier when the officers showed up after her initial 911 call, just one at first and then a few more trickling in, finally it felt like half the squad was there, but they all had one thing in common: this sad, pitying look on their faces. It didn't help that Veronica was nearly hysterical, most words coming out in halting phrases with deep sobs between.

It wasn't until the first responders had gotten her a drink of water and a soft-voiced female officer in plain clothes explained the importance of clear and concise communication that Veronica was able to get her terror under control and explain what had happened with some sort of coherence. But even when she'd calmed down and started to explain the events of the past twelve hours and found the composure to take out her phone with shaking hands and pull up the most recent picture of Sophie, that look of pity didn't leave. They pitied her because they knew that if they didn't find her baby soon, that was the last picture she'd ever take of her baby. They didn't think she'd ever see Sophie again. She hated that look.

But Veronica now realized there was something worse than their pity. Because now that look of compassion was gone and something else was in its place. It was hard to put a finger on it, but it scared her.

"Is it Sophie?" She half stood up behind the desk, hope adding some buoyancy to her movements.

The officer put up her hand and patted the air. "No, no. I'm sorry, we just need to ask a few more questions. That's all."

Veronica took a deep breath and blinked rapidly, her contacts sticking to her eyeballs after being slept in. She could hardly hold back her frustration. Any distraction, any red herring would take them away from finding her daughter.

"Officer Burdick wanted me to show you something on my computer. Come here. I'll show you." Veronica waved her hand, the anxiety growing inside her, her skin humming as if it were charged with electricity, panic building in her back and chest.

The female officer nodded. "Yes, you can leave it there and we will definitely look." She took a step forward and put out her hand aggressively. "But you'll need to come with us now. Please."

Veronica looked at the screen and then back at the officers, then back at the screen, her hands balling up on the paper-covered desktop, defeat pouring over her like a bucket of cold water. She glared at Officer Burdick, but he was staring at the floor. They weren't going to look. Damn it.

"Fine." She slammed one of her closed fists on the table, grabbed her phone, and stood up, a shower of white papers cascading to the ground. With the computer still open and screen paused, Veronica walked into the group of stiff and stern-faced law-enforcement officers, hoping that one of them would get curious enough to watch. Burdick passed Veronica, entering the office as she was leaving it. He tried not to look at her, but she didn't break her stare, hoping she could compel him to continue the path they'd started on together, hoping she could pull one person to her side. But then he did meet her gaze, and any thoughts of having a like-minded helper in this man disappeared. All she saw there was disgust.

*What the hell is going on?*

"Did you find my mom yet? She was here last night. She knows more than I do. I was out at . . ." She almost said, "at a bar," but then thought better of it. They already asked about the bottle of wine on the counter and how many drinks she'd had at dinner the night before. "I was out at dinner with my friend Gillian."

They didn't respond, just walked behind her in silence as she went down the hall, passing Sophie's taped-off room and descending the stairs. There was a palpable tension in the dining room, and nearly a dozen eyes focused on her when she walked in. The number of official-looking people seemed to multiply exponentially, a fact that should have brought relief, but for some reason the more investigators and detectives that poured into her house, the higher her pulse jumped. The anxiety she was already fighting with every weapon in her arsenal was now sitting on her shoulders like an invisible specter that grew with every set of eyes that stared her down. She didn't trust that monster; that monster hurt her mother and made Veronica act irrationally. She had to shake it off, stay calm, do it for Sophie.

"Mrs. Shelton, so nice to meet you." A heavyset man in a tan suit with a bad comb-over stretched his hand out to Veronica. There was no going back; the uniformed officers that had escorted her to the dining room made a wall behind her, and the doorway into the kitchen was behind the detective. She felt like that coyote from Gillian's husband's story, injured, rabid, scared, and trapped. "I'm Detective Perry. I'm heading up the investigation here. Maybe we could find somewhere quiet to talk. What do you think?"

"I . . ." Her mouth went dry, and she had to swallow before trying again. She didn't want anything to do with this man. He didn't want to help find Sophie, at least not in any way that would actually work— she could tell that already. He had his own story in his mind, and she wasn't going to change it. "I already talked to Officer Burdick. I was trying to show these officers some . . . uh . . . a video of my daughter's room. There was a home invasion earlier this week, or I think there was because the alarm went off in Sophie's room, and then on this video . . . I can show you." She pointed toward the top floor of the house and tried to take a step back but ran into the tall officer.

"I would love to, Mrs. Shelton, but first I'd like to chat." His voice was calm and gentle, as though he were talking to a five-year-old who didn't want to go into kindergarten for the first time. "I have a few questions that Officer Burdick didn't ask you. I'm really hoping you can help me out."

She had no other choice. They briefly passed the living room, where it seemed the slightly askew furniture and the bloodstain underneath it hadn't been noticed—yet. One positive, but the only one she could identify, and by the time she reached the overstuffed couches, Veronica was shaking.

"You should sit down," Detective Perry said, pointing to the love seat as though he had lived there his whole life and Veronica was just visiting. "I'm sure this has been a very difficult day for you, but there are a few items we are finding very difficult to understand. Perhaps you could clarify a few details."

Veronica kept her feet planted and grasped her hands in front of her, her phone clasped between, to hide the shaking. They found the blood. They found it and now they thought terrible things about her. They thought she hurt her mother and maybe even her baby.

"Listen, this is getting ridiculous. You need to listen to me *right* now. Someone has taken my daughter. It's not my mom. It's not me." Her voice caught in her throat momentarily at the thought of her mother. *Triage,* she reminded herself mentally. Sophie first, then Barb. She cleared her throat, refocused, and continued. "That person was in my house five days ago taking pictures of her room. Probably preparing for this crime."

There wasn't an ounce of real concern in the detective's eyes, only a suspicious look that lingered there like the smoke over a cake after the birthday candles had been blown out. He walked past her and found his own place on the couch that was kitty-corner to the love seat he kept pointing to.

"You can tell me all about it when you calm down." He talked to her like he already knew every bad thing she'd ever said or done. He pointed at the seat again. "Come. Sit."

She would break that condescending finger if he kept pointing it at a seat she was never going to sit in. She stomped her foot, tired of being "calm," tired of being the only one who seemed to give a shit that there was an empty nursery upstairs.

"I won't sit down. All of you are sitting down on the job right now." She raised her voice, hoping the clump of useless detectives and officers in the dining room could hear her. "My daughter is getting farther and farther away from me! I called you to help me, not to have a coffee break in my dining room. I've yet to hear anything about an Amber Alert or . . . or . . . closing down roads or . . ."

She didn't know much about child abductions, but she certainly expected more urgency than she'd seen so far. They were getting distracted by all the wrong things; she knew it. They had to stop looking at her mother and start looking at the recordings and interviewing all the random people in her life that might have something to do with this crime.

Detective Perry nodded his head slowly like he was trying to process her explosion and then placed his hands on his thighs, his calm demeanor only stoking Veronica's volatile emotions further.

"I'll put this simply, Ms. Shelton—unless you'd like to sit down and tell me about your mother, we'll be heading to the station."

"I can't leave," she said, putting her hands together in front of her is if she were praying. "I need to be here for Sophie when she gets home. You'll have to drag me out of here, I swear . . . I'll lose it . . . I'll . . . I'll . . ." Veronica's volume climaxed again as she searched for any threat that might work against a police officer. Who *could* she call for help?

It didn't seem to matter anyway. Detective Perry continued his interrogation, ignoring her outburst.

"We don't have to go anywhere yet, Ms. Shelton, but like I said before—you have to answer some questions. Where is your mother?"

She laid her phone flat, hot after being clutched so tightly, and then cracked each knuckle in her right hand and repeated the action with her left before placing them against her thighs. She sat down, back stiff and brain frantic. She'd answer his questions, but he didn't want to hear what she had to say. He didn't want to help her, not in the right way, not in the way that would find her baby and fix this mess before Sophie was lost forever.

Detective Perry asked her questions about her mother and about how long Veronica had owned the house, if Veronica was on any medication, how much she'd had to drink the night before, who went to the therapist on the appointment card they'd found, and why the neighbors never saw Veronica caring for her child, just her mother. And most important, he pressed her for why Barb and her car were missing but all her personal effects still sat untouched in her bedroom.

As the answers lined up side by side, even she began to see the writing on the wall—they all thought she was involved. That was why the looks had changed and the questions were cutting rather than careful. They thought she had done it, and the more she listened to herself speak, the more she started to understand the doubt. She had been drunk last night. She'd come home in such a state that she didn't remember what had happened. Without the recordings, how could she decisively say that Sophie had been there when Veronica got home if she couldn't remember? And her mother . . . oh God, her mother. Veronica actually *had* been the one to hurt her, and once they found that blood and realized her story that was full of holes . . . could Veronica blame them?

Then a far more frightening question entered her mind: If they thought she had hurt Sophie, then how were they ever going to find the person who walked her darkened halls and took pictures of an empty crib? That was the person who'd come into her home while her mother was sleeping and stolen her precious child. How could they not see her baby was in danger?

As the questions swirled around her and the hopelessness grew, Veronica started to build another plan. She shook off the internal doubt and confusion and focused on what she did know. She hadn't hurt her baby. She might not remember what happened last night, but she knew that harming Sophie was beyond her capacity, drunk or sober. There was no doubt in her mind that her mother was just as concerned as she was about Sophie, and she felt strongly her mother had a good reason for walking out the door that morning, even if Veronica couldn't figure out what it was. That was where her list of what she knew ended—but it was enough.

The police were on the wrong path. Nick wasn't there to help find Sophie. Her mother's practiced hands were missing. So now it was her turn. Today she would be the one to take care of her daughter.

# CHAPTER 14

Detective Perry was one of those unpleasant individuals who acted like any extra movement he had to make took years off his life. Same went for the number of words in the interrogations he asked. Short, curt questions and annoyed grunts after each of Veronica's responses. He had her retell the story of Sophie's disappearance. He asked for all the infant's vital information again and then several queries about her missing mother's height, weight, age, mental state. She was waiting for the opportunity to talk about the newer people in her life—Gillian, Lisa, Mark—who may or may not merit suspicion, but they never got there. The conversation turned quickly to a pile of journals on the table, multicolored tabs sticking out on each side of one of the notebooks.

"Where did you get those?" Veronica asked, her fingernails digging into her thighs. She'd filled those journals while fighting through her darkest moments. She'd numb her pain by pouring it out onto the page, writing and drawing obsessively for days on end sometimes. The idea of strangers looking at those pages made her want to douse them with gasoline and toss them in the fireplace.

"In a box in the baby's room," Perry said as he tapped his fingers on the pile. He didn't even say Sophie's name, like she was just some generic baby that he cared about as much as a child who'd gotten tired of a doll. She swore she could smell his breath from the armchair next to the loveseat—cigarette smoke and coffee.

"I never said you could read those." Veronica reached across Perry's protruding belly, trying to regain possession of the books. Perry shifted his hand to cover the journals protectively.

"You gave us permission to search your house, Ms. Shelton; we found these in the process. They are very . . . interesting."

"They are *private*," she said, letting her hand drop but outrage growing inside her at the idea of that man reading her most private thoughts, almost like he'd set up a camera in her bathroom and watched her shower, shave her legs, and wax her mustache.

"There's some very interesting artwork in here." He faked a shudder. "Dark stuff. But what I found most interesting was your writing. You're not just an artist, are you?"

The words "just an artist" were said in the same way her father used to say them when she told him about her major in college. In fact, most people gave her that same skeptical, condescending look until she landed Mia's Travels. Her father was dead by then, but he probably wouldn't have been very impressed.

"Those were never meant to be read by anyone but me. Please . . . stop . . ." She put her hand out, asking for the books back, but Detective Perry wasn't moved. Ignoring her shocked request, he plucked the tabbed journal off the top of the pile, slipped his index finger between the pages, and started to read.

"'Sometimes I think it would've been better if she'd never been born. God, I wanted her so badly. I took those damned shots and I cried at each negative test, but once I got her—I failed her. If Nick were here, it'd be different. I know it would. Ma says time and therapy will help, but I don't even think I want it to. I deserve this. When her cries break through the sound machine and the ear plugs and the Tylenol PM, I know why she cannot be calmed. She wants her mama and daddy, but

Daddy is gone and Mama wishes she were by his side. That poor baby. My poor baby, with no mama there to hold her.'"

The room was silent. Veronica was frozen by the sound of her own words coming out of another person's mouth. Without hesitation he turned to another page in the journal and started to read again.

"'Last night I took out all my prescription bottles and lined them up,'" he read. "'How many would it take to end my life? Which ones would cross into my breast milk so I could take Baby Sophie with me across that sleepy abyss to the eternities? Would it be too hard for my mom? Would it be more generous to give her the opportunity to take my hand and join us in the blissful nothingness of death? Why is it so hard to make that final decision?'" Perry paused and glanced at Veronica, who was frozen in terrified shame. He didn't speak to her; he just continued reading.

"'I put the bottles away in my office drawer and locked it, not to keep me from making the decision but to save it for another day when the pain is worse and nothing but a handful of pills will make it so I can hold my baby again.'"

He closed the journal and looked at her with the unspoken accusations filling his eyes.

"Listen." Veronica finally broke the tense silence buzzing through the room. "I kept those journals so I could see how far I'd come. I don't feel like that anymore. Those are old. I never think about those things anymore. I'm not mom of the year, but I'm working on it. I love my baby. I love my mom . . ."

"Who is Lisa Masters?"

Hearing Lisa's name was almost a relief to Veronica. Lisa would vouch for her. She knew Veronica didn't want to hurt her baby. But then Veronica remembered what happened at their last session, how she'd run out of the door without paying her copay or saying her goodbyes. Could they talk to Lisa without Veronica's permission?

"She's my therapist," she answered, honest but brief. Veronica didn't feel like she needed to lie about seeing the mental health professional, but in response to her brevity, a darkness passed over the detective's features, deepening the wrinkles in his bloated face.

"I'm starting to think this would go better down at the station, Mrs. Shelton." Perry looked over her shoulder to another detective who'd walked in from the front room where the bloodstain was hidden. He made a few motions and seemed to have some kind of secret method of communicating through eye movements and head nods. Oh God, had they found it? She didn't need a decoder ring to know one thing: if she didn't act fast, then they'd never let her go, and if they did—it might be too late to save Sophie.

"I can't go yet . . . I . . . I . . ." Veronica thought through her options. Her phone was on the table, just fingertips away, and one name came to her mind—Gillian. Gillian would help her. Veronica just needed a little time.

"My boobs are full," she said, rubbing the side of her right breast with a grimace on her face. "I need to pump before I go anywhere. When Sophie gets home, she'll be hungry."

Detective Perry cringed and glanced away from Veronica's breasts at the first mention of nursing. He did the secret eye-language thing with the other man and then sighed.

"Okay, please go . . . pump." He managed to get the term out of his mouth and then swallowed hard. "I'll have a squad car waiting for you."

"Thank you." Veronica stood, picked up her phone, and headed toward the bathroom, where she would normally *never* pump. "All I need is a little privacy."

"Of course . . ."

⌒

As soon as the electric whir of the breast pump mingled with the bathroom's ceiling fan, Veronica texted Gillian with a basic explanation of the situation and an urgent request to meet her in the backyard neighbor's driveway. Unsurprisingly, Gillian didn't hesitate, and Veronica realized she'd had no other plan if Gillian had said no.

Once, before letting down her guard with Gillian, she'd mentioned to Lisa her annoyance with the needy woman. Lisa had said, with some reserve, "Everyone is in that waiting room for a reason. Just remember that."

She was just glad to still have her phone. Officer Burdick had asked if they could take a look at it early on when the officers had first started filling her hallways. Veronica had consented even though she'd been told she didn't have to without a warrant. At that point, she wanted to do anything she could to help the investigation but asked that they wait to take possession of the phone in case she missed a text from her mother or maybe even a ransom call. Her consent changed when Detective Perry started in with his aggressive line of questioning. If permission to search her house had led to these journals, what would they find on her phone that they could twist a million different ways?

She should've tried to get a change of clothes, but after twenty minutes of fake pumping while waiting for Gillian's arrival text, Veronica was afraid to show her face for fear of being whisked off to the police station. So she was stuck in her dress from the night before. Shimmying out of the three-by-three bathroom window would be difficult enough in a pair of yoga pants and a tank top, but currently pantless, she had to turn off the part of her that cared that her nearly bare backside was hanging out of a window and instead turn on the mom instinct that kicked in when you are giving birth and half a hospital was looking up your gown at a baby coming out of your hoo-ha.

She had very little going for her right now, and pants were the least of her concerns. First was the fact that the police, the actual police, thought she had hurt her daughter and had something to do with her mother's disappearance. They wanted to take her to the police station and lock her in a room where she'd be no help to her baby. What was even worse, no one seemed to care to look anywhere but in her direction, which didn't make sense to Veronica, because her mind wouldn't stop running through possible scenarios and suspects.

The most common narrative churning through her imagination was that it was a terrible masked stranger who had taken Sophie. The "why" in that scenario was ever changing: The worst thought was that she'd been taken for dastardly and base intentions, and the best was that she'd been brought into a home and family that would care for her, having taken her in a misguided attempt to complete them.

The next suspect she'd considered was her mother. With her disappearing act and odd behavior, Veronica had to at least think through that possibility. But it didn't take too much to snip her off the list, because even with all the negatives of her behavior, the shock on her face that morning when they'd found Sophie missing had been genuine; Veronica could see that clearly. She hadn't hurt Sophie, but that didn't solve the puzzle of where Barb went and why she hadn't returned.

To be honest, she didn't really have any solid guesses as to the reasoning behind her mother's disappearance other than that she'd been so badly stunned she'd run away, afraid of Veronica in a way she used to be afraid of Veronica's father and the other men she allowed to lay hands on her. If so, she'd have to either return home or end up in a hospital eventually. By then hopefully Veronica would've found Sophie and this whole mess would be cleared up from every angle imaginable.

*Oh God, please let Sophie be alive,* Veronica thought as she let go of the window frame and dropped the eighteen inches to the ground. When she hit, she immediately scanned for any officers, feeling like a fugitive. If she could make it through the backyard without being seen, she could get to the small grove of trees that separated her house from her neighbors' house, the snowbirds Stella and Avery, where Gillian would meet her.

Veronica had no shoes at this point, and when she'd glanced in the bathroom mirror before taking the screen off the window, she'd had a brief thought that she looked like a girl who was taking the walk of shame back to her apartment after a one-night stand. Ready for the next step in her escape plan, Veronica checked her phone and made sure it was pushed deep into the cup of her bra. Thankfully, she'd stashed two twenties in the small wallet attached to the back of it the night before in preparation for her evening out. It would be enough to get her some pants and a pair of shoes at least.

Her heart pumping faster than she thought possible, Veronica gathered all her nerves into her calves and curled her toes under into the thick crabgrass of her backyard, trying to remember what it was like when she did track in high school. Those races were for a medal and some pride at being called "the best," but this dash was for her kid, and no way was anyone going to stop her. She needed to find out more about the break-in last week, maybe with a call to the insurance company or research about other break-ins in the area.

More than anything she needed some space from the chaos inside that house. She was running from all the confusion and accusatory looks almost as much as she was running toward her self-led investigation. If she didn't hurry, they'd notice how long she'd been gone "pumping" and break down the door.

One very brief check of the surrounding area and she bolted forward, remembering the exhilaration of sprinting rather than the deeply satisfying burn of the slow and long runs she was used to nowadays. It didn't end up being very difficult to get from the safety of her landing spot by the house to the cluster of trees. The pine needles poked through the thin fabric of her dress and grabbed at her hair, but she shoved her body farther into the mash of needles and branches, not caring that they scratched at her bare skin and poked at her feet.

Taking only a moment to look back, she checked the rear of the house. The bathroom window gaped open awkwardly, like someone had carved an eye out of a socket, leaving an uncomfortable emptiness behind. If she'd been more prepared, more cautious, she would've tried to replace the screen or close the window on her way out. But once she got in that room after too many questions, every single one inching closer to the accusation that Veronica refused to hear, she didn't think through everything as clearly as she should have.

No going back now. Now it was only forward, to Gillian, and after that . . . Veronica wasn't exactly sure. But she'd figure it out.

The back of the house was still clear, and her window for a clean escape was closing rapidly. Not even looking back this time, she pushed off the pine-covered ground and sped around the perimeter of the yard, keeping a close proximity to the grayish-brown fence on the Kensingtons' side of the property. Thankfully, Stella and Avery had no fence of their own and no gate, so she burst through to the other side in less than a minute, and Gillian's Civic was waiting, the loud hum of a barely working air-conditioning unit sounding like a freight train in Veronica's rattled state. Still on edge, but with more confidence this time, Veronica took in a shaky breath, combed her fingers through her wild hair, and sped toward the parked car.

Gillian looked to be sleeping inside the car, the sweat on her forehead nearly a match of the streams down Veronica's face and in dark circles under her armpits. When Veronica reached the car, the door handle flopped uselessly under her fingertips.

"Gillian, open the door," she growled through a fake smile, tapping on the glass gently in a hope she could pull off "casual pickup" even while wearing no shoes.

Gillian started and placed a hand on her chest before leaning over and popping the lock manually. "I'm so sorry, sweetie. Come in!"

The endearment sounded so motherly, like Gillian had taken some parental interest in Veronica. She didn't want a mom right now. She used her mother, hurt her mother; she lost her mother, maybe even pushed her away so hard that she would never come back. No, she didn't need a replacement mom. She didn't deserve one, and she'd probably ruin that relationship too.

"It's okay. We should probably get out of here as fast as possible." She buckled her seat belt and took the moist phone out of her bra.

"Where do you wanna go?" Gillian put the car into drive and did a slow U-turn till they were pointed toward Route 15, not asking any further questions despite that all she knew at that point was that Veronica's mom and Sophie were missing and that the police refused to help. A part of Veronica's mind thought that it was crazy for Gillian to be so willing to help her, but another had seen the loneliness in that woman's eyes last night. Loneliness was a difficult affliction to remedy alone.

"I need clothes and shoes and a charger for my phone," she said, checking her power levels again—twenty percent and a red battery indicator.

"Walmart okay?" Gillian asked, turning on her blinker in an action that seemed far too normal to Veronica given the current situation.

"Yeah, it's fine." She probably had ten, fifteen minutes tops before someone would come looking for her. Running made her look guilty, she knew that, but the first twenty-four hours were the most crucial in an abduction case; that's what the detective said, right?

"Do you have a plan?" Gillian asked, glancing at her while also trying to watch the road. "Do you think you know who took Sophie?"

Veronica filled Gillian in about the video and the flash and mulled over the question for the hundredth time that day.

"Whoever took that video took Sophie. Only problem is that I don't know who took the video," she admitted, the sentence sounding almost like a surrender.

But then there was a twinge in her foot where she'd scratched it against the peeling bark of a tree root, and she knew that she hadn't sneaked out of the house and literally run from authorities to surrender to her own insecurities now. They needed more help. Gillian was willing and eager but didn't have many tools to provide beyond a half-broken cell phone. Veronica flipped over her phone, taking stock of what she had and what she needed from the small wallet attached to the back where she kept her driver's license and a few unused gift cards from her birthday.

Her gaze landed on a newer addition to the collection of cards and cash: a stiff white business card. Mark DeVenuto from the waiting room looked back at her when she slipped the card from its hiding place. Mark. He seemed smart enough; he said that he had a friend in security; he had some money, that was clear; and he was interested enough to offer his help. He'd have access to computers and maybe even have an idea of how to proceed. But most important, he was a dad. That meant something to Veronica.

"I have an idea," she said to Gillian, who was pulling into the Walmart parking lot. "I think I'm going to call Mark." She cocked her eyebrow as Gillian put the car into park toward the back of the side parking lot.

"You mean that guy that's stalking you from Stacey's office? Do you really think you can trust him?" Gillian unbuckled her seat belt and grabbed her wallet from the middle console.

"He's not stalking me." She paused and put her hand out to stop Gillian. "What are you doing?"

"I'll go—just tell me your sizes. First thing the cops are going to do is ask if anybody saw you. There are video cameras everywhere."

Veronica rustled through her wallet and retrieved a neatly folded twenty, feeling guilty about involving Gillian in so much of her dysfunction. She passed the money over. "Don't worry about style. Just get me a pair of medium flip-flops, a simple pair of size-two pants, and an iPhone charger if you have enough."

Gillian took the money and smirked in response to Veronica's softening demeanor. "Size two? They're going to wonder who in the world I'm buying those pants for."

Veronica looked at her, not knowing how to respond, not knowing if it was a joke or a serious concern about keeping their connection a secret.

The hesitation seemed to register with Gillian. "I'm sorry, no more jokes. I get nervous and don't know what to say, and I want to help. I really am worried about your little girl. I want to help you the best I can. Maybe Mark can help, but I think we need to see him face-to-face. Nobody would believe this kind of thing over the phone."

"Uh . . . thank you, Gillian," Veronica responded. She was already unsure whether Mark was going to think they were insane or call the police himself. But she had an underlying sense that he was the kind of man who would help a damsel in distress, especially a damsel in distress who had a little girl just like he did. Gillian went to open the driver-side door.

"I'll lie in the back seat." Veronica maneuvered between the front seats and over the middle console. "Try to go as fast as you can . . . um . . . please."

"Sounds like a plan." Gillian smiled, then silently corrected her facial expression. She looked right into Veronica's eyes as she settled into the back seat, her legs cramped up till they were nearly touching her chest. "We're going to find your little girl if I have anything to do with it. I promise you."

Veronica swallowed hard, trying to hold back tears. That was all she'd wanted anyone to say to her: "We will get your daughter back." Gillian had been the one to say it. As her one friend walked away, Veronica realized the woman was her greatest ally.

Now it was time to get one more.

# CHAPTER 15

Gillian came out of the store with a pair of stretchy pants that slid easily underneath Veronica's knee-length dress and a pair of sparkly flip-flops with the clearance tag on them. Along with a discount charger, a bottle of diet soda, and another bottle of chilled generic water, Gillian had only spent $15.37. With their small budget, Veronica found herself grateful that she found a bargain shopper to help her escape from the police.

The bank where Mark worked was only two miles away from Walmart. The police were probably looking for her by now; who knew what terrible accusations and labels they were tossing around. Crazy mom. Baby killer. But even with the cops on her trail, she was way ahead of them. No way they'd know about Gillian or her car, and neither woman had any ties to MDB Bank.

"Maybe I should just call him after all. It's Saturday. He might not be there." Now that they were sitting around the corner from the bank, Veronica was starting to panic. It was a fancy institution, one that gave out loans and had bank accounts for people with far more zeros behind their salary than she had, so she had never set foot inside, and now that it sat in front of her, she wished she never had to.

"I'm not gonna tell you what to do, darlin', but I know you better than this Mark guy, and even I thought you sounded a little crazy when you texted me." Veronica started at Gillian's admission. She was tired of people thinking she was crazy for wanting to find her baby. Since when did saving your baby from kidnappers make you insane? Gillian could read the outrage in Veronica and patted the steering wheel. "Now don't get all steamy. As soon as I saw you, I knew you were serious and needed help. I just think this man needs to see you. Plus, his card says nine to one on Saturdays. I can go in and get him if you're worried. Want me to do that?"

Although Gillian was a timid woman in general, she seemed to have more gumption than Veronica had given her credit for previously.

"No, you're right—it needs to be me," Veronica said, remembering the way Mark had looked at her the night before, like she was the most interesting person he'd met in a long time. She straightened her hair in the visor mirror and made sure there were no remaining pine needles embedded in her dress. With a pinch of her cheeks, a swab of her half-melted tinted ChapStick, and the last-minute addition of Gillian's wide-brimmed sun visor to hide her face, Veronica headed inside the bank to find Mark while Gillian sat in the car, waiting. "Wish me luck."

"You've got this," she said with a thumbs-up that would normally have made Veronica roll her eyes but today gave her a boost of confidence.

The bank was one of the largest structures in Sanford. Veronica appreciated the grand nature of the Roman columns out front and the wide, sweeping staircase that led to the front door. When she and Nick would occasionally go into Sanford for date nights or any shopping she couldn't complete at online retailers, she used to imagine what it would look like for someone to pose for wedding pictures on those steps or to paint the masonry like she had on her trip to France as a young art student. But it seemed a bit grandiose for her more recent tastes.

Today, as she looked at the columns and the twenty or so steps, she saw the beauty and the statement of power those architectural decisions conveyed. And it all made her heart beat faster as she thought about walking through those doors and asking to speak to a man she'd only talked to twice, then convincing that man to help her find her daughter.

The front doors were made of a greenish glass with brass handles that pulled open easily. *This must be what it feels like to be a bank robber walking into a bank for a heist,* Veronica thought, trying to locate the cameras while keeping her head down and face hidden under the massive visor. She knew someone must be there watching, but she was finding it hard to avoid detection while also trying to look as average as possible. It was difficult for Veronica to feel normal on any given day, but today she thought she must stand out like a tall man in a lineup.

As she looked around the grand lobby, there were teller stations to her right and open desks to her left, and in the back, she could see some glass-wall offices occupied by men and women in business attire. The desks to her left were empty, and one teller stood at her station, watching Veronica as though she was ready to have her last client before she went on her lunch break.

"Can I help you?" The teller waved to Veronica, encouraging her forward. Seeing very few other options beyond barging into the walled-off offices at the back of the bank or just yelling *"Mark"* at the top of her lungs, Veronica went up to the station where the teller was waiting with her half smile and held out Mark's business card.

"Yes, I'm looking for Mark DeVenuto." She wondered if it would be awkward to mention he was the VP at this location. Instead, she let the card speak for itself. "He gave me this card. I don't know if he's working today, but I wanted to stop by and see if I could have a conversation with him. Privately."

The teller picked up the card and examined it carefully. She ran her finger over the logo and then placed a fingernail underneath Mark's name, her lips twisted to one side.

"I'm sorry, but I don't think I know who this is. Is he new?"

Veronica knew very little about Mark. He had a child. He worked at the bank. He was interested in Veronica in a way that men other than

Nick had not been interested in her in a long time. He made her feel safe. That was all.

"You know, I'm not sure. I met him at"—she almost said "our therapists' office" but then thought better of it—"the supermarket, and he said that he might be able to help me with some issues I'm having and gave me his card. I thought I would just stop by, but maybe I should've called first." Veronica reached for the card, but the teller snatched it up and stepped back from the counter.

"Oh, no worries! I'm sure that I'm just confused. I'm new here myself. Let me go ask my manager. I am sure he would know better than I would. Not like we're busy here today or anything." She chuckled, gesturing to the empty lobby, and then walked away with a little bounce in her step. It was possible that a new teller would have no reason to interact with someone as high up as a vice president. Maybe this was her chance to rub elbows with the higher-ups? Veronica hadn't considered what she'd do if Mark wasn't at work. It seemed strange to find him missing. She'd never seen him out of a suit, so she was sure he didn't take a day off often. She shook the suspicious thoughts off. If she let those feelings take her over, she'd never trust anyone again.

Once the business card was gone, Veronica started to get nervous. This was her only idea. If getting help from Mark didn't work out, what would she do? They could go to the library and try to search on a computer for a specialist that could analyze the video, but it seemed dangerous and very low-tech.

She could contact her editor. They'd been working together for years, and Carol had been very helpful and patient through Veronica's roughest hours, but that would mean letting her office know about the drama in her life. Working with children's books meant keeping a squeaky-clean reputation, or at least keeping her less-than-stellar qualities under wraps. Mia's Travels was her paycheck; she couldn't risk that. Then again, she could always call Lisa, but Lisa would advise her to call the police. And there was no way she was going to put her trust in the police again.

As Veronica examined her options, a man in a suit of the same caliber and style as Mark's from the night before came up to the counter. But it wasn't Mark. This man was shorter, with less hair, and was wearing a clunky wedding ring on his left hand. He held Mark's card in front of him as though he were examining a hundred-dollar bill to see if it was counterfeit.

"Hello, Miss . . . ?" He paused, waiting for Veronica to complete the sentence.

"Jane. Jane Nickel," she said, almost cringing at the money reference that was completely unintentional.

The manager gave her a brief smile and then looked down at the card again and then back up at her. "I'm sorry to tell you this, but I don't know any DeVenuto. I can help you with any of your account needs. But first . . ." He hesitated and then placed the business card on the counter. "Where did you get this card?"

Veronica swallowed and tugged at the visor again, a newly developing nervous twitch. What the hell? A spreading desperation filled her chest cavity and clutched at her throat. Did he lie about where he worked?

There was no time to think about that with the bank manager staring her down. She was in a very dangerous position that could lead to the police showing up in a matter of minutes. She *would* find out about the man on the card, but right now she needed to get out of the bank and back into the safety of Gillian's car.

"I met a man at the grocery store. He said he could help me with some financial issues and gave me his card. I'm sorry. Maybe I have the wrong bank."

The bank manager placed his hand on top of the card. "This is our updated logo, new as of a few months ago, and the address is for this branch. I'm concerned that you may have been approached by a con artist of some kind. I am going to call headquarters and see if there's been some mix-up. I'm sorry, miss, I'm afraid you may have been scammed. Did you give this man any personal information, things like your Social Security number or any information about your bank account?"

The concern on the bank manager's face was real. His questions about her bank account sent a pit of dark tar churning in her stomach. She wasn't worried about her money; she didn't even have an account here. She was more concerned with why Mark DeVenuto just happened to turn up in so many places in her life. He'd bought her a drink, and she'd felt more intoxicated after that cocktail hour than she should have. Did he slip her something? Maybe something far more nefarious than a scam to steal her identity? Could he have anything to do with taking Sophie?

The room spun around her. She had started to open up to this man. Perhaps it had been innocent, but still. Who talked to strange men at supermarkets? She let him buy her a drink without hesitation. And now her daughter was gone. She needed that card back. Her list of things she knew for sure was growing: Sophie was gone. Her mother was gone. Gillian was on her side. The police couldn't help her. Mark DeVenuto was a fraud.

"No, he didn't ask for anything like that. To be honest, I think he wanted to ask me for a date." She leaned against the counter and tried to giggle, but it came out hysterical, as if she were high. "Maybe he uses those cards to impress girls. I will have to give him a call and chew him out myself. Thanks so much for your help." She put her hand out for the card.

The bank manager shifted uncomfortably, ran his empty hand over his balding head, and then patted his cheek in thought.

"I'm not sure about this," he said, not giving up the card and starting to scan Veronica as though she held some clue as to what was really going on. "I really think you should wait right here while I look up your information and make sure your account has not been breached," he said, tapping the counter with the card.

Veronica glanced quickly from the teller to the manager, trying to figure out how to change the tone of the conversation. The new employee and her supervisor were not going to let this go, and if they looked up Jane Nickel, they'd know in less than a minute that she was lying.

"Thanks so much for your concern," Veronica crooned, "but I'm going to take a pass." In between his incessant taps, she snatched the card from his hand before he could stop her. "I'm positive this is all just a big misunderstanding."

"It will only take a moment. Your privacy is important to us," the manager pushed, his hand frozen in the same position as when she'd grabbed the card.

"I have an appointment I need to get to, so I have to go, but I'll come back if I see anything shady," she said, backing away quickly. The teller looked up at her manager like she was scared he might explode, but Veronica didn't hesitate. She kept her back to the exit until the very last minute, then turned and shoved the glass door open and stepped out into the steamy afternoon sun.

*They're going to call the police,* she thought to herself. *They're going to call the police, and they will pull the video tapes, and they will know I was here, and they'll know I was asking about Mark.* It all played out in her mind. This was a big mistake. She may have kept her face off the cameras at Walmart, but thanks to fictional Mark, this time she would be discovered.

At least Gillian had not been with her and there was still the hope that the outdoor cameras had missed Gillian's fairly generic car parked around the corner, so they still had a vehicle to use without being recognized. Now they would need it. She might not know where Mark worked, but she did have a phone number.

She saw the way he'd looked at her. He may have given her a fake name and a fake job, but he couldn't fake the attraction she'd read in his stare. Why would he give her a phone number unless it was in his best interest to get her to call him?

So she was going to do what the police were failing at—follow a lead in a direction that didn't point glowing arrows right back at her. Mark might be a con artist or a sex addict or a pathological liar or one of a million other things he could be seeing a therapist for—but he could also be involved in her daughter's kidnapping.

One way or another, she was going to find out.

# CHAPTER 16

She ran down the steps of the bank, skipping two or three at a time. She immediately located Gillian's car parked around the corner and ran as fast as she could for the second time that day. The door was thankfully unlocked, and she leaped into the passenger seat, slamming it shut and tossing the itchy visor into the cluttered back seat.

Gillian didn't even flinch this time. She must be getting used to the adrenaline rush. Instead she simply put down her phone—some game with geometric shapes adorned with human faces disappearing at the push of a button—glanced over at Veronica, and shrugged.

"So what did he say? Is he in?"

Veronica hesitated. She hadn't considered how to tell Gillian. After all, the woman had always been skeptical of the suited man—and it turned out she was right. Perhaps Veronica had spent too much time in isolation and had forgotten how to read good and bad intentions in other people. But somehow she knew Gillian was good. She knew Lisa genuinely wanted the best for her. She knew her mother loved her despite Veronica's failures as a daughter and, more currently, as a human being. She knew Detective Perry was an arrogant asshole. But then again, she'd also thought Mark was a kind banker with a teenaged daughter. Maybe Veronica should stop trusting her instincts and start following this trail that led her to Mark and, hopefully, Sophie. She pulled her legs underneath her, twisting them into a pretzel.

"There is no Mark," she said, having a harder time saying the words than she'd expected. "He's fake," she said matter-of-factly. "I'm not positive, but he might be involved."

Veronica had been afraid all day, panicked, scared even, but when she really considered what it would mean to have Mark involved in her daughter's disappearance, she felt a whole new terror overcome her. Who was this man? Was she right that someone had taken pictures in her daughter's room? Was it Mark? She'd balked when Gillian had called him a stalker, but with the waiting room, grocery store, and bar all lined up next to his lies about his job, it was looking more likely that she was a target rather than a potential love interest.

She'd always thought the people who took babies were family members trying to stop a custody order or crazy women who wanted to fake a pregnancy. Or at least that had been her hope, because at least the crazy-woman option meant Sophie was being taken care of until the police could find her. But what the hell was a grown man doing taking a child from her home? It just didn't make sense.

"That asshole," Gillian cursed with more venom than Veronica had ever heard from the quiet pleaser. Even when talking about her husband and their divorce, Gillian was measured and halting in reporting his lousy behavior toward her, but not today. Today she was pissed off and she didn't care who knew it. Veronica loved seeing strength in the docile woman, both because that fury was on Veronica's side and because if Gillian could learn to be strong, Veronica could as well. "So what are we going to do?" Gillian asked, just as baffled as Veronica. "Maybe you should tell the police?"

"No," she snapped. "They think I hurt my baby. They won't listen to me."

"Well, honey." Gillian paused thoughtfully and gripped the steering wheel. "Do you have any other ideas?"

Veronica didn't know if it felt good or terrible to have Gillian treating her like a child. If Gillian was the adult and Veronica the child, then the mother figure should be coming up with ideas. God, it shouldn't even be her mother by her side—it should be Nick. He'd know what to do. She missed him in the recesses of her too-empty bed. She missed the smell of his terrible instant coffee in the morning. She missed his arms comforting her when she was sad and his mind meeting hers in the spaces between confusion and reality when she was scared.

"I'm going to call Mark and see if I can get him to meet with me. I'll call him out on the bank thing, and hopefully that will open the door to asking about Sophie." She said it with a resolve she wasn't sure she possessed. "Let's get driving. They might call the police."

"The police?" Gillian's eyes went wide, and she put the car into drive. "Why does that bank want to call the police on you? You didn't tell them about the baby, did you? What in the world did you *do* in there?"

"There's too much to explain." She buckled her seat belt and tapped on the dashboard. "Just head east on Forty-Two. You'll be turning left just past the hospital."

"Oh yes, my Christopher is resting out there in the Millburn Cemetery too." During a less-than-legal U-turn, understanding flooded Gillian's features, and her shoulders relaxed under her tattered shirt, the dimples in her elbows less defined. "You're going to see your Nick, aren't you?"

Veronica nodded and pulled out her phone, ready to make one of the most important calls of her life. She might not be able to lean on Nick for help or guidance, but today she needed to be close to him if she could. Well, at least until she had a better idea of how she was going to find their little girl.

"I think this is a great idea." Gillian kept her eyes on the road, but there was a sad understanding in her voice. "Do you know what you're going to say to Mark?"

"Not really." She laid the phone on her leg and held the business card in her other hand. It was a strange sensation to feel like nobody could help you and to have absolutely no idea how to help yourself. It was a lot like when the depression started after Nick died and Sophie was still in the hospital after the car accident. Back then she didn't want to admit it to herself. Sophie was just fragile, so the nurses needed to do everything. And when she came home, it seemed safer for her mother's experienced hands to be the ones caring for the recovering infant. Her mother would give her suggestions like therapy and medication, but none of them seemed to be a viable solution to the crippling sadness and haunting ideations that injected themselves into Veronica's mind.

In those early times, she spent days on end in bed, emerging to do nothing but pump and watch the most recent videos of Sophie, living a life outside her arms and influence. She used to think that her biggest regrets in life would be listed among mistakes she had made or incorrect roads she had taken, but now she knew the truth. Her greatest regrets were found in the spaces between her choices, in the void of inaction that had slowly devoured her life.

Sooner rather than later, she might second-guess running away from the police or bringing Gillian into this fiasco. And this whole plan to track down Mark DeVenuto was a road that likely would lead to disaster and eventual remorse. But she told herself, at least she was *doing* something. And those actions, as misguided or dangerous as they might be, seemed far better than the heavy weight of regret over *not* doing it.

Veronica lifted the phone, dialed the number with ten taps at the screen, and hit send without letting herself dwell on all the crashes and burns that could be waiting at the other end of the chain of events she was about to set in motion. Instead, she let the movement of her fingers against the screen and the phone pressing against her face fill her with satisfaction and hoped that maybe this time doing something would make a difference.

# CHAPTER 17

The phone rang three times, and a masculine voice came on the other end in the middle of the fourth ring.

"Hello?" It was him. She knew right away. She'd only spoken to him twice, but for some reason his voice was embedded in her mind. The wild resolve that had urged her into dialing his number now clawed at the inside of her throat.

"Hi," she said in a slightly flirtatious voice, hoping that the nerves she could hear there sounded like a woman who wanted to get to know someone better rather than a suspicious mother. "I don't know if you remember me, but we had a drink last night. You gave me your card."

The silence continued for a few moments longer, and just when Veronica took a breath, considering another angle, Mark started to talk.

"Of course I remember you," he said, sounding sincerely pleased she'd called. "Veronica, right? Hey, do I get to buy you dinner this time?"

Veronica bit back her rebuttal. Instead, she took a deep breath and pressed forward.

"Not today," she said with a hitch in her voice, trying to decide how to dive in. Maybe she should go with his initial offer to help her, even if she now found it totally suspect. "I'm in trouble. Remember that alarm

I told you about last night? Well, my daughter . . . um . . . I know this is random, but I need your help."

She let the terror she'd been holding back bleed into her voice. She hoped to get him to buy into the fact that she wasn't suspicious and then corner him with her questions once they were face-to-face. As Gillian turned off the two-lane highway onto the gravel path that led to the cemetery, Veronica held the phone closer to her ear, bouncing along with the car.

"Oh my God, are you and Sophie okay?" There was an urgency in his voice that she liked. It gave her some control, and it let her know that he would show up if she asked him to.

"Uh, no, very not okay." He remembered her daughter's name a little too easily for Veronica's liking, and it reminded her of the potential dangers in this path of investigation. "But I don't want to explain over the phone. You said you had connections in security, and I need help. Is it too crazy to ask you to meet me?"

He was quiet for a moment as Gillian put the car in park down one of the grassy paths along the perimeter of the cemetery. She mimed to Veronica, first asking if she was okay and then pointing at her door and the gravestones over Veronica's shoulder, asking if she'd be all right alone.

"Go!" she mouthed and waved her off. The cemetery grass was a sickly greenish yellow, not well irrigated and becoming baked in the June sun. It was a place she'd come to when the ground was nearly frozen and her breath condensed in the fall air. It was close enough to her new home that she used to escape there on some of those early mornings and nights when she'd had to run as fast as she could away from her house to escape Sophie's screams.

Oftentimes she'd pace the rows, reading names, talking aloud, but she tried to stay away from the small headstones that inevitably sat above the graves of children. It felt like she was tempting fate when she read those out loud, like she was defiling something sacred.

It was the worst place on the planet because it reminded her of her loss, but it also was a place of refuge where she could sob her eyes out and no one would see her, and if they did, they wouldn't be surprised. It felt like a freedom, having permission to mourn openly.

"Yeah, I have a few connections. I can try to help. God, I hope you're okay," Mark finally responded. It sounded like he was walking, and then the sound of a car door slamming. "Can I come to you?"

"Yes. Where are you right now?" she asked, and then added with a little flash of self-satisfaction, "Work?"

"Yeah, work," he said, almost halfheartedly, like he wasn't interested in trying to fool her. "I'm in my car now, though. Where can I meet you?"

She considered her options carefully. Normally she'd say they should meet in a public place with lots of witnesses, but since she was more likely to be ID'd by police than he was, she had to go with a more secluded spot. It was risky, but she was owning risky right now.

"I'm at the Millburn Cemetery off Forty-Two, five rows up on the left side. Please come fast. I hate to sound dramatic, but it is life or death."

His car growled to life in the background, and she knew he meant it when he said he'd come.

"God, I think you should call the police," he said, obviously concerned.

Veronica cocked her head to one side and listened closely to the tension in his voice. He wasn't bluffing. He really wanted her to call for help, which made her wonder if he was even involved. For some reason it was depressing to consider the idea that he had nothing to do with the abduction. She might never find Sophie.

"No, no police. If you call them, I won't be here. I just want you," she said, hoping it would make him feel important and needed but also acknowledging a twinge of honesty in her words. She could hear his car rev in the background.

"I'll be there in ten minutes."

Too bad he wasn't the real Mark DeVenuto. Then she might be feeling relief right now and her muscles would relax enough that she could take a deep breath. But no matter how nice he seemed on the phone, Mark DeVenuto was a liar and couldn't be trusted.

# CHAPTER 18

Turned around backward in Gillian's front seat, Veronica watched Mark's white Lexus pull into the gravel parking lot of the cemetery, a cloud of dust following behind him. She'd been rethinking this plan since she'd hung up the phone a painstaking fourteen minutes earlier. He'd sounded genuine on the phone, but if he *was* the culprit, a man who was crazy enough to stalk her and take her child, then faking a few words on the phone would be easy for him. And the police—what better way to get Veronica to keep the police out of it than to offer to make the call himself?

And that was just one of her worries. What if Mark had a gun? What if he brought someone with him? What if she was too late? She'd tried to get up the courage to visit Nick's headstone but got too overwhelmed with anxiety about her impending confrontation to leave the car. She texted Gillian and asked her to return. Her face red and tear streaked, she showed up a few minutes later, equally as nervous about Veronica meeting the mysterious man.

"Now remember, don't get in his vehicle, whatever he says, and keep your phone in your hand." She took Veronica's phone and dialed a number. Gillian's phone buzzed on the console between them, and Veronica's name popped up. "I'll listen from here, and if there is any sign of distress, I'm calling 911." She hit the green "Talk" button on her phone and handed the iPhone back to Veronica, the connection left open.

"How are you so good at this stuff?" Veronica asked, her voice echoing out of Gillian's receiver.

"I watch a lot of TV," she said with a shrug, and then put a warm, moist hand on Veronica's forearm. "Good luck."

Veronica nodded, too nervous to talk, and headed toward Mark's running car. He was clearly visible in the driver's side, looking down as though he was texting. She squinted to see if by some outrageous stroke of luck he had a car seat strapped in the back seat, but from what she could tell, it was empty.

When her feet hit the gravel, he still had not noticed her approach, which made her nervous. She needed to see his reaction to her, read his expressions.

Veronica hesitated a few feet away, tears of anxiety rising in her eyes, but he continued to stare at his lap. Using a light touch, she tapped her fingernails on the hood of his car, the heat from the metal biting at her skin. Mark's head snapped up, and before she had time to prepare herself any further, he was standing in front of her, in a fancy suit once again. She pressed her hands against her thighs to hide how badly they were shaking.

"Hey there," he said simply, leaning against the car slightly like they were meeting up for a first date. He was handsome, that was for sure. She couldn't blame herself for falling for his facade. His dark hair swooped naturally to one side like he ran his fingers through it a thousand times a day, and his deep-blue eyes had a softness at the edges that seemed like empathy. But now that she knew he'd been lying to her about who knew how many things, these qualities seemed less like an indicator of the kind of person he was and more like a disguise. Seeing him in front of her was disarming. She'd expected to have the feelings of anger, betrayal, and suspicion follow her into the face-to-face meeting, but instead she was confused.

"Hi." The greeting stuck in her throat and came out garbled. She blinked back more tears, knowing that if she didn't push through, they'd come out along with sobs very soon.

"Oh, you're in bad shape, aren't you?" He took a step toward her with his hand out but stopped short of touching her. "What's going on? Can I help?"

The shaking from Veronica's hands spread up her arms and into her shoulders and torso. She blew out a breath and bounced her leg up and down, hoping to relieve some of the pressure. Where to start?

"My daughter . . . is missing." She barely got the words out, but once they hung in the air between them, she watched his reaction. She may have been imagining things, but he seemed to stumble backward, like he'd been shoved by unseen hands.

"Missing? Your daughter?"

"Yeah, my little girl, Sophie. I woke up this morning, and she was gone. Gone. The police—"

"You called the police?" he interrupted, regaining the ground he'd lost during her last revelation and putting himself so close she could feel his breath against her cheek.

"Yeah, Mark, that's what you tend to do when your baby goes missing." He was nearly six inches taller than she was, and she had to look up at a sharp angle to meet his eyes, but with her head tipped back, she stared him down, the vulnerability leaving her voice and a hardness firming it up instead.

"No, I get that, I mean . . ." He stuttered through a response, and she absolutely knew in that moment that he was hiding something.

"Why did you tell me you worked at MDB Bank?" The question was enough to make him stop bumbling through his explanation. She used his muted shock to her advantage, following the momentum like a car on a roller coaster. "I went there today. Talked to the manager. They don't know who the hell you are. Which makes me wonder why you've been lying and what else you know about my baby."

"I don't know anything about your baby," he said, slapping his hand against the hood of his car, regaining the power of speech more rapidly than Veronica had expected.

"Lies. *Lies.* You know something. I know you do."

Mark rubbed a hand over his face, lingering on his chin and neck, sighing deeply. "Did you give the police my name?"

Veronica was getting over her initial nerves and morphing into all-out anger. She didn't have one satisfactory answer, and now he was worrying about covering his own ass?

"No, asshole, the police think *I* hurt my baby, so we aren't exactly buddy-buddy. I went to find you at the bank so you could *help* me. Only to find out that this stranger who has taken a recent interest in me is not who he said he was."

"So you decided to meet a man you thought could be your child's abductor at a secluded location alone? Oh, Veronica." He shook his head and almost laughed.

"I'm not alone, so don't get any ideas," she added, realizing that he was right. This was a very dangerous position she'd put herself and Gillian in. At first she'd thought it was worth it if there was a small chance she could find out more information about her child's whereabouts even if it was a long shot or he was an out-of-work bank manager who used old cards to hit on girls or if he was dangerous, but now she realized it was a really great way to get herself killed.

"I'm not here to hurt you, Veronica." He patted at his pockets and pulled a thick wallet out of a pocket inside his suitcoat and flipped it open. "I'm not a bank VP. I'm sorry I misled you." He retrieved a small blue card about the size of a credit card and held it out. "I rarely have to show this to anyone, but I don't want you thinking I'm some criminal."

Skeptical and less than convinced by Mark's words, Veronica took the laminated paper and glanced at it without taking her eyes off him for too long. The blue square had a lot of information on it in small black lettering, and in the left-hand corner was Mark's picture with his name beside it.

"What the hell?" she gasped and pulled the ID closer, reading through all the fine print. He was Mark DeVenuto all right, but he wasn't a bank VP or anyone else who would wear a fancy suit and drive an even fancier car. He was a PI.

"I'm sorry; it's nothing personal. It's just my job." He took the card back and returned it to his wallet. "You were my assignment. At first it was following you to that therapist, going to that group." He kind of shrugged. "And then I followed you to the supermarket. Yesterday was a little different. I hadn't planned on buying you a drink and chatting about life, but I made a split-second decision to engage when I saw you driving around that restaurant parking lot when I was doing surveillance"—he hesitated before completing his sentence—"on you."

Veronica felt naked, like in a dream where she suddenly realized everyone else had their clothes on. She folded her arms across her chest and hugged her midsection; the phone in her hand was hot against her rib cage.

"You were following me?" Somehow the idea that someone had hired him was more devastating than the thought that he was working on his own. More people meant more power and more levels that she'd need to go through to find Sophie.

When she was a child, her mother had watched a Lifetime movie about a black-market adoption ring that stole babies from women they thought weren't fit mothers and sold them to wealthy couples who wanted a child. It had been a frightening concept to ten-year-old Veronica, but it was also a story that came from a made-for-TV movie, so she'd given it little weight once her mother had told her it was fiction. But now—who the hell knew?

"Who do you work for, and who hired you?" she demanded.

"I work for Rabbit Hole Investigations, but the other information is confidential." He put his wallet back in his suitcoat and gave a semi-shrug. "I'm sorry."

"You're sorry?" her voice pitched up, echoing in the silent cemetery. "My kid is missing and you are going to stand here and just say sorry? Were you watching me last night? Were you watching my house, or do you have a camera there or something?"

"My advice is to go back home and talk to the police. And no, I didn't follow you home last night. You were with Gillian, and she already seemed to be suspicious of me."

"You know her name too," she said under her breath, getting more frantic with every moment that passed. "I can't go to the police, or did you not hear that part? They think I'm crazy. They think I hurt my baby, and my mom is missing, so they think she's involved too. They've probably stopped looking for Sophie altogether at this point and are just looking for me, but I don't have her, Mark," she spat out his name, "and you might have information that could help and you won't tell me anything. Maybe I *should* call the police and tell them about how you're stalking me and how you took pictures inside of my house. Yeah, I know about that."

"I've never been in your house," Mark said with determination, his forehead wrinkling as he searched her face and then took in her shifty body movements. "This is why the police are suspicious of you, Veronica. You sound crazy right now. Between that and your issues with Sophie and your frequent visits to your therapist, I'm sure they have you right at the top of their list. You do know how rare it is for a stranger to abduct a baby, especially taking a baby from inside her home, don't you?" He regarded her with the same suspicious look the officers had given her, and a thousand defenses gathered at the back of her throat. It wasn't fair; they didn't know what it was like, this depression, this mourning. She was just a human, damn it, a human being who was trying to get help. "You said your mom is missing too; why aren't you worried about her at all? I was a police officer for ten years, and your story smells bad, really bad."

Veronica, who had glanced back to check on the car and get a moment to breathe without staring oh-so-superior Mark in the face, turned back with her finger pointed and a red heat scorching her cheeks.

"I am not crazy and I didn't hurt my baby. I'm trying to save her. And my mom? I'm scared to death about where she is. I'm so scared. They are all I have. Why would I hurt them? Why?" The memory of the crack and thud and the pool of blood on the carpet reminded her that she *had* hurt her mother, but she hadn't meant to. She would never hurt her on purpose.

The devastation that she'd pushed down after the bank threatened to breach her fortifications. Angry that she couldn't stop herself, Veronica covered her face and turned her body away from Mark and tried to hold back the sobs that built inside her and escaped like wind through an open door. "Why doesn't anyone want to help me?" she wailed, more defeated than ever before. Was she invisible? It was as if she were screaming at the top of her lungs and no one could hear her. She wanted to shake . . . everyone. Giving up wasn't an option, but she was so tired of convincing people to do the right thing.

Mark sighed, and a few seconds later his hands were on her shoulders. "I do want to help. I just don't know *how* I can help you. There are rules in my job. I'm not supposed to reveal anything except, maybe, to the police."

"Come on, Mark." She couldn't hold back the frustration in her voice. "This isn't some process service case, and I'm not someone skipping bail or whatever you do." She let his hands remain on her shoulders even after returning to her original position in front of him. He looked down on her, and there was some trace of protectiveness in his eyes, like he wanted to show her he was a good man, to convince her of it. She forced herself to soften and tried to match his tone. "This is about a missing child. Why were you following me, Mark? Tell me that. Who is so interested in me?"

He pressed his lips together. "I could get fired."

"I could lose my child," she rebutted.

Veronica wiped at her face and looked up into Mark's eyes, silent for a moment, hoping the sincerity there would move him. He stared at her deeply, blinking rapidly and then squeezing her shoulders like he wanted to pull her in for an all-encompassing hug.

"Damn it," he said under his breath. "Fine. Fine, I'll help you. I don't have a lot of info, and I'll have to keep it as general as possible. Like I said, I was supposed to follow you to therapy and then initiate contact. I recorded our conversations and turned them in to my boss. I know there was at least one other guy on the case, but you were mine. He was supposed to follow your mom. My boss said it had something to do with insurance but wouldn't share more."

The tears in her eyes evaporated, and she stood a little taller, raising Mark's hands along with her improved posture. "Insurance? What insurance? There was a payout after the crash, but I'm not sure why they'd be watching me. What was the company name?" She tried to recall the name of the insurance company on the payout checks that came every few months, hoping it would sound familiar.

"I don't know for sure, and it is really unethical for me to tell you anyway. I can tell you this—the point of contact on the brief was for a private home. Sometimes the client wants to be more anonymous, so we use codenames and info is given on a need-to-know basis. I just do what they tell me and don't ask questions." He let his hands fall from her shoulders, but slowly, like he wished they could stay there. "Listen, I can't give you any more information, but I could tell the police. I have the PDF of my orders on my phone, and maybe my boss would be able to give more details to law enforcement."

He retrieved a large smartphone from his pants pocket, and Veronica noticed a bead of sweat trickle down his neck and onto the collar of his shirt. *He must be burning up in that dark suit,* she thought, wishing she didn't feel empathy for him in that moment.

"I've already told you, Mark, I can't go to the police. If they knew I was involved in getting this info, I doubt they'd even take a second glance. I've *tried* to give them information and leads, but they don't care about a word that comes out of my mouth. They are wasting time, and my girl is getting farther and farther away. If you've been watching me, then you know, you *know* I couldn't hurt my baby. I'm not asking you to do anything other than put your phone on the hood of the car and let me look at it for five seconds. You can count. Maybe I'll recognize something?"

Mark switched the phone from one hand to the other and then stared at the screen for a moment. He took several deep breaths like he was trying to force himself to say something unpleasant and his voice box didn't want to let him. He looked at the device one more time and then put it on the hood of the car and turned his back to her.

"One . . . two . . . ," he started counting. Five seconds was almost nothing, and by the time she picked up the phone, he was already on his way to number three. She scanned the document. There was a code name and an address from Durham at the top, probably close to Duke. As Mark got to four, Veronica hit the "Share" button and typed in her phone number and hit "Send." The whoosh was louder than she'd hoped, but Mark didn't seem to flinch. At five, she clicked out of the screen and put the phone down on the hood of his car, her mind racing.

Durham. What would someone from Durham want with information about her and her baby? As he turned around, she started to type the address into Google Maps when Mark interrupted.

"I looked up the address, when I . . . uh . . . got to know you a little better and was getting curious about the reason behind the surveillance." He peeked at her with expert eyes, searching her reaction, and then grabbed the phone off his car and put it in his pocket. "It was a dead end, though. It's a rental. A nice rental, but still. Number listed online just goes to the old couple that rents it out, and they wouldn't give me any info on the current tenants."

"Well, I don't recognize the address, so no need to worry." No way she was going to tell Mark her thoughts—he might try to stop her—but a plan was starting to form, and it was a good one.

Mark stood up to his full height. "I'm going to be brutally honest right now. I feel like this is too much for you to do by yourself."

"Thanks for your concern." Her phone dinged and buzzed in her hand. She confirmed it was the information she needed. "But I have help."

"Who, Gillian? No, you need real help. Police help. Let me talk to them. I can help get them on the right track."

"Mark, you can't talk to the police without permission from your boss, and if your boss knew about this"—she pointed back and forth between them—"you'd probably get fired, so . . . if you don't want to help me, that's fine, but then you have to let me do it my way."

She started to walk away, up the slight hill toward the rows of headstones. The detectives said that the first twenty-four hours were the most important, so Veronica knew she had to hurry. Halfway up the berm, a hot hand wrapped around her wrist.

"Hold on for a sec," Mark said, rushing to catch up. "Listen, I know I said I can't go with you, but if you run into problems—you can call me. And." He paused and tugged on her fingers, bringing her forward momentum to a stop. "I'll look into this more. I'll talk to my boss, and maybe I can get more information about your case."

"Okay," Veronica said, scanning the building beads of perspiration on the sides of his face and forehead. His desire to help her was more dangerous than helpful. If he cared too much, he'd cause problems for sure. If the police knew they'd been in contact or the address she'd gotten from his phone, then they might stop her before she got the chance to find out who hired PIs to watch her every move. "Just be discreet, okay?"

"I can do discreet. It's kinda my job." He gave his sideways smile, like he couldn't stop himself from flirting.

It irritated Veronica that the gravity of the situation didn't seem to have settled on the private investigator. "Do you even have a child, or was that part of your cover too?"

Mark's smirk left, and he dropped her wrist. "Yeah, Kayla is real."

"I never would've guessed," she spat, but then rethought her aggressive response. She needed to keep Mark on her side. "I'm sorry, I didn't mean . . ." Veronica strained to keep her emotions under control. She could be hard and strong when someone was being suspicious or mysterious, but when they showed empathy and concern, it took her legs out from under her.

"No need to explain," Mark said, putting his hand on her shoulder and then tracing along the back of her neck around to the other shoulder like a side hug. It was also a stance where he could best support her if her knees did go out, and surprisingly, she allowed it. Only for a moment and a half, but it was enough to make her feel like Mark, who she'd thought was enemy number one moments ago, was now added to her very short list of allies.

Since Nick's accident, she hadn't found one man she wanted to let in. It had been hard enough to let Nick in, after growing up with such an unreliable father figure and the string of men in her mother's life. To think that there might be another man out there that she could trust—it was a groundbreaking new idea.

"Well, thank you," she said, taking a step back and breaking away from the half minute of comfort. "I'd better get back to Gillian."

"Yeah, and I'll make some calls. Be safe, okay?"

She nodded, filled with that same taken-care-of feeling again, like his concern had arms that stayed with her when his were gone.

"I'll try, but I'm going to do whatever it takes," she said, meeting his gaze.

"I know," he replied with a half-hearted laugh, trying to act casual again but failing. "That's what makes me nervous."

Without responding, she ran up the hill, not looking back. Her flip-flops strained with each dusty step, and sweat built up on her shins under the dark pants Gillian had picked out for her.

The car was running, and the frozen air that had gathered inside gave her instant relief, like she'd jumped into a cool pool of water. The chill in the air seemed to bring back some of the sanity that the sun and Mark's infuriatingly calm demeanor had pounded out of her.

"Well, that was interesting." Gillian sat in the car, still holding the phone in her hand.

"Did you hear the part about him being a PI?" Veronica asked, putting on her seat belt, ready to get on the road.

"I heard all of it. I'm guessing you want to go to that place he was talking about. How far away? Please don't say Canada."

"No, Durham. And I have to go. What other choice do I have at this point?"

Gillian nodded like she'd already guessed that was their next stop. "Do you want to say hi to Nick?"

Veronica looked down the rows of headstones. Nick's was up four rows and over seven, or was it up seven and over four? It had been a while since she'd visited. She used to come more often and walk the rows, feeling more comfortable with the dead than the living. She'd read the names and dates and wondered how many of those souls buried under the ground had someone who got choked up when they heard a certain song or saw a family playing at the park, remembering that those options were cruelly removed in one flash of a moment. Usually knowing others out there shared her pain made her feel like she belonged somewhere. But not today. Today she wanted action, not sorrow. She wanted change, not stasis.

"No." She shook her head. "He'll be here tomorrow. Right now, I need to find our girl."

# CHAPTER 19

"Do you think it's safe to stop by my house?" Gillian asked as they drove away from the cemetery. Mark had left just a few moments earlier, waiting longer than Veronica would've liked before exiting the gravel parking lot. He was taking this role of protector a little too seriously for her comfort. He might call the police, it was a real possibility, but dealing with law enforcement and their outrageous suspicions was something she had to put on the back burner for now. There was an overwhelming urgency that pushed her toward the house in Durham, and she wanted to get there as fast as possible.

"What do you need?" she asked, reluctant to give up any precious seconds that could be spent getting closer to some answers. As they pulled away, Veronica waved goodbye with a little tip of her fingers at the headstone she hadn't gotten to visit that day.

"You're going to think I'm crazy," Gillian said as she sped out of the cemetery right in front of an approaching car, going slightly faster than Veronica would've liked.

"I don't think I have a leg to stand on when it comes to crazy. I'm just worried about time; that's all." She was trying to be kind to Gillian, fully recognizing that routinely she'd been nothing less than terrible to the woman sitting beside her—a woman who had no obligation to her and who was putting herself at risk just staying by her side. Through all her judgments of Gillian's external appearance and the overly emotional moments in the waiting room of Lisa's office, it had taken Gillian's steadfast friendship during this chaos of a day to really see her. Behind the tattered, flashy clothes and sometimes needy exterior, inside she was one of the strongest people Veronica had ever met.

"You know what," Veronica said, tugging at her seat belt till the sliding buckle over her shoulder was in the right position. "Whatever you think is fine. I trust you."

Gillian's lips turned up, and she seemed to sit somewhat taller in her seat. Veronica wondered how long she'd been treated like a "less than" person in her life. Veronica promised herself that she wouldn't be one of those people ever again.

Gillian's home was close. They pulled into the neighborhood in a matter of minutes. Streets were lined with small, tidy houses from the 1950s. Well, some of the houses were tidy, with neatly painted wooden siding and large oak trees dripping with moss. But there were others protected by tall metal fences, with grass that was the color of straw.

There was one at the end of the street that stood out even among the variety of the homes. It had the same "bones" as the rest of the houses, the tattered ones and the neat ones, but this one wasn't just neglected—it was abused. Once upon a time, it had been a small white Cape Cod with blue shutters and a black tar roof, but now the shutters were faded so badly that they were nearly gray, the siding was missing streaks of paint that had sloughed off in great strips like a peeling sunburn, and the roof looked like it'd been struck by a windstorm, missing whole tiles in sections that must leak when it rained.

*Don't let that be her house,* Veronica thought, but somehow she already knew the truth. As Gillian barreled down that road, Veronica knew they were headed straight to the driveway that matched the house, cracked and threaded with sprouts of grass breaking through. A car covered with a tarp was up on blocks, obstructing the garage in the rear of the house.

That was probably one of the cars Christopher was working on before he died. Gillian said he was a mechanical whiz. Now all she had was a pile of metal and a house filled with reminders of what it used to be like when it was filled with the child who loved her. The thought made Veronica crazy. This could very easily be her future. If she lost Sophie forever, would she turn into Gillian? Not this strong, brave Gillian, but the woman Veronica had judged so harshly and labeled as a failure in life?

"Can we hurry?" she asked, the feeling of anxiety crawling up her like bugs on her skin.

"Just give me a second; that's all it'll take." Gillian looked at Veronica as she parked her car in the street in front of her house, leaving it running. Veronica had a momentary concern that they would run out of gas at some point because of all the idling, but the needle pointed to half a tank. She still had twenty-four dollars left, and that should at least get them back and forth from Durham if the car didn't sit running for much longer.

These were strange thoughts, ones that Veronica could never get used to. She didn't know how people planned out crimes and pursued them for excitement or profit, because this feeling of dread and anticipation was only made bearable by the thought of bringing her baby home and making things right with her mother.

"If we can leave in fifteen minutes, we should get there before it starts getting dark. I think it would be a lot easier to search for Sophie with the sun still up," she said, and wanted to add "and a lot less scary" but didn't want to lose the one person still willing to stay by her side.

"Sounds good. I'll hurry." Gillian hefted herself out of the car and jogged up her driveway. In a matter of seconds, she disappeared into a side door that could barely be seen from the street. Veronica took out her phone and plugged it into the charger that Gillian had purchased for her from Walmart.

The battery was already getting low, and that phone had to stay charged. It was their lifeline. It kept them connected to Mark, and it kept them on a path that hopefully would lead to Sophie. She quickly forwarded the information from Mark on her phone to Gillian's phone number with a brief spark of preservation; that way if anything happened to her phone, they'd have a backup.

As the battery began to fill and the messages pushed from her phone to Gillian's, she scanned her text messages, looking for something, anything from her mother. Nothing. A sinking feeling of dread clutched at her chest. Where in the hell did she go? If she was hurt, why didn't she get help? If she was angry, why didn't she at least reach out and yell or scream or accuse? The silence was lethal to any calm Veronica forced on her addled mind. Right now she'd take anything but silence. Anything.

She pulled the phone in as close as the charging cord would allow and started to type "Are you okay?" but then remembered her mom's phone was sitting in the middle of the nest of officers and detectives. The phone. Couldn't they track her with the phone? If Barb DeCarlo had come home, surely Veronica would've heard something by now. She knew that the police thought Veronica might be some sort of murderer or abuser, but her mother knew better. Her mother saw the way she cared for her child, provided food for her and clean clothing. She would tell them that, wouldn't she? She'd have to take the risk and turn off her phone, at least for now. Couldn't leave any possible trail behind her if she could help it.

Before pressing and holding the "Power" button on the side of the phone, her fingers hovered over the photo icon. She wanted to look at pictures of Sophie, to remember her smile and maybe watch the videos that her mother had taken of Sophie clapping and laughing, but the idea also cut at her and kept her from touching that screen. How could she look at that baby face without knowing where she was?

She curled her fingers back and shut the phone down completely until it felt dead in her hands and then rested it in the sticky cup holder on the passenger side of the car. She wasn't ready, not yet. Not until she knew these weren't the last videos she'd ever see of her baby's smile and chubby fingers shoving a teething ring into her mouth.

A loud pounding sounded on the passenger-side window. For the first time in hours, she'd let her guard down, and in the time it took for her eyes to travel from the phone to the window, she was sure she'd been caught. Heart in her throat, she didn't know whether to be relieved or frightened when she saw a large, heavyset man standing on the other side of her car door, wearing tan coveralls and his face a deeper shade of red than Veronica's burgundy dress.

"Who the hell are you?" the man demanded, pounding again on the window. "Where is Gillian? She locked me out of my own house. I have stuff in there, and I have a legal right to get it. Where the hell is she?"

This must be the delightful ex-husband. With a deep breath, she shouted through the window, mimicking his tone. "Who the hell are *you*?"

"I'm Gillian's husband. I pay for this goddamned house. She gets to stay here for free while I'm sleeping on some loser's couch. Is she acting like she's single now?"

Veronica was confused, not catching all the details the night before about Gillian's divorce, but this man sure seemed to match her description of Carl's charming personality and less-than-well-groomed appearance. Veronica found herself feeling impressed at the fact that Gillian had left this disaster of a human. God, she was proud of her.

Carl wasn't leaving, and if he kept pounding on the window, it would either break or someone from a neighboring house would call the police.

"You're causing a scene," she said through the glass, but that only made him shout louder.

"What?"

"Shut up!" she shouted, popping the door open and kicking it hard. It hit Carl in the belly, making him let out a string of swear words. She slammed the car door and took a step toward the man, her nose coming no higher than his chest.

"I'm Gillian's friend, and I don't think you have any say in her life anymore. As far as I can tell, you're nothing more to her than a bad memory." Veronica wished she were a man in that moment and could shove Carl back a little, but she recoiled, remembering the last time she shoved someone and the sickening crack after.

Carl did not take well to Veronica's show of strength. He was clearly a man who didn't like strong women. That was probably why he fell for Gillian in the first place—and why he didn't love the new Gillian at all.

"You have no idea what you're talking about. This is my house, and I have every right to be here. I've been waiting in my car since the sun came up, and she's been nowhere to be found. Then I went to take a piss and come back, and her shitty car is parked out front like she hadn't missed our appointment. Did she tell you that she finally got the divorce she wanted? She wanted all this but can't even show up. The judge said I could get my shit *today*. I'm tired of waiting. If that bitch doesn't get out here soon, then you should get your pretty little ass in there and tell her I'm going to burn the place down."

Veronica put her hand over her mouth and pretended she was coughing to hide her amusement. Today was not the day to cross Veronica Shelton. Today, anything that stood in her way was going to come crashing down one way or another.

"Yeah, I don't think I'm going to be telling her that. If this is all legal and aboveboard, maybe you should call the police instead of threatening arson," she bluffed. "But you don't want that, do you? I think you know that if the police get involved, she can get a restraining order."

He crossed his arms and scoffed. "Yeah, like she has the guts or the money for that."

Veronica let a sly smile bloom across her face.

"Well, she might not, but I certainly do," she said, gritting her teeth and standing as tall as her five-foot-two frame would allow her. After all, if this man came after her, she could run. She was a fast runner.

But instead of backing off or slinking away to his hidden vehicle, he looked Veronica up and down as if he knew what she looked like naked.

"I always knew Gillian was butch," he said, chuckling, "but I never knew she was a queer."

Veronica's fingernails dug into her skin, fury building with every second, her muscles tensing, and all the frustration and anger she had been pushing away now came to the surface and built up inside her muscles like a superpower. She raised her clenched fist, cleared her mind of the visions of blood on the floor and the sound her mother made when Veronica had pushed her; then she used all the power collected inside her biceps to hit Carl square in the jaw.

Her hand exploded with pain as the loud crack echoed in the air. Fighting back a wail, she grabbed her wrist and cradled it against her chest, rocking and trying to breathe slowly. Carl's head snapped back from the blow. He opened his mouth to test his jaw, rubbing the spot where her knuckles hit his skin, and then, with a deep sniff, he turned his head back and quickly stared down Veronica.

"Why, you little bitch," he said, letting his hand drop, revealing a red spot on his jawline. He said it with a fury that made Veronica wish her hand didn't hurt so badly or that the car wasn't directly behind her. He put his arms on either side of her body, hands resting beside her on the car. She was trapped.

"You think you can hit me? You think you can insult me? What the hell is wrong with women nowadays?" He started by talking low and slow and then building, like a tide crashing in on the shore. Veronica cringed, her muscles tightening like she was trying to become as compact as possible until she disappeared. No wonder Gillian had learned how to become a nothing person. This man made Veronica want to be nothing, because if she were nothing, then maybe he wouldn't hurt her.

"This is my house. *My* house. And I don't care what you and my nasty wife are doing together, but you are not going to keep me away from it. Let's go find Gillian." He wrapped his thick fingers around Veronica's arm at the elbow, pain reverberating down to her wrist and hand, still tender from her attempt at self-defense.

"You're hurting me," she gasped.

"Yeah, and your fist felt like butterfly wings," he replied under his breath, yanking her across the front yard with zero attempt at being covert. "Gillian!" he shouted. "Get your fat ass out here!"

Veronica started to struggle against Carl's iron grasp, but all it did was make him dig in harder. Her feet were having a hard time keeping up with his pace, every instinct telling them to run the other way but finding it impossible to go any way but forward. When they reached the front door, Carl jiggled the plain bronze doorknob and then pounded on the weathered front door with the side of his fist.

"Gillian, I'm not kidding. Get out here now." His shout was a little softer this time, deeper and somehow more threatening than the screaming. If Veronica knew Gillian at all, she'd open that door and let that man inside. Veronica had to do something.

"Carl, if this is your house like you keep saying, then why don't you have a key, huh?" She yanked on his arm as she spoke, hoping that Gillian would take the break in the assault to make a plan for escape before the neighbors called the police.

He lifted his fist again and pounded. "She stole it from me in the divorce. She stole it and all my shit and then had the locks changed."

Veronica's shoulder began to ache. "I doubt the police would see it that way," she said, clenching her teeth to keep the pain out of her voice. She deserved the pain after the way she'd treated her mother. "I'm sure someone has called 911 by now. You should cut your losses and leave."

Carl stared at her with his swollen lips half open and spittle gathered at the corners of his mouth, like the idea that the police could be involved had never crossed his mind. He opened and closed his carp-like mouth one, two times.

"She'd never call the police. She's a dimwit, but she's not that stupid." He looked at the door and then backed away, almost falling off the raised concrete slab of a front porch and taking Veronica with him.

"Are you so sure?" Veronica asked, poking at the small hole she'd made in his momentum.

The thoughts processed through his mind slowly. His eyes bugged out, and for a moment, between his mouth and the expression on his face, she was certain he knew Gillian was capable of much more than he was giving her credit for. But before he could change his mind, the lock on the front door clicked and the doorknob turned slowly.

"I told you so," he gloated, his mouth snapping shut and a thick, gross smile turning up the week-old stubble on his face. His hand tightened around her arm, and then he yanked her in close to his side, her arm against his bloated belly, strangely taut but pliable at the same time. He smelled of sweat, gasoline, and body odor. The scent made her stomach churn.

The door opened slowly at first until Carl put his hand on the painted metal and pushed. It swung inward toward a darkened hallway, a slight scent of potpourri and dust reminding Veronica of her grandmother's house on her dad's side, and she gagged. No way would she let this man drag her across that threshold into the unknown darkness. With a burst of energy, she threw all her body weight behind her as if she were trying to jump off the porch, hoping that gravity would give her enough force to break his grip. She didn't have much of a plan after that; Gillian had the keys and the police still might be on their way, but somehow she knew that going into a dark house with an angry man was a very, very bad idea.

The suddenness of her movements shocked Carl, and her leap of faith threw him off balance, but unfortunately did little other than make him stumble backward and curse even louder than he had before. It also made him mad. So, so mad.

"What the . . ." His attention shifted from the open door to Veronica, who had recovered from her leap and was now using her feet for leverage to pry herself away from Carl's grasp.

"You're gonna break your arm," he said, as if he were the only sane one.

"Let me go!" she screamed this time, completely forgetting about her fears of the police.

He yanked at her limb. "Get up and get in the *house!*" he shouted, and his voice echoed off the cookie-cutter houses down the street.

"Let her go." It was Gillian standing in the doorway, voice firm, feet spread apart. She'd changed into black shorts that cut just above the knee and a faded peach T-shirt that looked like it'd been worn for yardwork.

"I'll let her go when you give me a key to my house." He held Veronica to the side like a dog that'd rolled in poop and needed a bath.

"You're not going in my house," she said with a determined drawl, blocking the way into the front hall with her body. "A judge settled it all. You got your money. You got your things. It was handled all fair and proper. This is my property; now get off."

"If fair and proper means you are stealing every red cent of my hard-earned cash, then I guess you're right. First you go and get Christopher killed by talking to those goddamned hacks that didn't help him at all, and then you take my house and my livelihood too?"

"Leave. Now," she said, calm, with her feet on the threshold, one hand to her side and one behind her back. In the distance, Veronica swore she could hear sirens whining. Panic set in. They needed to go—right now.

"It's like you're deaf. The judge said you were supposed to let me get my stuff then, but you never showed. I'm getting what's mine now." With that declaration, he dropped Veronica onto the concrete, and she slammed onto the slab, hard. Her hip hit first, her skin scratched through the thin fabric of her dress and stretch pants. Throwing her hand down to catch her fall only added another flash of pain through the already-tortured limb and up to her shoulder. She pulled it in to her chest and crawled backward.

"No, you're not. Not without an officer present." Gillian pulled her hand out from behind her back. In it was a snub-nosed .22, small enough to look like a toy gun but glinting in the sun like only metal did.

A gun. How had this day gone so completely mad? Her father had had a big collection of guns, and when he got drunk, he'd take out his favorites and shoot at cans in the backyard. When he got really wasted, he'd try shooting at moving targets in the acre behind their house, things like squirrels or bunnies. He usually was too smashed to hit the cans, much less the animals unlucky enough to have made the wooded lot their home. But one time just before Veronica went to bed for the night, he came in with Fluffy, the neighbor's orange-and-white tabby, in his arms. She looked asleep until Veronica noticed the trail of blood on her side when her dad put her on the counter and called for Barb. They buried Fluffy in their backyard, and Veronica spent the next six months averting her gaze when she walked past the "missing" posters that filled the light posts of her neighborhood.

After that, Veronica couldn't stand guns or the power such a small handheld object could hold. She had considered getting a gun as protection as a single woman in a big, empty house but couldn't bring herself to do it, even though she'd learned how to manage a gun very early in her life. But today that fear of gunpowder and metal shifted a bit when she saw the device in Gillian's hands. They could use a little bit of portable power.

But then again, Gillian didn't seem like the kind of person who spent much time at the gun range, and though she pointed the gun at her husband with determination, her hand was shaking with a broad tremor that made the gun wobble up and down uncontrollably.

Veronica scrambled backward, intentionally tumbling off the porch this time. She wanted to get away from Carl, but there was no part of her that wanted to get stuck in Gillian's cross fire.

Veronica tossed herself behind an overgrown bush on the left side of the yard. She could feel her pulse racing in her nearly useless shoulder. Her phone was in the car, so even if she could make herself dial the numbers, 911 was a risky option. She glanced around at the neighboring houses. Maybe someone was home and watching, or maybe someone would answer the door if she pounded on it. Her attention was drawn back to the altercation at the front door as Carl took a half step forward.

"You don't even know how to load that thing," he scoffed, surer of himself than he had any right to be with a gun pointed in his face.

"I sure do," Gillian said firmly, and brought her other hand up to support the gun handle from underneath, and the shaking began to slow. "I know how to fire it too."

There must've been something about the way she said it, or maybe he could see the bullets loaded in the cylinder, because after another half second of consideration, he put up his hands and backed away from the door. Following his movement, Gillian exited her house and pulled the door shut behind her with one hand while keeping the gun lifted with her other. She tested the door to make sure it was locked and then returned her hand to the gun.

"Get off my porch, Carl. You got your due." She took another step and then another until Carl backed down the stairs and had his hands held chest level, begrudgingly resigned. "I won't let you bully me anymore, you hear me?"

Carl mumbled something that Veronica couldn't hear and then stormed off toward a car parked down the street. She fell to the ground, the dust from the dried-out grass coating her skin and gritting between her teeth. If it weren't for the sirens growing louder with every second, she would've stayed behind the shrub and made sure the crazy man who had just sped away wasn't going to loop back around with new resolve. Instead, she forced herself to her feet, wincing when her arm twisted slightly. Pulling it tightly to her side, she skirted around the foliage and ran toward the house. Gillian was sitting on the front steps, gun dangling between her bent legs, exhausted but wearing a look of relief that Veronica envied.

"Gillian, you were *amazing*." She patted her friend on the shoulder, needing a moment to fully process what she'd witnessed. Gillian had done what Veronica's mother had never been able to—stand up to a powerful man and say no. At first she hadn't known how to search for Sophie without her mom by her side, but it was turning out that Gillian might be a better option.

*Sophie,* Veronica thought the name again with urgency. They were getting off track. She quickly refocused.

"We need to go. I think someone called the cops." But Gillian didn't budge; she stared at the ground, the gun held loosely in her palm, swaying back and forth. The sirens were distinct now, and with each whir, Veronica's thinking focused into a sharper point. "You're holding a gun, Gillian. They think I'm a crazed psychopath. We have to go." When she still didn't flinch, something inside Veronica snapped, and she yelled. "Get your ass in the car!"

Gillian turned to look at Veronica, an amused wrinkle creasing her forehead. "What did you say to me?" she asked, almost chuckling.

Veronica was not laughing. Her arm throbbed, her heart was racing so fast she worried it was going to burst, and she was about to shove her hand into Gillian's pants pocket and fish out the keys herself.

"I said—get your ass in the car." She put out her hand, refusing to let down her intensity even for a second. "And give me your damn keys."

Strange expression still in place, Gillian fished the keys out and handed them over. Without waiting to see if Gillian was following, Veronica ran to the car, clicking the "Unlock" button several times. With a roar, she started the engine and put it into drive just as Gillian flopped into the car and slammed her own door closed. With Veronica's foot on the gas, they jolted forward. Maneuvering around a few parked cars and one abandoned trike, Veronica followed the street, letting the speedometer rise as rapidly as the four-cylinder engine would allow.

A loud thump came from Gillian's seat when Veronica turned a sharp corner so she could disappear from sight before anyone, including the police, could happen upon their speeding escape car.

"What was that?" Veronica searched Gillian for the source of the sound and then back at the road.

"What was what?"

"That thump? Was it my phone?" Veronica took a slightly more well-measured turn onto Highway 42 and glanced around the car for her phone so she could start the GPS app.

"Sorry, dropped it." Gillian, pale and calm despite the run-in with her ex, leaned over in her seat and retrieved an item from the floor and placed it in the cup holder between them. Veronica's gaze immediately fell on the heavy item—the gun.

"Oh my God, Gillian, you brought it with you?" The handgun rested casually in the cup holder like a ninety-nine-cent Diet Coke from the corner market. Gillian didn't respond at first, leaning forward in her seat and straining against the seat belt she must've put on in their high-speed escape.

"Yeah." She grunted a few times, straining forward, as Veronica tried to watch both her and the road. "I'm not letting you go in without some backup." Sitting back, she produced Veronica's missing phone and placed it in the empty cup holder closest to the steering wheel.

"You went back to your house to get that gun, didn't you?" she asked, not sure if she was impressed or scared by her friend's particularly aggressive turn.

"I sure did, sweetie." She plugged Veronica's dark phone into the iPhone charger lying between the seats like she owned the device. Then she passed over her own cracked phone with the GPS open on the screen. "Now put the pedal to the metal. We've got to get ourselves to Durham and find your girl."

# CHAPTER 20

Fifty-nine minutes isn't very much time when you have a million things on your mind. At first Gillian tried to talk about what had happened at her house, but that led down a path to her asking for forgiveness over and over again as though it were her fault Carl had assaulted Veronica.

Then, in an effort to refocus, Veronica would try to tell the story of Sophie's disappearance with a little more specificity than the rushed texts and brief spurts of information from earlier in the day. But she found that she couldn't bring herself to explain more than the basics of the morning without anxiety threatening to take over. It was much easier to answer a few questions about the discussion with Mark at the cemetery.

The rest of the journey she spent in her head, replaying each detail and trying to find any small item she may have missed on her first time working through the scene of Sophie's disappearance.

As far as she could tell, Sophie had vanished while Veronica was having dinner with Gillian. Her mom said she'd checked on her one more time at about 9:30 p.m. before heading to bed. If only Veronica could remember if she saw her during her drunken return home. She didn't remember going into Sophie's bedroom, so she couldn't know for sure, but the idea that someone took Sophie right out from under Veronica's sleeping nose didn't seem very likely.

There were still so many questions she couldn't answer, like why would someone want to take Sophie? Who would want to track Veronica's every movement and put a private investigator on her tail? Where was her mother, and why hadn't Veronica heard from her—was she angry or injured or both? How could the police give up so easily on finding who really took a six-month-old baby?

As they passed the welcome sign for Durham, Veronica's stomach began to squirm like it was filled with a thousand tiny insects. Not cute butterflies, but the large, juicy grub worms that used to live under her grass and eat at the roots before she got her yard treated.

"Are you ready?" Gillian asked, breaking the silence. Since confronting her ex-husband, a firm calmness had come over Veronica's friend. Gillian still had her soft and compassionate underbelly, but now she seemed to be wearing a plate of armor on her back.

"Of course," Veronica replied with confidence she didn't exactly feel. The gun in the cup holder rattled with each bump in the road. She knew Gillian was probably right and she shouldn't go into such a dangerous situation unarmed, but the day had already gotten so far out of control that she was concerned what she might do when faced with someone who had at the very least taken her baby and at the very worst hurt her.

The GPS on Gillian's phone gave her periodic warnings that grew more complicated. The speed limit had dropped progressively over the past few miles from fifty-five to thirty-five, and suddenly she felt like they were crawling along. The houses became closer and closer together and grew from tiny bungalows like Gillian lived in to more architecturally complicated and carefully maintained homes. If it'd been another day and another time, these houses and their history would've fascinated Veronica, and she would've spent days looking them up, and maybe even knocking on a door or two. But today it was all she could do to keep her foot from pressing harder on the gas pedal as she sped through the town, leaving those historical wonders in a blur behind her.

Soon the traffic increased, as did the number of stop signs and pedestrians. The town would have been tiny if it weren't for the bustling university at its center. In fact, from what Nick's sister had told her, much of Durham's population was made up of academics and other staff who ran Duke. After going to college in a metropolis like New York City, Veronica thought this college town had a homey feel to it that didn't match the tense anticipation inside the car.

All the turns were clustered together now, one swiftly following another. The passing houses became more and more like set pieces to Veronica, her anxiety building and making a high-pitched ringing sound in her ears that she was sure others could hear. Gillian must've read the growing tension in the car; she sat upright in her seat like a pole had been fused to her spine.

"When we get there, I'll park around the corner from the house, and I want you to stay in the car," Veronica said.

"I told you, I don't like the idea of you going in there alone. What if they hurt you? I mean, they clearly know who you are. Maybe I should go instead. They don't know me."

"You are not going. You don't know what to ask or what Sophie even looks like in person. If these people are involved in any way, they won't expect me to show up on their doorstep."

"Unless Mark warned them we were coming."

Veronica thought back to her discussions with Mark, how the look in his eye when he stared down at her hadn't changed even when she'd called him out or when he'd learned that she was a suspect in her child's own disappearance.

"I didn't tell Mark where we were headed," Veronica said, feeling like he had been on their side, but not wanting to bet on it. Her phone sounded, making her jump.

"You have reached your destination" echoed through the car as she drove past a beautiful new-construction two-story Victorian, brick along the front with white columns and a sweeping front step that led to a striking red door. A white picket fence that looked like it'd be about hip high on Veronica lined the yard, and there was an arch of climbing roses curving over the driveway that went far past the house toward what must've been a detached garage in the rear of the property.

It was lovely, picturesque even, the kind of place you imagined children playing as their mother darned socks on the front porch. For some reason it didn't look like the beginning of an unusually hot summer. Here it seemed summer's heat only brought out roses faster and gave children a reason to run in the sprinklers.

She squinted to see through the gauzy curtains hanging on the other side of the front picture window and only saw the outline of what she imagined was a dining room table. Another light illuminated an empty sitting room where two sofas and a table with a floral centerpiece were clearly visible from the street.

"Looks like someone is home," she said, questioning herself only slightly. This place looked so normal, not like a den of child-stealing psychopaths. But it was her only lead. She tapped the screen of her phone to turn off the map and then pulled around the corner, two houses down from the dreamy house with yellowish lights in the window glowing in the early twilight.

"I don't like this, Veronica. I don't like this at all. Can we call someone? If you don't want to call the police, maybe you can get Mark to come? Or maybe we should call Lisa—"

"No." Veronica turned off the car and started to collect her few belongings. "I'll turn on the phone and leave it on like with Mark, but if we get disconnected and I don't come back or respond to texts or calls . . . then you can call the police, okay? Give me fifteen minutes."

"*Fifteen minutes?* That's enough time to kill you and start making a suit out of your skin. Five minutes—or you screaming bloody murder—is plenty."

She hesitated, knowing her plan was very limited, including only "bring Sophie home" or "here is another lead." But she also knew she wasn't going to leave that house until she knew why these people were having her followed and whether they knew anything about her child.

"Ten minutes if everything sounds normal and then you can call 911, okay? Good enough?" Without a purse or pockets, Veronica put her phone in her bra and tried to adjust it so the outline wasn't as obvious against the clingy fabric.

"Good enough." Gillian nodded, slumping in her seat for a second before sitting upright again. "If you take the gun. Good enough, *if* you take the gun. In case of an emergency."

Veronica sighed. "Where am I supposed to put a gun, in my bra with my phone? You're going to be listening to everything; why do you need me to take a loaded firearm?"

Gillian reached behind the seat and yanked out a grungy-looking bag, pink with white polka dots, stained by what looked like a tan liquid. With an exaggerated shake, she dumped the bag out onto the back seat of the car with a reddish-brown puff of dust, leaving an impact mark on the gray fabric. Scooping up the gun with no trepidation, she flipped a switch on the back of the gun, tossed it into the bag, and forced the zipper shut.

"Just in case, that's why." She held the gun bag out toward Veronica.

"I don't feel comfortable . . ."

But Gillian shook her head, the same look she'd had when Carl tried to get past her into her house earlier pressing into the lines of her face. "Take it or I call the police."

"You wouldn't . . ."

Gillian shoved the bag toward her. "I would."

The streetlight above the car flashed on, and the rest down the street followed like they were playing a game of tag. She wanted to get into the house before it got too late for a knock on the door to still be normal. All this bickering was wasting time. She put out her hand, angrier at Gillian's stubbornness than resigned to the fact that she was walking into a quite possibly dangerous situation.

"Fine. Give it to me." The bag landed heavy in her palm, and Veronica wondered if the gun was pointing right at her. "Please tell me I just saw you put the safety on."

"Yeah." She cocked her head to one side. "Need me to show you how to take it off?"

"No, I've got it." She placed the bag under her armpit like a clutch purse and opened the car door.

Just as she was about to slam the door shut on Gillian's eager face, the other woman called out, "Be safe!" and a deep throb of regret pounded through Veronica. Her feelings had been turned off for so long, numbed by routine and avoidance in an effort to keep away the deep sadness of grief, that any emotions like the ones she'd experienced today felt foreign and overwhelming. The terror and panic that followed Sophie's disappearance were intense, yet to be expected, but the way she felt toward Gillian was different and uncomfortable. Gillian was her friend. How had that happened in all this madness? Veronica leaned down one more time and made contact with the increasingly hardening eyes of her companion.

"Thank you for taking care of me." She patted the lump under her arm, only one of more than a dozen evidences of Gillian looking out for her. "I'll be out soon; I promise."

She closed the door and walked boldly forward, following the gray trail of sidewalk that traced the perimeter of the block of impeccable houses. There was something so wrong about this setting. It didn't give her hope for finding her girl. The tall black streetlamps kept the street nearly as bright as midday. The houses had the curtains open like there were no secrets inside them, ever. She'd been so focused on getting to that dot on the map that she hadn't thought about what would happen if it was a dead end.

It could be a bad lead. Maybe Mark got the address wrong or the information was as fake as the code names on the file. Was she walking up to a stranger's home with a gun under her arm? This could be some sweet old couple that was more likely to sit on the porch swing than steal babies.

She pushed the swinging gate open with her fingertips and crossed into the well-kept yard, not letting her doubts hold her back while also allowing them to hold her up, comfort her, keep her from utter devastation if at the end of this terrible day she didn't have anywhere else to go but a home with an empty crib and a mother she'd scared off when she needed her most.

# CHAPTER 21

The steps didn't even creak as Veronica ascended them. It was universally peaceful throughout the neighborhood, and the target house didn't break the mold. As she approached the door, Veronica could hear the soft murmur of voices and smell something savory cooking inside. The more exposure she got to this town and this home and the people who probably lived inside, the more she began to wonder just what the hell she was doing here.

Veronica took a moment to readjust the heavy bag under her arm, feeling foolish for what was inside. She'd brought a gun to the house of some unsuspecting family off of some information on a PI's phone. Great. What was she going to do next, bring a knife to a schoolyard and just drop it somewhere in the playground for the kids to fight over?

With a gun under one arm and an active phone tucked into the cup of her bra, Veronica was feeling a bit like a sideshow freak who was trying to fit into the real world. She straightened her hair with the palm of her hand and bit her lips a few times, one of her mom's old suggestions for getting color when you had no lip gloss. She rang the doorbell.

The bell that sounded was one of those pretty chimes. It didn't just ring up and down with the familiar dingdong but trilled a tiny melody that lasted a full second longer than expected and probably echoed through the remote corners of the spacious house. If she'd lived in that house, she'd find reasons to ring the doorbell every day. It must be such an exciting sound for those who lived inside. The odd thoughts felt a little manic and did little to bring down her blood pressure.

Short but determined footsteps headed toward her, clomping on what must be a hardwood floor. The steps sounded light and feminine, which both relieved Veronica and confused her. For some reason she had pictured a large man dressed in black who had come to steal her daughter away in the middle of the night.

As the dainty steps grew closer, her mouth went dry. She suddenly wished she'd had something more to eat or drink that day than the Diet Coke Gillian had offered her from Walmart.

The woman turned the knob without taking any time to mess with a lock. The smell of warm pot roast and something sweet baking in the oven burst out from the house like a puff of smoke. A young woman with slight hips and dishwater-blond hair swung the door open wide like she was expecting family, unlike the way Veronica greeted people, opening the door just a crack to see who might stand behind it, friend or foe. The woman looked more like a teenage babysitter or nanny than the homeowner, but a platinum band and large diamond winked at Veronica from the woman's left hand.

The woman's face, which had been warm and welcoming, immediately crunched down so that all her features smooshed together into the middle of her face. Her smile was gone.

"Hi," Veronica blurted, and searched her mind for what she planned to say if she got this far. Most of her strategy had been based on there being some reason for confrontation at the front door, not a totally innocent-looking young woman who seemed to be willing to trust anyone who was going to ring her doorbell. "I'm looking for Suzanne Reynolds. Is she home?" Using the name of a childhood friend, she hoped that at least she could open some sort of dialogue.

"Veronica? Why are you here?" Her voice was as dead and still as her features.

Hearing her name come out of the stranger's mouth sent stab of terror through Veronica's midsection and made colors swim in front of her eyes so that she could barely see through the haze. It was all real. These people had been watching her. They knew who she was. They were interested in her life and in her child.

"Who the hell are you?" Veronica demanded, low, angry.

"Get off my property. I'm calling the police." The childlike woman was now glaring at her, closing the door instead of holding it open. Veronica couldn't let that happen.

"I'd like to see you call the police. I'm sure they'd love to hear how you've been stalking me. I know that you hired a private investigator to follow me. Why? Where is my baby?"

The woman didn't respond, just shoved the door closed, but Veronica put her foot against the bottom and her hand flat against the wooden panels. Ramming from the other side, the panicked woman spoke.

"I will not talk to you. Get off my front porch." She was frightened in a way that reminded Veronica of that trapped-animal feeling again. She was hiding something, and it was more than the fact that someone at this address was tracking Veronica and her life. The waifish woman was hiding and protecting something inside the house.

"You sure as hell *are* going to talk to me. You're stalking me and my kid. Where is Sophie? Where is she?" Veronica's voice rose to a near shriek. Maybe now it was time to call the police, but if she didn't act fast on her own, then this woman would get away and hide. Veronica wouldn't get answers.

Pushing on the door, Veronica tried to place her body over the threshold so it could not click shut. The other woman had her whole body leaning against the other side.

"Get off my porch . . . or else . . ."

With one more shove against her already-aching shoulder, Veronica stumbled back enough that her foot moved and the door slammed shut.

Then there was the sound of someone fiddling with the lock, trying to get it closed.

This woman wouldn't listen to her. She didn't want to talk, and Veronica didn't have time to wait for the police to come. If the woman wouldn't listen to a desperate mother on her own, perhaps Veronica would have to be more compelling.

With a quick flip, she took the bag out from under her arm, unzipped it, and let the gun fall into her hand, heavy but comforting.

With the gun in her right hand, and racing against the scratching sounds of the frantic woman on the other side, Veronica used all the force of her body to ram into the door. Pain shot through her injured arm and up into her neck and head, but the oak door swung open easier than she'd expected it to. On the other side was the wisp of a woman, her knee-length floral skirt up around her hips, sprawled out on the floor like a discarded rag doll. Veronica pointed the gun at her, shaking in her hands.

"Answer my questions and everything will be okay. I don't want to hurt you. I just want my little girl back."

The woman seemed stunned, like perhaps she hit her head when Veronica broke down the door. She raised herself up on her elbows and shook her head a few times like she was trying to get water out of her ears.

"Don't shoot me," she pleaded. "We didn't mean to scare you. Your mother was worried about you and . . ."

"My mother?" A wave of nausea threatened to pull her under. It was a deep, sickening feeling, like when she got a call about the accident and already knew what they were going to say on the other end. Her mother was involved. It all came together into a blurry mess that almost made sense. That's why she disappeared after the fight, not because she was scared or angry at Veronica but because she was *involved*.

Every molecule of guilt and worry transformed into outrage, like they'd gone through an instant chemical reaction. It pounded through Veronica's veins, her blood burning her from the inside out with every heartbeat.

She pointed the gun with a renewed resolve at the woman cowering on floor. "Where is my little girl?" she asked, ignoring all the other possible questions she could have posed at that moment. "Tell me where Sophie is right now."

The woman sat up slowly, pulling her skirt down over her thighs. "I don't have your daughter, Veronica." She touched the back of her head, and her hand came back bloody. The dark swoosh of red seemed to shift her focus. Veronica ignored the blood so it didn't remind her of the other times she'd resorted to violence today. Instead she took in her surroundings.

The wooden floor reached through all the rooms that Veronica could see. No one else seemed to be rushing in to investigate the sounds of their altercation at the door. A maroon runner went up the stairs and turned at a platform to follow the stairs back up to a long hall that disappeared into the recesses of the upper level. On the floor at the foot of the stairs was a phone with a shattered screen, dark but calling to her.

She held the gun up high enough that it would still be a threat to the woman on the floor. The weight of the weapon brought her back to target practice with her dad before she'd learned to run out the door anytime he wanted to be alone with her. It was terrifying holding up a gun and pointing it at another human being. She didn't know if she'd be able to pull the trigger like she had when she was a child and had learned to put a hole in the middle of nearly every paper target put in front of her. She tried to erase the blood and fear from the face in front of her and instead imagine the blank white and black of copy-paper targets instead. If there was anyone she was willing to pull the trigger for, it would be Sophie.

With a steadied mind, Veronica moved over inch by inch, trying to get closer to the device without letting on to her plan. The woman was still tending to her injuries when Veronica reached the phone, but as she leaned over to grab it, a sound pulled her attention away. It wasn't the angelic trill of the doorbell, and it wasn't a timer from the kitchen—it was the sound of a baby crying. Veronica's heart exploded, sending electricity through her limbs and to every corner of her body, leaving her feeling supercharged.

Immediately she aimed the gun again, this time pointing it directly at the woman's head.

"You bitch," she spat. If it weren't for the extra step of taking off the safety, she might have let her finger slip. If she'd hurt her mother and fought against a madman and shoved down a woman she'd never met, it would be nothing to let her finger loosen against the trigger and pull. Instead, she kept the gun held high and backed toward the kitchen, where the crying seemed to originate.

"No!" the woman shouted. "Don't you dare touch her."

Veronica glared at the cowering woman and continued to follow the swell of the baby's wails. "You shut your mouth." She waved the gun like she'd lost any apprehensions to shoot anyone who stood in her way . . . and she was a little afraid she had.

"Don't you touch her!" the woman screamed, scrambling up onto her knees, her skirt going askew again, wrapping around her body. Veronica had two choices: shoot or run. The baby cried again; this time it wasn't a fussy cry but sounded more like a wail of pain or fear. It was Sophie; she was sure of it.

The gun fell to her side, and she forced her feet to run, fast, one flip-flop flying off her foot as she pushed off the hard floor and dived toward the kitchen. The light there called to her like a homing beacon. No one was going to keep her from her baby.

The woman was charging from behind, her feet pounding despite her small frame. But Veronica was fast, and there was no way she'd let this woman get past her. There was no door to the kitchen, just an open entry with white trim around it. She was moving so fast her hand holding the gun slammed against the wooden frame, causing stabbing pain that barely registered because she was so focused on getting to the child in the kitchen.

There she was, little blond-haired, blue-eyed Sophie Shelton, tears streaming down her face, screaming now in a swing that was ticking but barely moving. Veronica's throat clinched shut, fighting back a scream, making it hard to breathe.

"Oh, my sweet baby!" she sobbed, rushing forward and putting the gun down by her side as she knelt in front of the swing. There wasn't time to unlatch the seat buckles and lift the tray keeping her secure in the seat. Instead, without thinking, Veronica put one hand under her daughter's arms and the other pinched the white buckle on her right hip and then pulled, gently but firmly. Sophie popped out of the seat, her left foot tangling for a moment in the seat straps but breaking free after two tugs. Then she was in Veronica's arms and pressed into her hip like they'd been hanging out that way every day while doing chores or making dinner. She felt perfect.

But her awe lasted only a moment before the woman barreled into her and dived toward the gun. It skittered across the floor. The woman grabbed for the weapon and looped an arm around one of Veronica's legs.

"Get off me," Veronica said, kicking hard, trying to free herself. Several hard, shoeless kicks against the woman's shoulder and one final one against her cheek set Veronica free as she slipped out, almost losing her balance, with Sophie held tightly in her arms.

"No!" The woman let out a high, shrill scream and, instead of going after the gun, lunged again at Veronica.

Finally free, Veronica ran. She was a distance runner, but she was still light and fast even on short stretches. The muscle tone was there whether she was running a marathon or escaping a kidnapper who now had a gun. Holding Sophie tight against her chest, Veronica ran barefoot through the dining room and out through the front hall. The front door still stood wide open, so she leaped through it and slammed it shut, hoping it would give her just a few seconds more to get to the car.

Veronica yelled, hoping that Gillian could hear her on the phone through her dress and bra. "Gillian, I don't know if you're still there, but if you heard all of that, I have Sophie. Be ready. We need to go now."

The grass was spongelike under her bare feet, and as soon as she reached the sidewalk, she let her soles smack against the rough cement and pulled Sophie in closer. Her baby was crying, clearly picking up on the drama of the moment. Veronica held her even closer, trying to comfort her while also running for their lives.

Even in the panic of the moment, her daughter's scent filled Veronica's nostrils, the same smell from the blankets Sophie sometimes slept with. Her blond hair brushed Veronica lips like feathers. It had been so long since she'd held her baby in her arms. At eight and a half months, Sophie felt so substantial now. When Sophie was a tiny infant, Veronica used to be afraid she'd break her, that she would just turn Sophie the wrong way and she would crumble into a million pieces.

But this new version of Sophie was full of life. She had a layer of baby fat underneath her skin that welcomed Veronica's fingers and congratulated her for her part in its existence. For one brief second before diving into the back seat of Gillian's car, she let herself feel accomplished that the baby had those rolls. It was because of her milk, her middle-of-the-night pumping sessions and daily devotion to a lactation routine, that she was so healthy. Some part of Veronica *had* been taking care of her daughter.

That made her proud now that she was holding the product of her efforts in her arms. Most women carried their babies inside them for nine months. Veronica perhaps needed longer. Perhaps her timeline was closer to sixteen months minus a week or two. Whatever the reason, now she had her baby. Now she could hold her. There was no anxiety threatening to take her under. There was only the desire to bring Sophie home and to get away from the woman running after them.

The car was already running. Gillian must've heard something, because she was ready. Veronica flung the back door open and jumped inside, landing on top of some shopping bags and piles of old mail.

"Go! Go now! Fast as you can!"

Gillian didn't hesitate—they shot out like a rocket. Veronica looked over her shoulder. The kidnapper was running at full speed, her dishwater-blond hair blowing out behind her even though there was no breeze on the still-warm summer evening. In her hand was the gun pointed at the ground, and even though the sight of it gave Veronica chills, she was certain the woman wouldn't shoot.

The kidnapper had taken Baby Sophie for a reason. She'd taken very good care of her. Her onesie smelled of fresh laundry, and with a pat on her bottom, Veronica discovered a clean diaper. A woman who took such good care of a baby wouldn't shoot at the car she was riding in.

Two seconds later, Gillian turned onto the main highway that would take them home, and Veronica took a moment to assess the situation. Sophie's cries were slowing as Veronica patted her back and snuggled her in tight against her chest.

How did she never realize that holding their daughter in her arms would bring her some sort of peace about Nick's passing? How did she not know that considering his eyes through their daughter's eyes could make her heart rate steady? But today was not a day for regrets. She had her girl. Now that she'd conquered her anxieties, she could be a real mom and take care of the baby like she always wanted to. She should have been worried she didn't have a car seat for the baby, but instead she just slumped down lower in her seat and prayed that Gillian's safe driving would get them home without incident. They might be on the run from kidnappers, and there might be angry and confused police officers waiting at her house, but none of it mattered. She was a mom again, a real mom, and she was never going to let that go again.

"We found Sophie." She finally said the phrase out loud, her voice heavy with tears. Gillian's overemotional quality used to annoy Veronica, but now she couldn't hold back a few tears herself.

"You know who those people are? Do you think it's safe to go home? Think your mother will be there?"

Veronica forgot Gillian had heard nearly everything. She didn't know why or how her mother was involved, but the idea was unsettling. And now they were heading home—to the house of not just Veronica and her daughter but also the woman who had possibly betrayed them.

"I don't really know."

"So where am I headed then?" Gillian asked as she came to a stop at the intersection that took them out of town and toward Sanford or north toward Washington, DC.

As she watched her baby wiggling in her arms, Veronica tried to imagine running away and leaving everything behind. Eventually the police would figure out that Sophie was alive and someone else was responsible, right? Running away to DC seemed like a beautiful dream, but that's all it was—a dream. It was probably safest to walk up to that house with a baby in her arms and say to the police, "I told you I didn't hurt my child."

"First things first, let's get my car. Sound good?"

"Yeah, that's a great idea," Gillian responded, and pressed down harder on the accelerator. "Off to Dave's Ale House, eh?"

"Dave's Ale House it is." Veronica shifted down even lower in the seat and snuggled the dozing baby against her cheek. The movement of the car and the way that Veronica patted her back must have worked a soothing magic, because soon Sophie's dusty-blue eyes were closed and her perfect Cupid's bow lips partially open, letting out fragrant little breaths. With her mouth against her daughter's hair, Veronica smiled.

# CHAPTER 22

Veronica started awake. Rather groggy, she took in their surroundings. They were just a few miles from the center of town.

Just before Veronica fell completely asleep, she had asked Gillian to go the speed limit as to not attract unwanted attention. Veronica was anxious to get home but couldn't help wondering if there was a vehicle speeding along behind them, trying to catch up. Perhaps there was, but they hadn't been caught and somehow Veronica didn't believe that they would be.

She'd turned her phone off again after leaving Durham, but now that she had Sophie and they were safely back in town, it seemed like the necessity for hiding had passed. Plus, she wanted to see if her mother had tried to reach out to her yet. She fished the phone from her bra and readjusted the baby into the crook of her arm, where she settled back to sleep easily.

She turned on the phone and waited for the official chime to let her know it was launched again. As soon as the apps developed on the screen, notifications began to ding through at a ferocious pace. All from her mother in the past hour.

Ronnie, where are you? Come home.

No one is mad at you. Bring the baby and come home.

Ronnie. I'm serious. I can't help you if you don't let me. Come home now!

Where are you????

*Damn it,* Veronica thought, her heart sinking. Her mother really was involved. What in the hell was she going to do? What if they were walking into an ambush?

Veronica was about to present the problem to Gillian when the phone started to ring in her hands. She checked the caller ID. No name, but the number was familiar.

"It's Mark," she said, her stomach jumping as she pulled herself up to sitting, relieved it wasn't her mom but still nervous. "What do I do? Do I answer it?"

"What do we have to lose?" Gillian made eye contact through the rearview mirror, her eyes illuminated by the light of the oncoming cars. Veronica nodded and pushed the "Talk" button.

"Hello?" she answered.

"Veronica? I've been worried sick about you." It was reassuring to hear the masculine voice on the other side of the phone sound sincerely concerned. "Give me an update."

"How about *you* give *me* an update instead." She didn't want to sound suspicious still, but if she wasn't sure she could trust her own mother, whom *could* she trust?

"Well, I have some good news and some bad news. The good news is that I found some information. It's not the names you wanted, but I do have more info about that break-in four days ago."

"Pull over. Pull over!" Veronica ordered to Gillian in a hushed shout, pointing at the parking lot of Dave's Ale House. The car thumped as they made their way over the transition from the road to the full lot. Gillian made her way around to a side lot of the neighboring strip mall where there were signs that said, "Verizon Customers Only."

"Okay, go ahead," Veronica said, and put the phone on speaker so Gillian could hear. She'd turned around in her seat, biting her bottom lip.

"I was trying to do some additional research on the code name connected to your case. Before I get your hopes up, that lead was a dead end."

"That's okay, I have more information about that. But first," she interjected quickly, stalling, "tell me about the break-in."

Mark blew out a soft sigh on the other end of the phone before responding. "It wasn't a break-in."

"What do you mean? An alarm was triggered. The police came out."

A long silence hung in the air, Sophie's soft breathing the only rebellious sound, and Veronica was worried that Gillian might nibble a hole in her lip if the dramatic pause went on any longer when Mark spoke up.

"I found the paperwork and some prints. We did take pictures inside your residence, but no one broke in." He paused again, some papers shuffled in the background. "It says here in the report from the PI that a key was left in a pot by the back door."

"That's where we keep our spare key," Veronica said, immediately feeling stupid that she kept her hide-a-key in such an obvious place, but even more ridiculous that she hadn't remembered until now. "Oh God. I know what happened. My mother told them where it was." Even Veronica could hear the malice coating those words.

Gillian's eyes went wide, and she slumped down in her seat as if it were *her* mother who had broken all possible trust between a parent and a child. Veronica stretched her shoulders backward, trying to decide whether she was ready to let him in on everything, when the movement woke Sophie. She wiggled against Veronica's arm, and suddenly her little fist flew up and hit her own cheek. Veronica bounced her slightly, knowing what was coming next. Baby screams always started with a silent, frozen mouth, like the Munch painting. When the wail hit, it was loud and made both women flinch.

"Shhhh, Sophie. It's okay. Shhhh," she whispered, comforting the baby by taking her balled-up fist in her own hand and then rocking back and forth, pulling her close enough to give a gentle kiss to the spot Sophie had smacked herself.

"Oh my God, you found her?" Mark gasped through the phone.

She couldn't help letting a smile spread her pursed lips against Sophie's face. She wanted to say, "Hell yeah, we did!" But instead she attempted to keep a level head, knowing this disaster of a day was not over yet.

"We did. She was at the address I saw on your phone."

"*That's* where you found her? What the hell? Who are those people?"

"You're asking me? Maybe you should ask your boss about that one. It was some waify-looking woman. She seemed to know who I was, but once I heard Sophie, I wasn't leaving till she was in my arms."

"Why didn't we start with *that* update? That is some good news. Damn, you are one strong lady, Veronica Shelton."

Gillian waggled her eyebrows at Veronica, and a blush crept into her cheeks. "Well, let's not get ahead of ourselves. I've got Sophie and we are heading home." Or at least that was the plan till those texts popped up.

"Oh." He got serious again. "You feel like it's safe? If those people hired RHI to watch you, they know where you live. And you said you think your mom is involved? Why do you think that? Don't you think she would've given my guys the code to the house?"

"I . . . I don't know," she stumbled through her thoughts, the question throwing her off for a moment. "All I know is that the woman that had Sophie told me that she'd talked to my mom. I mean, I didn't exactly stay to chat, but it makes sense why she wasn't as worried this morning and why she up and disappeared before the police came." Veronica hesitated, finding it difficult to explain why her mom would steal her baby without revealing her own failures as a mother. On the ride back to Sanford, her brain tried to make sense of this kind of betrayal, and the only logical option was that Barb must have believed she was protecting her granddaughter. "I'm sure she thinks she's doing the right thing, but this is insane. Now she's texting me incessantly."

Gillian turned around in her seat, surprised at the latest update on her mother's manipulations. Veronica shrugged at her, still not sure if they should alter their plans to return to the house.

Mark sighed into the phone like he was considering all options. "Good intentions or not, this can't be good. You need to be cautious going home."

"I . . . I don't know what else to do," Veronica said, very matter-of-fact, hoping Mark had a viable plan.

"Hm," he replied, drawing it out in a hum, "it seems a little dangerous to me."

Gillian and Veronica locked eyes, and she knew what she had to do.

"I think it's time to talk to the police," Veronica suggested. The idea was risky, no doubt, but with Sophie in her arms and the information from Mark's agency, they'd likely at least listen.

"Well, how about the police station, then? Not sure your place is safe, Veronica." He said her name protectively. Veronica cringed at the idea of walking into her mind's version of a dirty, chaotic police station where they'd likely take Sophie away from her, at least initially. Now that she had her daughter back, and she could touch her, all Veronica wanted to do was take care of Sophie's every need.

"Sophie at least needs a diaper change and a bottle. Anyway, what can my mom do with the police there? Nothing. Who are they going to listen to?"

He took a loud breath, and she heard more shuffling on the other end of the phone. "How about I go with you, you know, just to be safe?" he asked with so much hesitancy he sounded like a kid asking his grandma for money.

Veronica studied Gillian's facial features, realizing that she was coming to rely upon her input more and more. Her friend scrunched up her shoulder to her cheek and mouthed, "I don't know!"

Bottom line was Veronica couldn't hide away with Sophie until the police figured this all out, because she held too many of the missing pieces like, for one, the child in her arms. No one would figure out this puzzle without her. But even though it was a less frightening option than the police station, it was still terrifying to walk in that front door to a firing squad whose weapons may have been loaded by a saboteur from her own family.

"You'd really do that?" Veronica asked. "I thought you didn't want to get involved. Thought you were worried about your job." Gillian nodded at her like she'd said something profound.

"I've been thinking about it a lot, and if you want my help, I'll be there. You're worth the risk."

Those words couldn't have been more meaningful if he'd said she was the most beautiful woman he'd ever seen. Worth the risk. Both Gillian and Mark were filling spaces in her life that had been achingly empty for a long time. Deciding to trust him was a leap, but his information had led her to Sophie.

"Okay, can you get to Dave's Ale House? I'm going to grab my car and Sophie's car seat and then . . . I guess . . . we can go home together." She nodded at Gillian, who gave a thumbs-up.

"Yes," he responded quickly. "I'm five minutes away. I'll be there as soon as possible. This is definitely the right choice, Veronica."

"I sure hope so," she said almost as much to herself as to Mark. "See you soon."

Veronica bit her lip and kissed the top of Sophie's head as the phone went dark.

"Well then, I guess we should get your car." For just a moment before Gillian began collecting Veronica's things, they sat in a comfortable pause. The calm was filled with a feeling of security and impending conclusion.

As Gillian started up her caregiving fervor, asking a million and one questions, Veronica thought about the first time she'd brought Sophie home. She'd been filled with worries about diaper rash, jaundice, and breastfeeding. Nick had reassured her with a gentle squeeze of her knee and a knowing calm in his eyes that said he thought she could do anything. This time she believed that look he used to give her. She couldn't do anything back then; she barely survived losing the man she loved, leaving her child nearly parentless in the aftermath. But tonight she felt confident and sure of her new future. She kissed the sleeping babe again, letting her lips linger on the long, fine golden strands of hair lying flat on her daughter's head and whispered.

"Let's go home, sweetheart."

# CHAPTER 23

Mark pulled up seven minutes after they'd ended the call. His fancy car slipped right next to Veronica's running Prius, which she'd moved next to Gillian's car. Sophie was sleeping soundly in her car seat, with the air conditioner set at just the right temperature. Both Gillian and Veronica sat in the front seat, trying to hide from the Saturday-night rush of dinner patrons.

Once his car was in park, Mark jumped out like someone had fired the starting pistol. Veronica rolled down the glass, and the hot, humid night breeze poured in, fighting against the cooled air shooting from her dashboard.

"Hey," he said simply, as though he were meeting her casually on a street. His hands were in his jeans pockets, and a nearly tight green T-shirt made her guess his age as younger than she'd guessed before—late thirties rather than midforties.

"Thanks for coming," she said, her eyes only darting up for a moment. "Are you okay with riding together?"

"Why don't you and your friend head over and I'll meet you there if you'll text me the address."

"Oh no," Veronica rushed to add. "We decided that Gillian isn't going with us. I was hoping you'd ride with me instead." Gillian had enough going on with her divorce; she didn't need any more legal issues, and though the gun wasn't registered in her name, Veronica thought it was best for her to be cautious. And driving up to the house with Mark by her side sounded more palatable than going alone.

Before Mark had arrived, Veronica had won that argument, and instead of Gillian sitting in a car for the fourth time that day, waiting for something to happen and listening through a phone, she was going to a hotel. Gillian scoffed at the idea of Veronica paying for a room when she had a "perfectly good house to go to," but there was too much of a chance that Carl could be there, and since Gillian no longer had a gun, Veronica wasn't sure how things would end for her friend this time around. She'd promised to help her resolve that situation in the morning, after Gillian had enjoyed a shower and a good night's sleep and Sophie had spent the first night in eight months cradled in her mother's arms. Plus, what better place to find help than a house full of police officers?

"Yeah, I need some freshening-up time," Gillian said, putting on her daintiest Southern accent, and then wrapped her hand around her waist and unclicked the seat belt. Her hair had flattened throughout the day, and her short hairdo was nearly as fine as Sophie's. As Gillian reached for the door handle, Veronica grabbed her arm at the wrist.

"Hey, lady." Veronica clutched gently, the give of Gillian's skin now something that made her feel safe. "I'll see you soon. Thank you for everything. You saved me today."

"Nah, sweetie, you saved me." She took her hand off the door and gave Veronica a brief squeeze. "I stood up to Carl, I helped you find your baby." Then she added, shyly, "I have a real friend. I owe you."

Veronica shook her head. "Not even close. I'll owe *you* till the day I die." Getting more emotional than she had the energy to manage, Veronica broke away from Gillian and blinked back the gathering moisture in her eyes. "The reservation is in your name. I texted you the confirmation number from the website. I don't think there will be a problem, but if there is, you can call me."

Gillian seemed to catch on to the shift in her tone and gave her a knowing nod. She ducked her head so she could look up through the open window at Mark.

"Good luck to both of you."

Gillian drove away to her hotel room while Mark took his place next to Veronica in the Prius, making it look more like a clown car than a functional vehicle. He looked very uncomfortable, with his knees pressed up against the dashboard, but if he was squished, he didn't let on. Instead, he buckled his seat belt and then looked back at the baby in the car seat.

"I cannot believe you found her on your own." He looked at Veronica and then back at Sophie. "You're pretty amazing, you know that?"

His assessment humbled and annoyed her at the same time.

"You don't really know what I am, Mark. Just like I don't know much about the real you. I found my baby. I think any mother would do the same if she could." Well, maybe not her own mother. The pang of betrayal was still fresh and painful. But most mothers would crawl through fire for their child. How did he know anything about her beyond what his funded snooping had provided? She put both hands on the steering wheel, pulling herself back to reality and away from the draw of Mark's eyes and his barely noticeable but distinctly masculine scent.

"You ready?" Veronica asked, anxious to get things cleared up once and for all. He nodded.

She put the car in reverse and put her hand on the back of the passenger seat. With her arm behind Mark, the car seemed to get even smaller, and for one moment, with the car seat behind her and the protective and helpful man at her side, she realized they looked like a real family—a mommy and a daddy and a little tiny baby snuggled up in the back seat. It wasn't Nick by her side, it would never be Nick, but it felt nice having Mark there, interested, helpful, caring. She put the car back into drive and let her hand graze his shoulder as she placed it back on the steering wheel.

"I'll tell you the whole story on the way."

# CHAPTER 24

It only took a few minutes to get to Veronica's street. After hearing a significantly abbreviated version of Sophie's rescue, not including the confrontation with Gillian's ex or the handgun, Mark suggested that she take one drive past her house to assess the situation before heading in. She agreed and turned tentatively onto Mayfair Lane. The streetlights were different from the black iron ones in Durham and didn't have the same romantic effect. These lights were tall with sliver posts and yellow light that washed out the surrounding greenery into a sickly jaundiced color and turned Veronica's pale arms into sallow appendages.

The small, counterfeit family drove past Veronica's house, going the exact speed limit. Veronica had expected the car-lined street of that morning, unmarked vehicles and squad cars alike up and down the road in front of 7380 Mayfair like kids waiting with their empty candy bags for a parade to start.

But even before reaching her bungalow, it was clear that the street was empty. All that remained was the broken-down Buick two houses down that probably hadn't left its parking spot on the street since well before Veronica had signed the mortgage on the house and, on the other side of the road, a bike that some kid had ditched hastily, maybe too late for dinner to put it away in the garage. No squad cars, lights flashing. No uniformed police officers pacing in front of the house. No curious, suited detectives discussing strategy on the front porch. In fact, as they passed the house, not one light was on. It looked completely empty.

"What the hell?" Veronica cursed under her breath, wondering if she was imagining things or had somehow forgotten where she lived. But no, it was her house and it was her empty driveway and dark windows.

"I thought you said the place was crawling with police?" Mark asked, scanning the house even as they passed it.

"It was when I left this morning." She turned her eyes forward again, trying to think through it all. "Maybe it's a ruse? Maybe they want me to think it's safe to come home so they can trap me."

"Damn, maybe. You said your mom has been texting you?" Mark asked. Sophie started to fuss, small whining grunts that grew into louder sounds of displeasure. With the instincts of a seemingly well-practiced mother, Veronica reached back and rocked the car seat with one arm while continuing to debate with Mark.

"Yeah, but I didn't think the police would just leave. Or God, it could be the police pretending to be my mom. I didn't even think of that." It was sad to Veronica that this idea of the police setting a baited lure was more comforting than the idea of her mother asking her to come home.

The rocking wasn't helping. Sophie's whimpers turned into full-on cries, and instead of running away, Veronica felt the urge to pick up the baby and comfort her. Mark continued, but it was hard to listen with Sophie's wails.

"Yeah, it's not procedure to let a person of interest leave the scene of the crime. I mean, if we were in New York, this would be all-out manhunt, tracking you down in different counties, following the location of your phone using cell towers. But I'm here now. I can corroborate your story. You have Sophie. This will all work itself out, I promise."

"You know what?" Veronica put both hands back on the steering wheel. It was time to finally put her child's needs first in her life. "You're right. We've got the baby; that's enough information. If it's a trap, then all we have to do is tell them about the house in Durham. My baby is hungry; we are going in one way or another." Veronica looked up and down the road and then made a slow U-turn in the middle of the intersection. They traveled the street again, and this time Veronica pulled up into her driveway as if she were coming home from a trip to the store.

"Do you think we should go through the garage rather than the front door, just to be safe?"

"Yeah, good idea." He scanned the front of the house like the officer had earlier that week when the alarm had been tripped. How had she missed these protective traits in him when she thought he worked at a boring bank job all day? "Wait till you have the baby out just in case they don't know we're here yet."

"Okay," Veronica agreed. After parking in the driveway, she quickly unbuckled Sophie, who was screaming desperately now, her fists flailing and face red. Sad little trails of tears streamed down the side of Sophie's face, and Veronica wiped them away, the wetness soaking in and healing some broken part of her. She wrapped her arms around Sophie and held her tight but not suffocatingly so, hoping just the beating of her mother's heart against hers would bring comfort before she could get a bottle warmed and her diaper changed.

Mark stood behind Veronica every step of the way, like he was blocking her from some sort of invisible threat, close enough that she could smell his fabric softener or deodorant. After retrieving Sophie, she leaned inside the car and pressed the garage-door button. It lifted with a whir, just as empty as it had been that morning.

"Here, take my key." Veronica passed her keys to Mark.

"Uh, why don't you let me do that?" He put himself in front of her again, slipped in the key, and tested the doorknob before she could protest at his overprotectiveness. The door opened on his first try, and he swung it wide and put up his palm and a finger over his lips, reminding Veronica that he used to do this for a living. He disappeared inside the darkness as she shushed Sophie and considered how ridiculous it was to tiptoe into her own home with a screaming baby.

Without waiting, she crossed into the house. Her baby was hungry, and she wasn't going to be able to nurse her, so it was time to pay the piper, swallow the pill, face the music, or whatever other silly idiom that could define her life right now.

"Shhhh, sweetie. Mama is here. Let's get you some food." Hearing Sophie's cries echo through her main floor, Veronica felt a sudden shame hit her in the gut; she remembered once again all the time she'd lost with this little girl but made herself push forward into the kitchen. She grabbed a teething ring from the freezer and placed it gently into Sophie's open mouth. Her gums slowly worked at the cool plastic, and she soon started sucking. "There you go."

Trying not to think about what Mark might find elsewhere in the dwelling, she opened the fridge and grabbed the first bottle on the top row.

"Hm." She inspected it closer. Empty. It was strange, but the whole day had been strange, so Veronica dropped the bottle in the sink, wondering if it had been returned by her mother after a feeding, and grabbed the next bottle. Empty. "What in the world?" she whispered. Sophie dropped the teether on Veronica's third trip to the fridge and started to fuss again. This time Veronica took out each of the last three bottles one at a time and then tossed them in the sink. They were all dry as a bone. Every last one.

Angry but trying to stay calm for Sophie's sake, she yanked down a new, sterile bottle from the cabinet by the sink and then slid the can of formula over from its hiding place behind the paper-towel holder. She'd made a few bottles for Sophie since getting the can, but the slightly sweet smell of the dust still made her feel conflicted. Right now, she didn't have time for those feelings; Sophie was close to exploding, so she blocked them out. It was like closing a door, and before, the pushback on the other side kept her from ever getting it completely shut, but today, for some reason, she got it slammed closed.

Shaking the bottle to mix the powder and purified water, Veronica put Sophie into a cradle hold and wormed the bottle's nipple into her mouth. Sophie's tongue played with the plastic tip until a drop fell onto her tongue, and she wrapped her mouth around it gratefully. As she sucked blissfully on the off-white liquid, she locked her eyes on Veronica's face like she was trying to memorize it. Veronica smiled.

"I'm going to be here all the time now, baby. I promise." Like she'd been waiting to hear those words her whole life, Sophie's eyelids started to droop, and her sucking slowed slightly as she dream-ate her good-night meal. No matter where the milk came from, Veronica felt immense satisfaction at personally participating in feeding her child.

With Sophie taken care of, a new concern came to the front of her mind. Where the hell was Mark? There couldn't be police in the house, or they would've come when Veronica walked in with a crying baby, so where was he?

She left the kitchen, still holding the bottle to Sophie's mouth with one hand and cradling her body with the other. Veronica's feet were still bare, and the cool tile of the kitchen sent a shiver through her that made her want a hot shower. Yes, that's what she needed once she got Sophie fed and changed—hot shower, new clothes, some real food. She wished going to bed were on that list, but bed wasn't an option until she'd found out what had happened to her mom and why she let those people take Sophie.

"Mark," she said, not sure if she was whispering because of the non-existent police or the possibility that her mother might be still hiding out in the house. "Mark?"

She listened closely after each call, hoping that she'd hear his deep voice calling to her or telling her everything was going to be all right. Nothing, not even the shifting movements of someone walking through the house. It was like she had made him up. He wasn't in the front room, where the chairs were in their altered positions from when she'd moved them to cover the blood from her mother's fall. The dining room looked like someone had come in with a laser beam and disintegrated everyone in the middle of a meeting, the table filled with scraps of paper, a random pen, empty coffee cups, one with lipstick on the lid, and chairs pushed out in all directions. The house was a ghost town, and it seemed that anyone who walked into it disappeared into thin air.

A rumbling erupted in Sophie's diaper, and even with little hands-on experience, Veronica knew that sound. Her search for Mark would need to wait. He was probably doing that overprotective thing again and searching every corner of the house. She was finding it less and less annoying. The bottle was empty, so she dropped it in the sink with the other five empty bottles, shifted sleepy-eyed Sophie to her shoulder for a burp, and then headed upstairs.

The third stair creaked, and a nervous, excited feeling bubbled up inside Veronica's midsection. This was real life. She'd been hiding from it for a long time, but now it was finally here. Somehow the euphoria of finding Sophie and holding her numbed the confusion and concern about her mother. As she reached the top of the stairs, something made her slow down. The door to Sophie's room was closed, and a yellow light cast a pale net on the floor in front of it. The whole house was dark; she hadn't dared to turn on a light yet just in case the police drove by and changed their minds about her guilt. Sophie let out a soft burp and hiccup, and a warm gush flowed over Veronica's shoulder.

"Oh, sweetie," she gasped. She put Sophie on her clean shoulder, rubbed her back, and ran up the last few stairs, even more ready for a shower than before.

The door swung open easily, and after being in near darkness since the sun went down, Veronica was disoriented by the light in the room. She blinked rapidly, the room coming into focus. Mark was standing on the far side of the room with his back to the door, facing closed curtains.

"Mark. There you are." He spun around on one foot, a look on his face that said he didn't expect to see her there. He seemed—off. It scared her.

"Veronica," he started, but she interrupted.

"Are you okay? What's going on?" she asked, taking another step forward into the room, but then she stopped in her tracks. Mark was not alone. Sitting in the rocking chair was Barb DeCarlo.

She was fully dressed, hair and makeup done like she hadn't run out of the house in her pajamas, a white bandage on her temple the only sign of their fight that morning. She slid her bottom to the edge of the seat and sighed a deep, sad, meaningful sigh.

"Mom," Veronica said flatly, not sure if she should run out the door or call 911. "Where is your car? What the hell do you think you're doing here?"

"My car isn't important right now. I'm here to help you, Ronnie," she said, her eyebrows hanging low and mouth turned down so drastically it looked like she was faking a frown. "I'm sorry this got so out of hand."

"Help me? That's cute." An internal fury bubbled and brewed, growing till it burned her from the inside out. "You sure helped me a lot when the police were here this morning, or when you let strangers come into my house and take pictures of Sophie's room, or when you helped crazy people take away my child."

"Half of what you just said is total drivel," her mother shot back. She ran a careful gaze over Sophie. "You know you can't keep her, right?"

"Damn you," Veronica growled. "Damn you to hell. How dare you. Look, Ma, I'm holding her. I fed her a bottle, of formula, no less. Thanks for dumping my breast milk, by the way. That was below you, Ma."

Barb shook her head and then covered her face as though she couldn't stand to look at her daughter holding her grandchild. Sophie started to squirm in Veronica's arms. She needed a diaper change and to go to bed. Barb wasn't going to stop Veronica from taking care of her baby. Maybe if she saw it with her own eyes, things would change.

With a desperate glance at Mark, who seemed caught between wanting to help Veronica and not knowing what was going on, she turned her back on her mother, praying that he would protect her if Barb tried anything crazy. Just twenty-four hours earlier, she would've placed a million dollars on the fact that her mother would never do anything to betray her, but until she heard a better explanation for what had happened that morning and why her mom still wanted to take Sophie away, Veronica was going to keep up her guard.

Veronica laid Sophie on the changing table, keeping one hand on her belly and grabbing the supplies from the open shelf underneath. With wipes and clean diapers at Sophie's feet, Veronica unbuttoned Sophie's onesie and started on the process of changing her daughter. She hadn't done it in so long, and back then it'd been a tiny newborn's bottom and not a wiggly, smiley, curious eight-month-old's bottom.

"Hey, darling. Mama's got you. I'll never let you go. I promise." She started to sing as she worked. It felt so right, so natural, like she'd done it a million times before.

When Sophie stopped wiggling and looked up into her face, Veronica hummed a soft, slow version of "You Are My Sunshine," the same song Nick used to sing while rocking Sophie through her colic. She drew the last words of the verse out, their meaning more profound than ever before because she'd almost lost her "sunshine" that day. As she finished up the diaper change and slipped a layette gown over Sophie's head and wormed her arms into the sleeves.

"There you go, darling. You are ready for bed." Veronica kissed her daughter's cheek and then sterilized her hands with the pump under the changing table. Veronica turned then, holding Sophie up for her mother to see, almost like when she was a little girl and started to love art and would bring home her special pictures for her mother's approval.

But tonight, her mother didn't smile and tell her, *Good work, baby!* Tonight, Barb DeCarlo was crying.

"I told you I could do it, Mom. See. I don't know what happened, but I can do it now. I can take care of her. I'm cured!"

"I can't do this," Barb cried and covered her face with her hands again. "I can't take the baby away. Don't ask me to."

Veronica, about to put Sophie in her crib and rub her back till she fell asleep, stopped. A sickening feeling came over her like her insides had been pulled out through her throat in one massive yank. She backed away from the crib and, more specifically, from Mark.

"What the hell is she talking about, Mark?" Veronica's voice was now as cold and hard as a stone in a mountain river. She glared at the man she'd let into her life, first because of what seemed like a coincidence and then out of desperation. Mark, who had been leaning back against the window frame, stood tall, so much taller than she'd remembered. He was more well muscled than she'd let herself notice before when she'd been playing around with ridiculous flutters of romantic interest.

"Don't panic, Veronica. Your mom explained everything. It is a big misunderstanding, and it's all going to be okay," he said, and if it'd been twenty minutes earlier, she might have believed him. But not now, not with the slow and determined way he was walking across the room with his hands outstretched and his focus always shifting between Veronica's face and the baby. "All you need to do is give me the baby."

# CHAPTER 25

Veronica lunged backward as if a poisonous snake were trying to bite her child, but her feet tangled in the multicolored carpet, and she stumbled and fell, hard, turning her body so that Sophie was protected. When she hit the floor, all the air rushed out of her, lungs empty of oxygen, she tried to take a breath but couldn't.

The world spun around her, and she could feel Sophie slipping from her fingers. The more she grasped for the baby, the closer she came to losing consciousness completely. On the edge of her awareness, Veronica could hear Mark talking to her mother. Sophie was not in her arms anymore.

"Go, take her back to Daisy. We'll be in touch soon."

Air started to return to Veronica's deflated lungs, and as the oxygen hit her brain, she rolled to her side and attempted to get on her knees. Her mother held Sophie in her arms.

"Please don't let anyone hurt her, okay? This isn't her fault."

"I would never let anyone hurt Veronica, I promise." Mark put a hand on Barb's shoulder but, seeing Veronica's movements, pointed to the door. "Hurry."

With one deep breath, or at least the deepest she could manage, Veronica wailed out to her mother as Barb rushed out the door, once again taking her daughter away.

"*You bitch!*" she cried, a sob cutting off half of her scream. She scrambled to her knees and then stumbled to her feet, tripping over herself. The pinks and yellows of the room twisted into a pastel swirl as she rushed for the door, but before she could reach it, Mark had a tight grip around her waist. He dragged her back into the room, her feet unable to get any traction on the loose shag of the nursery carpet. It felt like all the good in the world was being swept away when Sophie left in her mother's arms. The injured animal inside her riled up again like its wounds had been stabbed, and she lashed out, pulling at Mark's arm, a fierce wail rising in her throat.

"Veronica, shhhh, Veronica. I'm so sorry, but you have to let her go. They're going to call the police if you don't."

She used her nails this time, digging into the flesh and hair of his forearm, wishing it were high enough that she could bite him and get free. She'd been so close to having her baby back, her life back, and now it was gone—again.

"Don't you touch me. You're with them. You're a liar. Get off me." She wrestled against his arms, but the more she fought, the tighter they clamped down like a Chinese finger trap.

"Listen to me; I'm on your side. I'm on your side, Veronica." He whispered in her ear, his breath moist against her face. He spun her around like a ballerina and held her in front of him, leaning down so his face was in front of hers. "Your mom wants what is best for you. She told me everything. You'll see; it is going to be okay."

She was going to vomit. His words didn't compute, and the sympathetic look on his face confused her rather than calmed her. She shook her head, lost in panic and horror and wishing she could contact Gillian. She was still safe, or at least Veronica hoped she was. Every time she turned around, someone else betrayed her. And now Sophie was gone.

"Whatever that woman told you to make you help her, it's a lie." Spit built up at the corners of Veronica's mouth. Her hair stuck to the tears spreading across her cheeks, and a strand stuck to her bottom lip. Mark had been reasoned with before. Maybe she could get through to him again. She grabbed on to the front of his shirt and pulled him in till she could see the stubble on his chin. Each phrase was interrupted with a gasping breath like she couldn't get enough air. "I'm sure she told you I was sick and I wasn't a good mom to Sophie, but I'm better now. You saw me—I took care of her. She was completely safe with me. I'm a good mom, Mark. I swear I am. I swear I am."

She stood there with his hands on her shoulders, exposed, vulnerable, her eyes meeting with his in open desperation. His looked back, his gaze soft and concerned. It was working. She was getting through to him.

"I believe you," he said convincingly, and then slid his arms around Veronica and pulled her into an embrace. She wanted to wrench back and run after her mother, but if this was what he needed to decide for himself that she was sane enough to be helped, then she would surrender to his embrace. There was something in his voice and touch that let her know that he wanted to help her even if he was doing it in all the wrong ways. She placed her cheek against his chest and flattened her hands against his sides. His body was different from Nick's, longer, leaner, and his arms were strong like they could fight off any obstacle standing in their way. And he was on her side.

"Then let's go stop her." She slid her flat hands around his firm waist till they met and her body was leaning against his. "Together."

"I wish I could." Mark rested his cheek on the top of Veronica's head and took a deep breath, his arms tightening around her in a whole different way than before. He rocked his head back and forth on top of hers. "But your mother is right. You can't keep her."

A harsh gust of betrayal blew away any of the warm, comforting feelings his arms and words had provided. She didn't feel safe now. Now, she was trapped.

"Let me go," she said coolly, and went stiff, releasing her embrace.

He wasn't going to help her. Her mother had said some magic words that had burrowed into his brain like a parasite, and now he wasn't going to help her. He couldn't be involved directly or else he wouldn't have sent her to get Sophie the first time, but how did he turn on her so quickly?

He was still holding her close, despite her demand. "There's a hospital your mom found for you. She didn't get to tell you about it, but it sounds nice."

"You've got to be kidding me. You all are taking crazy pills." She wriggled against his now-suffocating encirclement. "I'm better now. I'm better."

He held her tighter till her arms were pinned against her sides. "I can't let you go until you promise you won't run away. Promise me you'll listen."

"I'm not listening to a word you say." She dropped her voice an octave and stood completely still. "You are just a creepy stranger I never should've talked to."

All the warmth went out of his half hug, half prison, and he put his hands back on her upper arms and stood up so their bodies were no longer touching.

"So that's a no?" he asked. When she found the courage to glare up into his face, she saw hurt there, and a tiny pang of regret nagged at her consciousness.

"That's a hell no and a get your hands off me this second," she growled, unable to stop herself despite hating what her voice sounded like when it played in her own ears.

"They thought you'd listen to me better, but they were wrong." Mark shook his head and then looked up at a spot over her shoulder before speaking. "It's not working. You do your own dirty work." With that, he released her, and she almost collapsed standing on her own. There was a charge to the air that was unfamiliar to Veronica. She'd walked into a trap set by her mother and whomever Mark was talking to. Was it an earpiece? A mic in the room? But Mark was staring in a very specific direction. Veronica's fists clenched at her side, and she tried to follow his eye line.

"What the hell? Who are you talking to?" she asked, and glanced around the room.

Then she saw it, and everything came together—the camera. Someone was watching through the camera. Her knees went weak. Someone really had been stalking her. Someone had entered the safety of her home to spy on her. Someone had brainwashed her mother and taken her baby, and now they were doing it again. She wasn't delusional or paranoid—it was real.

Mark folded his arms and leaned back against the covered window. As soon as he disengaged, Veronica dived across the room and reached the door in two giant leaps, not even checking to see if Mark was following her. The stairs were to her right, but this time she wasn't trying to leave the house. This time she was certain that whoever was behind all this insanity was here under her own roof and sitting in the one place where there was a direct feed from the camera in Sophie's room to a screen.

The room was, not surprisingly, shut up tight, but a closed door wasn't going to stop her. Getting Sophie back wasn't good enough if she couldn't keep her safe. Veronica had to find out who was relentlessly trying to screw up her life.

Whoever the intruder was probably didn't know that there was a key to this door hidden on the frame surrounding it. She'd had to put it there when her mom moved in and Veronica would fall asleep at her worktable. Her mom was always worried that she'd been lost in her grief and had hurt herself on purpose. Once she pried off the doorknob and forced her way inside, only to find Veronica sound asleep on top of a pile of charcoal drawings. After that, they came up with a new plan to save her mother's sanity and save money on broken doorknobs.

Today, with a quick pop of the lock, the door to the studio flew open easily, forcing a gush of wind through the room, sending all the papers rustling and curling toward the ceiling, making the walls look alive. The room was dark except for the one screen glowing on her work desk, where she'd work and watch Sophie. Sitting there, behind the table where she'd been creating since her mom dragged it in off the Canns' driveway on garbage day twenty years earlier, was the one person she never would've expected.

He stood slowly behind the desk and gave her a stiff, forced smile. He was taller than she'd remembered and thinner, but his voice sounded the same as when he'd said *I do* or *I love you* or *Good night, beautiful.*

Today her husband said simply, "Hello, Veronica."

# CHAPTER 26

She'd calculated it at one point. Since meeting Nick at NYU in her freshman dorm, she'd spent 546 weeks sleeping by his side, 3,822 days hearing his voice, 11,466 meals eating across from him, 53,789 miles traveling with him, and, the most devastating statistic, 345,600 minutes without his hand in hers, the last time she counted.

But there he was in front of her, a whole man, with arms that used to hold her and fingers that used to dry her tears. He didn't run to her and pull her into his chest and say, "I've missed you. How did I ever live without you?" Instead, he stood there, hands in his pockets, his hair lighter than she remembered, buzzed on the sides and longer on the top, his shirt one of those button-up athletic-fit ones she used to buy for him when he started his CrossFit phase.

"Nick!" She stumbled forward, slipping on a few loose papers on the floor but willing to go through anything, conquer anything, to touch him again. It was possible he wasn't real. She had to touch him to know. "Nick!"

She flew across the room, expecting him to crawl over the table to scoop her up and tell her everything was going to be okay now that he was home, but he just stood there as she collided with him, her arms going around him, pinning his arms to his sides, her face buried in his chest. He smelled the same, like soap and deodorant and skin, and she wanted to be closer to him, somehow closer. She wanted to melt into him, blend together, go back in time to before he went away.

"Oh, sweetheart." She put her hands on his face, one on each side, and relished the stubble scratching against her palm and the smoothness of his cheekbones. He stood eerily still. "You're alive." She went onto her tiptoes and placed a light kiss on his parted mouth. "I love you. Oh my God, I love you," she whispered against his mouth and then leaned in, pressing her lips fully against his, trying to get closer in any way possible. Nick flinched back like she'd bit his lip and held his chin up like she smelled bad.

"Stop, Veronica." He wriggled his way out of her embrace, backward, bumping into the rolling chair and sending it shooting out behind him and into the back wall. "Stop!" His voice echoed through the room, and he held his hands up like she was holding him hostage.

All her confusion started to swirl together in a blur of whites and reds and blacks, like the papers in the room were twisting around her in a giant cyclone. Why was Nick here? How was he alive? Where had he been all these months? Why was he watching through the camera? Why was he trying to take their baby?

The internal chaos of whys all gathered into a pinpoint of clarity: This was messed up. Completely and totally messed up. Nick wasn't dead. Her life for the past seven months had been a lie, a lie that led to paralyzing sorrow and devastating grief. He'd stolen seven months from her as a real, loving, dedicated mother, and now he was trying to take her child away for good.

"What the *hell* is going on here, Nick? I thought you were dead, and now here you are, fit as a fiddle. How did you pull this off, huh? Just couldn't take the responsibility of a wife and a kid anymore, could you? So you ran away." She charged forward and slammed into him with both hands, shoving him backward, empowered by a red rage that sucked all the light and sound out of the room.

"You know that's not true," he responded, hands still up, deflecting her next blow with his forearm. With a slight stumble, he took another step back.

She came at him again, this time keeping her hands to herself but stepping as far into Nick's personal space as she could without touching him. "If it's not true, why don't you explain it?"

He looked into her eyes, searching with his far-too-familiar blue gaze. She loved those eyes. They were Sophie's eyes, and they looked at her now like she was a stranger he was trying to figure out rather than his wife of eleven years. She used to say that she'd know he didn't love her anymore without him saying a word, because she could see his love in the way he looked at her. But that loving look, the softening of the corners of his eyes, the way each glance lingered on the lines of her face and the curve of her lips, it was gone. This new look was diagnostic at best, hypercritical at worst.

"Veronica, you are not well," he said with very little feeling. "We are going to take you to Green Oaks. They are waiting and ready for you. I can call the police and have them come help, but I didn't want to involve them unless absolutely necessary."

Veronica ignored the words that only half made sense and kept waiting for that spark to happen when they were together, the playful smile, the knowing laugh. "Why did you leave me, Nicky? I've missed you so, so much. Why . . . why did you leave?"

The details of how and where and what in the world had gotten into him could wait till later, but right now all she wanted to know was what she had done to deserve such cruelty.

"Oh, Ronnie, I can't go through all this again. You know why I left. Come on, you always knew why I left."

"Because of the baby," Veronica answered, trying to replay that night in her mind. She'd been sleeping. She'd been exhausted and mentally worn-out; the baby had been crying. Nick had gone to get gas drops and wipes. He'd taken the baby. He'd never come home.

"Yeah." Nick nodded, looking relieved he didn't have to say it out loud. "The baby."

Veronica sniffled loudly and ran her arm across her nose and used her fingertips to clear her cheeks of the angry tears that had flooded everywhere. Her mind seemed to be clicking pieces into place; she swore she could hear it, the click, every time another important piece of information came together, still hodgepodged and confusing but clearing up minute by minute, like when the eye doctor clicked different prescriptions into place. The baby.

"You went to the store . . . for the baby," she added, hoping that adding some detail would pull her story together in some way that made sense. Movement behind Veronica made her check over her shoulder. Mark was standing inside the threshold, looking both like a guard and her guardian. She wasn't sure which he was just yet. Surely she'd find out soon enough. "I got your text that night. You said you were sorry. I thought you died."

She looked back at Nick, hoping he could clarify, but he shook his head.

"No, no, Ronnie. No." He rubbed his face and scratched at his light beard and then slashed at the air. "That's not what I'm talking about."

"Then I have no idea what you mean." She slapped her leg and whimpered. "I don't know what you've been told about me, but I'm better now, damn it. I mean, how the hell can you give a shit now when you've been in hiding or whatever for all this time? I just want Sophie back, okay?"

Nick's features softened, his eyebrows tipped in and his forehead smoothed, and his mouth worked hard to hold in what sounded like a sob. Tears gathered on his bottom lids, and one fell down his cheek and got lost in his beard.

"I want her back too, Ronnie. I want her back too." He covered his mouth again, this time making a noise that sounded like choking. Nick didn't cry. Ever. And the shock that went through Veronica at his tears glued her feet to the ground and made her more scared than she'd been all day.

"So . . . you're just going to take her away from me? We could have her together. We could be a family. You aren't making any sense." She looked to Mark as some bastion of sanity in this ever-spiraling "fun-house," but he was staring at his feet, shaking his head like he wished he'd never gotten up this morning.

Nick made a sudden movement, pushing past Veronica and stopping at her workstation. He shuffled through a pile of papers there, some of them bills, some sketches, one or two dried watercolors that she wanted to add some details to. He picked one up and then went to the wall, filtering through the overlapping pages that hung from pins, lining the walls like three-dimensional wallpaper. All his searching made the papers move in unpredictable ways, as though the room were alive, a bird fluffing its feathers.

"What are you doing? That's my work."

She touched his arm, but he ignored her and kept searching, pulling down selected pages one at a time, stopping at her portfolios where her full-color mock-ups were for Mia's Travels. He rummaged through the stiff pages, filled with brilliant watercolors. Without a word, he yanked out three pages, full spread, final draft, and ready to send to her publisher.

"Hey, stop it! I need those." Veronica reached for the pages, but Nick held them high enough that only her fingertips brushed at them.

"Sit down, Veronica," he ordered and rolled the desk chair toward her and pointed at it with great flourish. "Sit."

And for some reason, even with all the bewilderment and betrayal, she responded to his voice. She still wanted him to love her, and some part of her addled brain thought there must be an explanation. Her darling Nick, her college sweetheart, her best friend, the father of her child. He wasn't the kind of person to do any of this. So she sat.

"You still haven't answered any of my questions, Nick," she said, sitting in the chair. Her bare feet dragged on the floor as he pushed her to the cluttered desktop. He used his empty hand to clear a spot until only wood showed. "Where is Sophie?"

Nick placed a four-by-six piece of cardstock in front of her, a simple pencil drawing of a little girl picking a flower.

"What is this?" he asked her.

"I don't know, a little girl. I was working on ideas for a friend for Mia, and this was an attempt. I used to pick flowers in my backyard on Main. I guess that's where the idea came from," she explained and shrugged. "What does this have to do with anything?"

He placed another picture in front of her. This one was made with oil pastels of a little girl with blond hair, her back to the viewer. She was holding hands with a grown-up, but only his or her hand was visible. The girl was looking up just slightly at the adult in the drawing, just enough so you could see a flash of blue in her eyes. She'd only noticed the ones with the girl running before. What the hell were these?

"What about this one?"

"I don't know, Nick. I illustrate children's books. Another child for another story, I guess. What the hell is going on?"

He tossed down two more pictures right in a row, both of the same or a similar little girl, one dancing in a tutu, her hair swirling across her face, her blue eyes the only thing showing, and the other sleeping, arm across her eye, lips in a soft pout. In every picture, the girl was young but not a baby, maybe five or six years old, a little younger than Mia.

"This is not going to distract me from the real questions, Nick. You don't get to ask me about any of this. You left us. I thought you were dead. I'm not going to forget. I'm going to get Sophie back no matter what you say or do or what that fancy hospital does. I swear I will . . ."

He dropped one last picture, and it fluttered to the table with a finality she wasn't expecting. This was one she'd seen before, a little girl with blond hair running away, her hair trailing behind her in the wind.

She didn't like this picture. She didn't like the pink fluffy skirt of the girl's dress or the little sliver headband in her hair. She didn't like that she was wearing a purple backpack that looked too big for her little body. She didn't like anything about the picture, including the swirling leaves at her feet and the shine of rain on the road. But most of all, she hated the boots on that little girl's feet. They sparkled, even through the paint. Even though they were created with watercolors, she could see the brilliant sparkles as if the sun were shining off of them right in front of her. Those boots . . . She touched them in the picture and then looked up at Nick, knowing but also not knowing at the same time.

"Where is Sophie, Nick?"

"Sweetheart, you know where she is." He put his hand on her shoulder and held it there, firm but gentle, like he knew she was about to fall apart and he wanted to hold her together. "Sophie is dead."

# CHAPTER 27

*Two years earlier*

"Time to get up, sweetie," Veronica said, leaning over Sophie's body. Her little girl loved to sleep curled up like a cat in the middle of the bed, and as a result had plenty of prettily coifed pillows at the head of her bed that never needed to be rearranged. Veronica patted Sophie's back, whispering in her ear, "I made you cheesy eggs."

Sophie rolled over and rubbed her tightly closed eyes. "I love cheesy eggs."

"I know you do. But you know what you don't like?"

Sophie shook her head and squinted between partially opened eyelids at her mom, waiting for the response.

"You don't like *cold* cheesy eggs. Let's get dressed."

Veronica took the wake-up call a step further and pulled the covers down as an incentive to get her daughter up and moving. It didn't work. Sophie turned over and covered her face, a notoriously slow starter.

"Mommy, I'm still tired. Can I just skip school this one time?" she asked with a knowing smirk.

"No, my little bluebird. You are in kindergarten now, and an official big girl. Big girls go to school every day. You're so smart; we gotta keep that big ol' brain growing." She tapped lightly on Sophie's temple and then smoothed her bedhead hair. "Daddy has to take you to school today—I have a meeting in the city."

"Oh," she said, and smiled. "Is Mia going on a new story? We read Mia's Travels at circle time yesterday, and I told the class those were your books." She sat up, the discussion working some powers of waking. She wriggled in place, pulling a strand of hair out of the corner of her mouth, making a face like it was the grossest thing she'd ever experienced. Then she continued. "They didn't believe me, because you have a different name now. Will you call Mrs. Hanson and tell her? Chrissy P. said I was lying."

Veronica laughed. She only felt like a celebrity when Sophie talked about her. She'd used a pen name to keep some anonymity years earlier when she first signed on to the project but had never thought it could cause kindergarten drama.

"Sure, sweetie, I'll see what I can do." Surely it was far too uncouth to go to a kindergarten teacher and claim to be the illustrator of a well-known picture book without it looking like bragging or a power play. She'd have to get Nick's thoughts. At least the story got Sophie up and moving.

The bed was tall enough that the six-year-old needed the help of a step stool to get in and out. She shimmied down the side of the bed, refusing Veronica's assistance. She was in an independent phase brought on by the start of all-day kindergarten. Now she found any opportunity to show how very mature she was. Still a little groggy, Sophie staggered to her dresser and pulled open the bottom drawer where her underwear and pajamas were half-folded, half-rummaged through. After retrieving a pair of purple underwear, she turned to her mother and wiggled her fingers dismissively.

"Can I have some privacy, please?"

"Of course. I'm so sorry," Veronica said as seriously as possible and then tried to cover her smile as she walked out. "It's rainy today, chilly too, so you'll need long pants and sleeves. Okay?"

"I got it, Mom," Sophie responded, sounding closer to a teenager than a kindergartener.

"Pj's in the laundry basket!" Veronica reminded as she backed out and closed the door. The smell of eggs, bacon, and coffee wafted up the stairs, making her stomach growl. She'd been tempted to sneak a little sliver of bacon or nugget of eggs, but the doctor said to come in fasting. Four years of trying. The doctor had looked at her like she'd lost her mind. *Why didn't you come sooner?* she'd asked, as though walking through the doors could've brought forth a miracle baby. Today she'd get those tests, the ones that she should've had years ago, the ones she feared so much because they could tell her definitively if she would ever have another baby. Maybe that's why she didn't come sooner—she didn't want to know if the answer was no.

Nick sat at the table, dressed for work, glasses on the bridge of his nose, reading the newspaper. She was pretty certain he was the only person in the Raleigh-Durham area who still got and read the newspaper every morning. She'd purchased him an iPad and an online subscription to the *New York Times* for Christmas a few years ago, but he insisted that there was no replacement for the oversize pages and smudgy print. Veronica watched him wrestle a page turn and smiled.

"Hey, babe!" Nick put the paper down on the table next to him, giving Veronica a broad, flirty, knowing smile. He'd caught her staring and he knew it. She swore that even after all these years, he was blushing.

"Hey, handsome. How's the news?"

"Dire, as always. Then again, would I read it if the headlines were all 'Lollipop Farms Yield Biggest Crop in Years' or 'Everyone Gets Along!'?"

"Ha, probably not." Veronica put her arm around Nick's shoulders and kissed his smooth cheek. He smelled of shaving cream and soap and had on a freshly pressed shirt straight from the dry cleaner. "You sure look nice today. Anything special on the docket?"

"I have an interview at Duke. I got a text from Stan last night saying that he pulled some strings and got me in to the first round of face-to-face interviews. You remember Stan, right? The associate professor I met last month when I went to my conference? Anyway, I didn't have a chance to tell you last night 'cause you were asleep. But good surprise, right? I gotta get out of here. It's over an hour away, and I'm supposed to talk to him and get prepped before I go in and present to the committee." He glanced at his watch and folded up the newspaper.

Veronica was more hurt than she'd expected to be. He didn't remember. When they talked about more babies, he said he wanted them but then never seemed to want to do anything extraordinary to make it happen. It was a weight she was tired of carrying.

"Yeah, you've wanted that for . . . forever . . . but, hon . . . you were supposed to take Sophie to school today. I have that doctor's appointment, the one with the specialist. You were going to get Sophie to school."

"Oh, damn it." He pounded his fist on the table and rolled his eyes at himself. "I'm so sorry. I totally forgot." He looked at his watch again and then back at Veronica, hesitant. "This is just a once-in-a-lifetime opportunity, babe. It's for our family."

"No, this doctor's appointment is for our family," Veronica snapped, but then took a breath, reminding herself that she was going on zero calories and high stress. "Sorry, it's just that I had to wait for three months to get into this specialist. I've been fasting for the past twelve hours so they can run tests. I can't cancel it. I just need you to get Sophie to school. Can you do that for me?"

Nick lowered his voice. "Those hormones mess with you, Ronnie. I thought you were going to talk to a therapist or something first so we can avoid what happened last time."

"Don't make this about me," Veronica snapped, filling a mug full of coffee and heading to the fridge for the creamer, refusing to be shamed for her brief bout with postpartum depression after Sophie was born.

"I told you about this months ago. You are the one that needs to step up here."

"And months ago you said you'd see a counselor first."

Veronica looked at the cup in her hand and, remembering that she was fasting, dumped it in the sink.

"I can see someone next week, maybe sooner. But I *can't* reschedule this appointment, Nick."

"Can't I take the bus?" Sophie asked, standing at the bottom of the stairs, wearing a fluffy pink skirt, a blue top that almost matched, hair brushed into a bit of a frizz ball but still brushed. Nick and Veronica looked at each other like they'd been caught with their hands in the cash register, fists full of money.

"Good morning, my sunshine!" Nick called out to Sophie in a false, singsong voice that he had perfected in his time as a father. He didn't want Sophie to know about any of the ups and downs of their marriage. Veronica couldn't tell if that was healthy or sheltering. Whatever it was, Sophie reacted to the syrupy voice with a bounce in her step. She ran across the room and climbed into his lap, nearly spilling his coffee.

"Good morning, Daddy. Do you like my skirt?"

"I do! You look like a ballerina. I bet you'll show everyone at school how to spin on one foot, won't you?"

Sophie scrunched up her nose and shook her head like she smelled something bad. "Not a ballerina, Daddy. I want to be an ice skater. Can I take lessons? Chrissy P. takes ice-skating lessons even when it's not cold outside."

Veronica abandoned the disagreement with Nick momentarily and loaded a plate with eggs and bacon and a sliver of toast with peanut butter and half a cut-up banana, just like Sophie liked it. She slid it in front of Nick and Sophie and put the fork directly in Sophie's hand so she didn't have to interrupt their conversation. Through mouthfuls of eggs and great gulps of juice, Sophie and Nick planned her future as an Olympic skater: "In pairs not singles, because then the guy got to throw you in the air."

"Well, sunshine, we've got to get going. Grab your coat and backpack, and let's get in the car," Nick said. The clock on the microwave read 7:30 a.m.

"Hey, the school doors don't open for another twenty minutes," Veronica reminded Nick in a hushed whisper, trying to mask her annoyance, not as practiced as Nick. "You can't drop her off early. No one is outside waiting."

Nick looked at his watch again and pushed away from the table, clearing his plates and leaving without any answers to her ever-growing list of concerns. He wasn't the only one running out of time; if she was going to get to her appointment in the middle of rush-hour traffic, she had to leave now.

"Guys." Sophie interrupted the silent mulling of the two adults in her life. "I seriously can take the bus."

Veronica had started to drive her precocious six-year-old after she came off the bus crying about the big kids using "naughty words," but it could be a good option this particular morning.

"Your call," Veronica said, raising her eyebrows at Nick. "It comes in four minutes. What do you think?"

Nick, who had been gathering his belongings, put his bag on his shoulder and held out his hand for Sophie.

"I think that you are a very big girl today," Nick said as she wrapped her hand in his. "Why don't you kiss your mommy, and I'll stand with you at the bus stop."

Sophie nodded and stood a little taller, and Veronica closed the distance between them, hand on her daughter's shoulder and a lingering kiss on her wild hair.

"Oh, wait one second," Veronica said, giving a playful glance at both family members before rummaging around in her bag.

"Hurry, Mommy, I gotta go!"

"I know, I know. It's in here somewhere . . ." She searched through loose sketches and a zippered pouch of art supplies until she landed on metal. "Ah, your new headband! You left it in the car last week. It goes well with that fancy skirt you're wearing."

Veronica placed the headband in her hair with practiced ease, somewhat taming Sophie's long blond mane. Sophie examined it with her expert fingers and seemed to approve. She tipped her head up and looked right into her mom's face.

"It's perfect," she sighed happily.

"You're perfect," Veronica bantered back, sneaking a pair of sneakers into Sophie's backpack, knowing she was going to wear "the boots" to school if there was even a whiff of moisture in the air.

"No, you are," Sophie said with a giggle, slipping on her sparkly pink rain boots, her most favorite clothing item and the only reason she loved rainy days. Each foot popped as it slipped into place.

"You both are the most perfect ladies I've ever set eyes on—now, let's go!" Nick tugged on Sophie's little arm and opened the front door. It whistled as the cool, wet fall breeze whipped through the entry. "Good luck, babe," Nick said only to Veronica, with a lingering glance.

She nodded noncommittally. She'd thought Nick wanted baby number two as much as she did, but maybe she was wrong. All their discussions ended in *If it happens it happens* or *I'd love to have another child with you*, but now that she was really thinking back, he'd never said, *I'm all in*. And he wasn't all in, because he was worried she'd lose it again. The PPD with Sophie was bad, but not as bad as never having another child.

She watched his hand in Sophie's, so much bigger, stronger, the same hand that held their wedding ring and held her hand while she was in labor and cradled her face when her father died and she realized his promises to get sober would never be a reality. She'd go get the tests done, maybe even give some treatments a try, but if they didn't work, she knew deep down it was going to be okay because she had them—Nick and Sophie—they were her everything.

"Bye, Mom!" Sophie shouted back at Veronica, a gust of wind catching her hair so it whipped out behind her like she was running. Veronica waved back, wishing she could recapture the joy for life her daughter embodied every single day.

"Bye, sweetheart!" Veronica returned the wave, and when they turned the corner to the communal bus stop at the end of the street, she fished her keys out of her purse and headed to the car. No music on her drive this morning, just serene silence that was hard to find in a home with a little person.

As she pulled up to the stop sign at the end of Hanson Drive, she glanced left and then right, checking to make sure it was safe to turn. The bus was there, blinking lights, red stop sign out halting traffic and causing a slight hesitation in Veronica's commute. Nick stood back with the group of parents watching their children get on the bus. When it was Sophie's turn, she blew him a kiss, which he caught, making Veronica's heart swell. Sophie was lucky to have such a good dad; it was one of the reasons Veronica had married Nick: his ability to love unconditionally. Her father didn't know how to love anyone but himself and alcohol, and all the men her mother had dated either demanded all her mother's attention or left without warning. She'd wanted different for her children.

And then Sophie ascended the stairs and was swallowed up by the great yellow machine, off to have a life outside the safety of Veronica's care. It made her both proud and frightened.

There were a lot of marvelous things in that world her child was headed into—Veronica knew that from traveling all over and meeting just about every kind of person you could imagine—but there were also monsters out there. There were traps covered by leaves, sinkholes that looked like a safe passage, and bolts of lightning that could hit at any moment, without warning. It was a stunning world filled with beauty and goodness; she'd seen it in her travels and in artwork and within her life with Nick and Sophie. But it was a dangerous world too, filled with gargoyles guarding the beauties and dangerous creatures hiding in the hallways of even the safest homes.

Veronica blinked a few times as she watched the bus drive away in a cloud of exhaust and swirling leaves before turning in the opposite direction. Today was a big day—today she found out if they could have another child, and today Nick found out if his dream of becoming an associate professor at Duke was just a dream or a real possibility. Today would put them on a new path, a new future, a new trajectory, and Veronica just had to hope it was the angels that would be waiting along the way, not the monsters. She'd always been afraid of monsters.

# CHAPTER 28

"The bus," Veronica whispered, putting down the painting in front of her. Why did she have to remember? Regret and guilt, they were twin pains that filled her body like liquid lead. "Why did we put her on the bus?"

Nick rubbed her shoulders knowingly, without the same reluctance as when she tried to kiss him earlier. She remembered that day now. She'd gone for her tests but gotten a call from Nick. There had been an accident. The bus . . . a drunk driver . . . the overpass . . . Sophie . . . It all came through in bits and pieces. The police asked all the parents to come to the hospital. There were injuries but, Nick added, not everyone made it. His voice was shaking, and she could hear his car rev in the background.

Not everyone made it—like it was an audition or something. Not everyone made it—from a bus full of children. She had leaned over and vomited into a wastebasket in the doctor's office as she stumbled out, only half aware of the hopeful and somewhat jealous looks from a woman who must've thought Veronica was one of the lucky ones to have gotten pregnant.

The drive to the hospital in Sanford had been a giant blur. She knew she should call her mother or the other parents on the block or the hospital, but she couldn't do anything but drive as fast as she could. She got there before Nick, and she should've waited—she should've waited for him. But she didn't. She wanted to see her baby, she wanted to see Sophie, so they took her back, past the rooms where worried parents held their frightened children, past the halls where moaning patients waited for medication, past all the hope that sloughed off behind her like scales from a snake.

A pair of double doors had led her to a room where doctors said something about identifying the children inside. She couldn't really hear; there was an infernal ringing in her ears and a voice in her head that told her if she didn't look, it wouldn't be real. She should've waited for Nick. But she didn't.

Inside a large, bare room, there had been six tables covered in sheets. Six small forms with just their tiny feet sticking out. Six lives stopped too soon, far, far too soon. One pair of shoes had laces untied, pooled on the stainless-steel tabletop. Veronica wanted to tie them for him, make him ready for his day at school. Start over two hours earlier and stop all these shoes from walking onto that bus. But she only thought about the loose laces for a moment because then she saw them, the shoes that took the tragedy from being a general loss of beautiful potential to the loss of her everything—her world. They sparkled even in that terrible cave of a place—Sophie's favorite pink boots.

Veronica's feet had frozen in place, and without saying a word, she had turned back and run, shoving the doctor out of the way with both hands. He called something after her, but she didn't listen—she bolted through the swinging double doors and ran past all the lucky parents who were still parents, then out the front door into the cold fall air as far away from the shine of those boots as possible. She couldn't breathe. She couldn't even vomit anymore; her stomach was too empty. She wanted to cry, but if she cried, it would be real.

She should've waited for Nick.

"I don't want to remember," Veronica shouted, clearing the papers off the table with one broad sweep of her arm and then clearing off all her supplies with another massive stroke. Standing, she turned to Nick and grabbed him by the front of his shirt. "Please stop. I don't want to remember. I don't want to remember . . ."

Mark stood silent in the background, staring at his feet like he was trying not to intrude on the private moment.

"I know." Nick pulled her into his arms, and there must've been learned muscle memory, because her body relaxed against him. He held her tighter, like he'd forgotten who she was and was suddenly remembering.

"Listen, Ronnie, you don't have to let it all back in right now," Nick said, pulling away slightly so he could get a look at her face. He put his hands around her cheeks and smoothed her hair like he used to do with Sophie. "That's what Green Oaks is for. They can help you remember slowly, safely. They can help you do this right."

"No," she interjected, not willing to leave Nick's arms but also not willing to give in to his plan. "I can't do it, Nick. It hurts too much. I can't. I can't remember it all. Plus, I've got to take care of my baby."

"Oh, Veronica." Nick sighed like she'd disappointed him in a way he'd never known was possible, backing up and leaving a cold spot where his chest had pressed against her. "You've got to stop with this baby thing. You've got to stop. It's one thing living in this fantasy world on your own, but you've got your mom doing it too. You need help."

"What the hell? My mom was here when you weren't. My mom was here to help me when I couldn't hold my . . ." The words stopped, and more memories started to flood back in. They were painful, like they were being injected into her brain with a hypodermic needle. Her mom finding her half-dead in her bed, empty pill bottle in her hand. Buying the new house in Sanford. Painting the nursery. Getting all the supplies. Feeling hope again. "Stop it, Nick!" This time it was more like a scream. "I told you I don't want to remember!"

"You can't live like this anymore, Ronnie. You are a danger to yourself, and you are running your mom ragged, and you are lying to everyone you know whether you realize it or not, your mom and your therapist and even Mark here."

"I'm not lying," she growled, backing up until she bumped into the desk. She looked back at Mark, who was now pacing by the door like he didn't know if he should help Nick or help Veronica. "Mark, I never lied to you. I didn't know any of this . . . really . . . I'm not a liar . . . I'm not . . ."

"This is so messed up," Mark said, half to Veronica, half to himself, looking both sympathetic and devastated at the same time.

"You saw my baby. You saw her—you know she's real, Mark. I don't know what Nick is playing at, but my baby is real."

"That little girl you stole at gunpoint? That is *my* baby, Ronnie," Nick said with a possessive edge to his voice and hard lines on his usually peaceful face. "My baby with Daisy. She's my wife. Chloe is my baby."

It all came flooding back, and this time she couldn't stop it. It washed over her like the pounding waves of the ocean, knocking her off her feet, waiting till she got her footing again and then slamming her down one more time. All those gauzy memories of building a life for Sophie came into focus. The empty crib. The empty bottles. The crying her mother never seemed to hear. Laundry that was never dirty. Diapers that didn't smell. A baby she couldn't touch . . . because she was only a memory.

"Your baby wasn't kidnapped today—*my* baby was kidnapped today. I didn't die—*you* died, or at least the woman you used to be died and was buried along with our daughter two and a half years ago. You are the criminal. You, Ronnie Crawford—or should I call you Veronica Shelton?"

Veronica crumpled to the floor, hands over her ears, knees up against her forehead, mumbling repeatedly. "I don't want to listen. I don't want to listen. I don't want to listen."

Nick fell to the floor in front of her on his knees and ripped her hands off her ears. She writhed under his grip, cowering, feeling powerless. Mark shouted out from behind them.

"Hey, hey, that's a bit rough. Knock it off."

But Nick didn't flinch. His eyes, Sophie's blue eyes with tiny pinpricks for pupils, bored into her.

"You are going to listen." He was angry now. It was an emotion she wasn't used to seeing on the normally levelheaded man. "I lost my daughter on that bus too. And then you blamed me for putting her on that morning instead of driving her, and so I lost you to grief and anger. But I've found some measure of happiness with Daisy and Chloe, and I'm not going to let you mess that up for me. Daisy wants to call the police, and I honestly can't blame her. At first it was just stealing pictures of Chloe from Facebook, but, Ronnie, you stole her baby today."

Veronica whimpered, trying not to listen, Nick's fingernails starting to cut into the flesh around her wrists. "You're hurting me."

"I'm serious, man, let her go." Mark was only inches away. "Now."

Nick, his breathing heavy and sweat beading up at his hairline, released her slowly, his fingers leaving white, then red marks on her skin. Veronica scrambled away, confused and frightened and totally lost as to what reality was and whom to trust. With the two men making a triangle with her at the apex, she felt cornered. Nick continued, calmer now, maybe a little ashamed at hurting her.

"Listen, you can find it again too, happiness, that is. You just need help." He stepped toward her, but when she flinched and Mark made a move in his direction letting them all know he wasn't going to allow another finger on Veronica, he returned to his spot behind the desk. "I don't want you to go to jail, Ronnie," he said, almost sweetly. "I still love you."

"I love you too, but it's too late for us," Veronica replied, surprised that she didn't just say the words but also meant them. She loved the memory of Nick, the imaginary man she'd been mourning, not this near stranger in front of her who had a daughter with another woman.

"Oh no, that's not what I meant." He choked on the words and then rushed to clarify. "I will always love you just like I will always love Sophie, but I've moved on. I can love Chloe and Daisy and still want what is best for you. That's why I hired Mark's boss. Your mom refused to do anything but enable you. You always said that enabling was her superpower, and look what a stellar job she's done around here." His sarcasm hurt Veronica, and she flinched away. Nick paused and forced himself to speak in an overly compassionate tone. "You need help, Ronnie, but if you don't take it this time, if you don't take it right this second, I will let Daisy call the police and we will have you involuntarily committed. We have plenty of evidence to your mental state; that's why I got the PIs. I tried not to tell them everything, I tried to protect you, but it's not easy to get someone committed, believe it or not. But even without knowing how far off the deep end you've gone, it clearly wasn't a surprise, even to strangers. Why do you think Mark here has been so quiet?"

He pointed at Mark, who gave Veronica an apologetic grimace. "When I told him just now, it didn't take much convincing that you have lost your ever-loving mind. The police figured out they were looking for a nonexistent baby fast too, and once your mom came home from urgent care, they called off the investigation. Take my offer, please. You can find life again. Real life, Ronnie."

"I don't know what is real anymore," she said, her body collapsing in on itself, knees pulling up to her chest and head hanging low. "I don't know."

Real—the word held little meaning for her. Baby Sophie had seemed so real, and Nick being dead felt real, and the search for kidnapped Sophie felt real, and her mother disappearing felt real, and holding little Chloe like she had her baby felt real and . . . How could it all be nothing more than her mind trying to protect her from a horrible truth? In the downward spiral of Veronica's despairing thoughts, she became aware of a voice calling her back.

"Hey," Mark greeted softly as he settled next to her on the floor. "Crazy day, huh?" He said it like they'd left a wallet in the back seat of a cab and had to find it before their plane took off. "If I'm confused, I know you're confused, right?"

"Understatement of the year," she said, the grief she'd been running from nibbling at her consciousness. She couldn't let it in; it was a ravaging creature. She rocked back and forth, her head hitting against the wall behind her, lightly at first and then a little harder with each tap once she noticed the pain of each crack took away the pain of remembering. Nick had backed off and was texting but also seemed to be watching Mark's interaction with Veronica. Mark's shoulder pressed lightly against hers.

"I think you need to go to this place, this Green Oaks."

Veronica bristled and shifted away from him, resuming her injurious self-soothing. "I'll be fine now. I can see Lisa. I'll be fine." Tap, tap, tap, tap. Each thump made another memory go away, another remembered pain dissolve into a physical one.

Mark shook his head and put his hand over hers where it rested on the floor. "No, I don't think you will. This"—he gestured to the room and the pictures on the floor, the rocking, and Nick—"is too much for Lisa, and, Veronica, be honest with yourself, this is too much for you too."

She didn't want to go. Tap. Her home was her safe place. Tap. She could make the rules here. Tap. She could hide from the demons. Tap. She could let in who she wanted and shut out all the rest. Tap. And Lisa, she didn't need to know everything. Tap. She liked "postpartum" Veronica. Tap. The Veronica she'd been living as could give her just enough information to work through some of the grief and learn how to get back out in the world. She could start over as her again. Tap. Maybe she'd take medicine this time. Tap. Tap. Tap.

It took a lot of energy to form any words, but when she did, they were low and firm. "You don't know me." She slid her hand out from under his and crossed her arms on her chest, hitting her head hard enough to make the paper-covered window rattle. "You don't know what I can or can't do. And you don't know Lisa, despite all your stalking and snooping. What the hell were you doing at that office anyway? Did you even go to the support group?"

She leaned forward to let her head crash backward again when Mark put his arm against the wall, taking the brunt of her impact. Mark flinched, and Nick butted in, pointing at his phone. "Ronnie, I don't care who you think knows you or doesn't know you—it's time. You come now or Daisy is calling. She's frantic. I can't hold her back anymore."

"You've got to go with him," Mark said with finality, not losing an ounce of intensity. He turned on his side and tried to draw all Veronica's attention to him, keeping his hand firmly in place behind her skull. "This is not a game. This is not about you going to jail or staying out of jail. This is also about Gillian."

"What about her?" Gillian. Veronica froze. She'd nearly forgotten about Gillian, which made sense, sadly, because most of the world had forgotten about her as well. What was it like to be so forgettable? Veronica never wanted to know.

"You got her involved in this mess. She's an accessory to kidnapping. She drove the car. She helped you plan the abduction . . ."

"She provided the gun," Veronica added, catching on to his reasoning.

"Oh my God, you had a gun?" He shook his head and continued as though he wanted to forget he'd heard that information. "You might have other options like treatment because of everything you've been through, but she will not. You can't let them call the police, Veronica. It will not only ruin your life, but it will ruin Gillian's."

It was all coming together, all the horrible truths of her life that she'd tried to keep behind her mental walls. She'd built a house of safety here. Within these walls, she could still be a mother, a cherished wife to a tragically lost husband. She could be a good daughter and re-create herself as the name she used on her artwork and picture books. When Nick's baby was born, she didn't want it to be true, didn't want him to have moved on so fully. He could move on from her but not from Sophie. How could he forget about Sophie? How could he have a child with another woman when he didn't want to make another child with her? Even thinking through the imagined life of Nick and Daisy and their perfect baby, Chloe, made her want to go back to the fake life she'd slipped into after Nick's baby's birth.

But in this house for the past eight months since Sophie . . . or Chloe had been born, she wasn't Ronnie Crawford, stay-at-home mom and flighty artist whose daughter was killed in the tragedy on Route 42, whose husband was gone because she was crazy, who had to live alone in the house that was a graveyard of memories. She was Veronica Shelton, successful illustrator, mother, widow, cherished daughter, working her damnedest to do what was right for her family.

It wasn't hard to pretend. Moving helped. Then Ronnie invited the ghosts in and asked them to stay for dinner, and now she had a full-blown delusion for a life and she was hurting more people she cared about. If there was one thing she seemed to excel at, it was hurting people.

Veronica let her legs stretch out into the scattered papers that now covered the floor and crinkled as she shifted on top of them. Her gaze fixed on one of the drawings of Sophie that lay by her hand. She was dancing. How she missed seeing her daughter dance.

"She would've been a beautiful figure skater," she said to herself, her voice echoing in the nothingness she was trying to force her mind to accept. She hadn't talked about Sophie in a long, long time. In fact, it was hard to remember very much of life before she'd built her fantasy world.

"Yeah, I know," Nick responded, letting his head bounce in agreement and once again holding back tears.

"No," she growled. She grasped the picture by her side until it crumbled into a ball. She fumbled to her feet, hand clenched tightly around the memory of their daughter. "You don't get to cry anymore. You moved on. You have Daisy and Chloe and a fairy tale life. You don't get to have the same tears as me."

"Damn you, Ronnie," Nick said with complete disdain, eyes wrinkled at the corners like they did when he forgot his glasses or was mad at some politician on the nightly news. "You aren't the only one who lost your daughter, remember? And then you blamed me for putting her on that bus. You kicked me out of the house. *You* divorced *me*, remember?"

"Liar. I loved you. I never would've—"

"You called me a murderer. Called me selfish. Called me every name in the book. And now I can't cry? Damn you!" He was shouting now. Nick never used to shout. Veronica's muscles twitched with each word, not sure if they were true but questioning herself more and more. "You deserve this hell you've built for yourself. Let's go."

He slipped his phone in his pocket and pointed to the door, two and a half years' worth of exhaustion showing in every movement. But Veronica didn't move. She wasn't ready to go and face it all just yet. Like she was shuffling through low tide at the seashore, she waded through the discarded memories that surrounded her until she stood in front of the statue of a man that used to be her husband.

He had a new ring on his left hand, one she didn't buy for him. His glasses were slightly different, the frames brown instead of black and some metal showing on the arms. His body was different too, thicker in places he'd been trim before, the short beard hiding some fullness to his face. And those tears that she'd banished moments earlier still stood perched on his eyelashes like they were waiting for her to look away before they could fall without reproach.

"Will it ever stop hurting?" she asked, wanting to touch his face, feel his arms around her, and wishing more than anything that she could say sorry but feeling at a loss for those words.

He blinked and a tear fell. "It's not going to stop hurting, Ronnie. You eventually learn to live with the pain. That's what grief is—living with pain. Time doesn't heal all wounds; it just builds up your resistance."

"Fine," she said, finding it harder and harder to say anything at all, "I'll go."

"Good," Nick responded, nearly patting her knee, but then retreating.

The anger was gone; he could never stay mad long, it wasn't in his makeup. She'd loved it and hated it about him when they were married. Sometimes you need a good, full-blown rager of an argument to work out all the kinks.

"Why don't you go pack a bag. They're waiting for us," he said, slipping his hands in his pockets and sliding past Veronica and moving toward the door. "Mark, could you go with her?"

"Of course," he replied, now by her side. Mark didn't say a word as he escorted her to her bedroom, watching silently as she took out a bag and packed it as if she were heading for vacation rather than a mental institution. But somehow it didn't feel like a judging gaze, or even a pitying one, which was perhaps worse, more like he understood or maybe even like he was impressed with her. As they walked down the stairs and out of the house together, Veronica robotically put in the code on the alarm system and carefully locked the door behind her, not sure when she'd cross that threshold again and who she would be when she did. Her mom was gone, presumably with Sophie . . . Chloe, heading back to Durham.

Green Oaks would have medication. They might even sedate her; she could drift into an abyss of emptiness. It might not be as comfortable as the life she'd convinced herself of for the past seven months, but it would be better than being out in the real world, alone. Her body released all the fight she'd been holding on to, the effort it took to live her life every day; her joints loosened and her mind started to darken again.

"Could you make sure my car makes it back in the garage? I left the keys on the counter in the kitchen." It felt strange to be talking about such normal things.

"Sure, I can do that."

"Can you check up on the house occasionally?" She hesitated slightly and continued. "Make sure my mom is okay? I forgot to ask."

Mark nodded, glancing at the side of her face more than once, probably thinking she wouldn't notice. "I'd love to."

Her limbs were heavy, and she had to force every footfall. It was as though the house were holding on to her, as if she were stuck in its tractor beam. She just wanted it all to go away. Why the hell did she have to feel anything anymore?

They were almost at Nick's car, the same Jeep Cherokee he'd been driving for the past ten years. Well . . . twelve. It was already running, and Nick was on the phone inside. Mark reached across her to open the door, but she stopped him, touching his shoulder.

"Will you take care of Gillian?" The question came out of nowhere, her mind as jumbled as a toddler's toy box. "She's going to be worried when I don't show up. Can you think of something to tell her—not the truth, not yet—and make sure she's safe? I'll have Nick text you all the info."

She was too ashamed for Gillian to know how broken she was. Weak, pathetic Gillian had lost her son and her husband and, unlike Veronica, hadn't lost her mind. In fact, she turned out to be one of the strongest people Veronica had ever met. God, she wished she could be more like her unexpected friend.

The lines on Mark's face were exaggerated by the yellow streetlights, and his irises nearly blended into the whites of his eyes, but Veronica could still read a deep sincerity there. He placed a hand on the space between her shoulder blades and spread his fingers wide like he was measuring it.

"You focus on getting better, and I'll take care of everything else out here, okay?"

Veronica couldn't find the muscles in her face that should make her smile, but if things were different, she would've tried to at least. She squinted up at him. "Why aren't you running away? Most men would be sprinting for the exit right now, and I can't say I'd blame them."

"I don't know," he said, looking up at the clear, moonless sky filled with a blanket of blinking stars. "I guess sometimes you run away from the flames, and other times"—he looked back down at Veronica and into her eyes, his hand leaving her back, making her shiver—"you stay and help put out the fire."

Without waiting for a response, he opened the car door and helped her inside, passing over the bag he'd been carrying on his shoulder. When the door closed, she settled in and clicked the seat belt like she had a million and one times, including the day Sophie had been strapped in the back seat in her infant seat as they headed home from the hospital and the day they drove away from her funeral, parents without a child. Those memories were nibbling at the edges of her consciousness, but she was holding them back, carefully at bay.

She couldn't take it all in today. It would overwhelm her. She needed to wait till she got to Greek Oaks, till she got the real help she needed. Until then, she could only let it in a bit at a time. She could only mourn in inches.

The pain would never go away; Nick's words echoed in her mind, feeling more like a warning than a comfort now. At Green Oaks she'd find out a lot of things, like the memories she'd tried to erase of Sophie and the grief she'd tried to bury, but she'd also find out if it was worth it, living with this pain. She'd learn if there really was any way she could ever "move on."

# CHAPTER 29

*Four months later*

"I know it's a lot to take in, and I'm not asking you to trust me or believe me, but if you'd give me another chance, I promise that I'm willing to work. Dr. Klein seems to think I'm not a total lost cause," Veronica said, sitting on the edge of her seat, trying to lighten the tone of the room.

"Well, looks like we have a lot to work on," Lisa half laughed, half grimaced. The look of surprise she'd tried to hide behind her hand during Veronica's monologue, divulging the whole truth of her life and lies, had almost disappeared.

At first, Lisa was ecstatic to see her again. She'd gotten a brief message from Veronica's mother four months earlier explaining that Veronica wouldn't be attending sessions anymore, but that was it. When Veronica walked in, there were hugs and loud welcomes as she left the empty waiting room and followed Lisa to her office. But once she started in on confession time, Lisa became somber and, soon, silent. Veronica was expecting a lecture or maybe even rejection, though Dr. Klein at Green Oaks seemed to think that worry was unlikely. It had taken a long time for Veronica to be willing to sign the consent form so Dr. Klein could talk to Lisa. She'd thought about letting that therapeutic relationship die and starting a new one. But she'd felt connected to Lisa, and that was hard to find in a therapist, so she finally consented. And now she was back.

"Clearly," Veronica agreed, bouncing her foot over her crossed leg. Just like Lisa had predicted in their first session, Veronica was sitting in the same chair even after a four-month absence. Hopefully, though the chair was the same, the outcome would be different now that Veronica was on a healthier path. "So you'll keep working with me even though I'm a total mess?"

Lisa clutched her pen in the palm of her hand and put her notebook to the side on the small table to her left. Her dark hair fell around her face as she fixed her lips into a firm but kind line.

"Veronica," she said and then hesitated, "or Ronnie . . . which would you like to go by?"

"I'm sticking with Veronica. New life, new name, new outlook, I guess."

"Okay, we can chat about that next time." She fought against another smile. "Veronica, what kind of people do you think walk through those doors?" She pointed to the office door and figuratively to all the other doors Veronica had to go through to get into this office. "Do you think they are perfect people? 'Cause they aren't. They are messes. We are all messes. You know that, right?"

"I'm a bit messier than most, you have to admit." She'd been angry at herself for being the kind of person who was the most screwed-up woman in a hospital of screwed-up women. "I bet none of the nice people sitting in your waiting room spent four months in a mental institution after committing a felony. Four months, Lisa. That is a long time. Most of the people were there for a week or maybe a month. I'm a special kind of screwed up."

"You know I don't like that kind of self-talk, Veronica," Lisa said, as close to scolding her as she'd ever come.

"I know, I know. I'm working on it. Green Oaks was terrible and wonderful at the same time. Don't get me wrong, I never want to go back there, but they helped me find myself again, and somehow I learned that I am still Sophie's mom even if she's not here with me. Doesn't stop me from feeling like a crazy person sometimes," Veronica added, trying to make a joke.

Lisa shook her head and then cocked it to one side. She really wanted to get through to Veronica—she could see it in the way Lisa thought through what she was going to say next so carefully instead of spitting it out or following a script like some other counselors she'd met over the past months. It made her feel like she wasn't a lost cause, like even if she told her whole story, someone could still find value in her.

Besides grief, shame was the emotion Veronica had to wrestle with as the memories came back. Shame for how she'd treated Nick and for how she'd used her mother and how selfish she'd been in her grief. Shame made her want to hide more, afraid no one would ever be able to love her again because she wasn't lovable. But then her mom visited her at Green Oaks, week after week, month after month.

And eventually, Mark came too, at first to give updates on all the items she'd left in his care and, finally, to sit and talk until he hustled her out of her bubble-gum stash while playing gin rummy and was forced out by a well-meaning nurse. He asked her if Gillian could come, but that was a shame she wasn't ready to face yet. Gillian had lost a child and gone through a divorce without crumbling, and to top it all off, Veronica used to look down on her. She'd pulled the poor woman into a kidnapping scheme and almost gotten her killed by her ex-husband. As far as Gillian knew, Veronica had moved as a part of her job and would be back soon. She wanted to tell her the rest face-to-face.

"The fact that you are trying so hard to organize and work on your own chaos shows me you are one of the best to sit in my waiting room, cry into my tissues, and rest in your very own special chair. Pains and struggles are not comparable. I don't have some measuring stick I take out when you leave to see who has the most heartbreaking story. You get to feel what you feel, Veronica. And then we work on what we can control. That's it. You are an artist—when you look at a palette of paint blobs or a lump of clay or random shapes on a page, what do you see?"

Veronica made a sincere effort to really think through the question and put herself into that moment of creation. She rarely looked at any raw materials and saw a helpless medium. One of her first art professors at NYU had assigned the use of only found items in their next project. When Sophie was little, they'd collect random items—leaves, candy wrappers, toilet paper rolls—and figure out how to make masterpieces out of them.

"Potential," she said honestly, almost forgetting that this "mess" analogy was about her until Lisa sat back in her seat, satisfied.

"Exactly," she said, grabbing her appointment book and putting it on her lap. "Potential. Now, does this time work for you next week, or do you want to meet sooner?"

"I have a follow-up at Green Oaks later this week, so I'm fine for next Thursday," Veronica said, allowing herself to feel like she had "potential" for at least a few minutes that day.

Lisa wrote whatever she wrote in her magic appointment book, closed it up, and put it on the table beside her. "Welcome back, Veronica."

They headed to the front desk together, and after another round of goodbyes, Veronica went through the heavy wooden door that separated the offices from the waiting room. On the other side, Mark sat reading a magazine. She'd only been out a week, so he'd offered to drive her to her appointment, and Veronica had decided to let him. She was doing that a lot more often lately, letting Mark into her life. When she was at Green Oaks, it had been once a week, but now that she was home, she'd seen him every day.

She cleared her throat and waited for Mark to look up, but he kept his head down, apparently engrossed in some *Good Housekeeping* article. He licked his finger slowly and turned the page. Veronica bit her lip, trying not to look too amused.

"Ahem," she said, clearer this time.

Mark put up one finger, mouthing the words he was reading on the page in front of him, and then with some flourish, he closed the magazine with a slap. "Oh, I didn't even see you there," he said with mock surprise.

"I know, you were far too interested in learning how to make lemon-and-lavender scones." She glanced down at the cover of the magazine, wondering how long he'd been planning his little prank.

"Strawberry and rosemary, get it right," Mark corrected, jumping to his feet. "Ready to go?"

"Um-hm," she said with pressed lips. He wouldn't ask what they talked about; he was good like that, and she probably wouldn't tell him. Not everything. He wasn't *that* kind of a friend. Not yet at least.

"Well, I don't know about you, but I need to go grocery shopping. First thing on my list—strawberries." He held the door open to the hallway, and Veronica left without even one self-conscious glance over her shoulder to see if anyone had been watching.

"As long as it's not tampons, I'm fine," she joked, remembering the first time he talked to her in Piggly Wiggly. She'd thought he was objectively handsome then, like you can think a celebrity on TV handsome. But now, she glanced at him as he held yet another door open to the stairwell and took in the little scar on his cheek that he said he'd gotten when he was a kid from a skateboarding accident and the arch in his eyebrow that she knew meant he was having fun playing around with her. Now she thought he might be one of the most attractive men she'd ever met. Not that she was going to tell him that anytime soon.

Mark grimaced. "I'm the ultimate romantic, aren't I? You were just so pretty, I didn't know what to say once I got the chance."

"Yeah, yeah, yeah, pretty, my ass. You were getting paid to talk to me about feminine hygiene products." She allowed herself to be playful, enjoying his compliment more than she wanted to admit to herself. After remembering how she'd shut Nick out of her life and then the pain when he'd moved on, she thought she could never be loved again. Mark might not love her, but she couldn't deny that he sure liked her, and that was a good enough start. "You know I'm telling Kayla that story one day, right?"

"You'd better not!"

They exited the building to the chill of the fall air. It was cool but not cold, and the trees were finally starting to turn colors. Before losing Sophie, fall had been Veronica's favorite time of year. She was trying to rewire the fuses in her brain to remember why she loved fall and not the one reason she now hated it.

"Yeah, it's gonna be a fun pizza Friday." She flapped her hand at him and then put it in her jeans pocket, glad she'd worn a sweatshirt over her cotton T. Lost in her laughter, Veronica jumped when she heard a familiar voice.

"Veronica? Veronica Shelton, is that you?"

Gillian. When she'd decided to put her off until she was a little stronger, a little healthier, Veronica didn't think it would be today. There was so much to confess and explain. It couldn't all be done on the lawn of her medical clinic, but she also couldn't walk away. Her days of treating Gillian poorly were over. Gillian deserved a real friend.

"Hey! You look great!" Veronica called out across the patch of grass behind the offices. Gillian's hair was a little longer and a uniform color, and her waistline was a little trimmer, but something beyond style or numbers on a scale had changed, something that meant more than those outward things ever could.

"You too, lady! God, I've missed you. Where have you been?" She dropped the large black handbag she'd been carrying and rushed across the lawn, her legs moving fast beneath her, and no worry of dignity lost. When she landed on the same sidewalk Veronica was standing on, Gillian wrapped her up into a warm and comforting embrace. Her homey smell, the way her arms just felt safe like she'd love Veronica no matter what, they made Veronica's body go from stiff and frozen by surprise to a deep calm, like she would be safe forever with Gillian's arms around her. Christopher must've loved his mom's hugs.

"Uh, it's a long story. I'm sorry I've been MIA. I hope Mark explained what he could."

"Yeah, he said . . . some stuff." She gave her nervous chuckle that Veronica missed. "I still have a million questions."

"Well, so do I. How is life?" Veronica asked, trying to steer the conversation away from herself. Gillian hesitated but then seemed to make an internal decision to let Veronica off the hook for now.

"Pretty good. I got a real job now, actually at Mark's agency. I do clerical work, but I also get to do research and stuff. Mark put in a good word after seeing us in action, right, bud?" Gillian wiggled her eyebrows and pointed at Mark. "But I'm sure Mark told you about all this if you two have been hanging out. Though he forgot to mention that little detail, you naughty young man. You said she was out of town and needed 'space.'"

"I was. I just got in a few days ago," Veronica rushed in to pad Gillian's feelings and rescue Mark.

Mark blushed, which surprised Veronica and made her blush a little too. "You caught me. I wanted to keep her all to myself for a little bit. Can you blame me? She is pretty awesome."

"Gosh, there is only so much gushing I can take in one day. I can't take the two of you." A pit formed in Veronica's stomach. She couldn't sit here and joke around and pretend everything was okay when there were so many things that she'd have to start lying about if she didn't clear up a few things with Gillian. Maybe not everything but . . . something. More than this playful banter. She cleared her throat and got serious. "Uh, Mark, if you'd give us ladies a few minutes, I'd be incredibly grateful. I'll meet you at the car?"

She gave him a look that hopefully transmitted her intentions. He seemed to read in between the lines, because he stopped laughing and gave her a look that said, "Are you sure?" She nodded, sure of two things: she wanted to talk to Gillian and she wanted to do it alone.

"All right, I know when I'm not wanted. I'll be waiting in the car, I guess," Mark said with a shrug and then pointed at Gillian. "I'll see *you* in the office."

"Not if I see you first," Gillian shot back as Mark walked away waving her off. It was good to see that no matter how cheesy the interaction, Gillian was finding her place in the world. She'd been through plenty of loss, a child and a husband just like Veronica, but somehow she was working through it all. With a lingering smile on her face, Gillian faced Veronica and gave her arm a meaningful squeeze.

"How *are* you? You kinda disappeared on me. I know you're a fancy illustrator and all that, but I have so many questions. How was your trip? Thanks for your text and covering the hotel; you didn't have to do that."

"Hey, it was the least I could do. I'm sorry I wasn't here to give it to you in person. Mark said you sold your house and got a nice townhouse. You must be feeling like a new woman."

"Well, I wish Mark had as much to say about you as he's had to say about me. My life is boring, sweetie. Tell me about you! What about your mama? And I'm dying to hear about Sophie. She was so adorable, she must be so big by now."

"Don't blame Mark. I asked him to keep quiet. There are some things I needed to talk to you about in person. But now is probably not the time." At Green Oaks, Veronica had learned that it was easier to face these difficult moments with preparation, so she was acutely aware that an impromptu discussion outside Lisa's office was not the right atmosphere to delve into her toolbox and come out successful. "I'm sorry I've been so distant. You were an amazing friend and you didn't deserve that." The words stopped there, her mouth snapping shut, Veronica unsure of what to say next.

"That's okay, hon," she said in that sweet, caring Southern drawl that made Veronica feel like Gillian was a loving relative rather than a newish friend. She looked at Gillian's watch, the same tarnished fake-gold one that used to cut into her skin but now hung a little loose around her wrist. "I have an appointment with Stacey in five minutes, so we don't have to do all this now. We can grab drinks later this week or somethin'."

"Yeah, yeah, that's a great idea. I'm open pretty much any night." Veronica let out a heavy breath of relief. She could plan for a meeting; this was all a little too sudden.

"How about tomorrow? We can meet at Dave's Ale House again. Seems right to go back there where all this craziness started, don't you think?"

"Tomorrow is great. I'll text you later, and we can figure out the details."

"Perfect," Gillian said, clearly relieved. "Well, hon, I gotta run, but tell me one thing real fast—How's little Sophie? She's been in my prayers every night, you know."

Gillian's gentle brown eyes were full of a very real care and concern. There was no doubt in Veronica's mind that she'd been praying for Veronica's daughter every night without knowing that the real Sophie had been buried in the Millburn Cemetery for nearly three years and the fake Sophie was a one-year-old little girl named Chloe. Veronica swallowed hard and told the truth.

"Uh, there are a lot of things I haven't told you about Sophie . . . and Nick, for that matter. I've been very sick and sad, and I said things that weren't true and . . ." This is why she was supposed to prepare. The truth started to spill out in a chaotic deluge of information.

"Oh, shhhh, hon." Gillian shushed Veronica and put her hands on Veronica's upper arms, holding her in tight as if she were stopping a toddler from touching the red-hot stove. "We've all got our secrets.

You don't have to spill them out right now, out here on the lawn, like a shook-up soda pop."

That's exactly how she felt, like carbonation all bubbly and frothy built up like it was going to explode at any moment—yet also like exploding could be more than just messy and inconvenient but also very relieving.

"These aren't any run-of-the-mill secrets." Veronica stopped again, finding it harder and harder to keep it all in now that she'd started. It felt good to tell the truth to Gillian. Maybe she'd be one of the ones to stick around, to love her not just despite her faults but because of them. Mark saw her craziness firsthand and then stayed and watched her work out of the dark hole of delusion one rung at a time over the past four months. But would Gillian?

"Oh, I've got some doozies myself. I promise you that." Gillian rubbed her hands together and then took one last look at her watch before gathering her purse off the ground and returning it to her shoulder. She settled back into her spot and met Veronica's eyes. Her face went from happy and soft to lined with worry. "Christopher didn't die of cancer."

Veronica could tell she was sharing something she didn't tell many people, and it was like she'd fallen off a high ledge or belly flopped into a pool. If it had been a year ago or maybe even a few months, Veronica would've let the shock show, but instead she tried to respond the way she'd want someone to treat her in the same situation. Like Gillian would have the opportunity to respond when Veronica was ready to tell her everything.

"You don't have to tell me anything you don't want to. I trust you; you don't have to prove yourself to me," Veronica said, expecting some nuanced version of Christopher's death story, like maybe Gillian had helped him commit suicide when the treatments got too rough or perhaps he'd died of a more embarrassing illness but she'd decided to call it cancer so no one would know. When it came down to it, it was none of Veronica's business.

"No, I've wanted to tell you for a long time, and now it's good you know. To tell the truth, I need someone to know. Someone besides Stacey, who gets paid to tell me I'm not a terrible mother." She pointed at the second-floor window where Stacey's and Lisa's offices were located.

Veronica put her hands in her pockets and stood silent and allowed Gillian to collect her thoughts. It was the least she could do in the face of such bravery.

"Chris did die, like I said, and he *was* sick but not with cancer. It's been nearly three years now. God, that's so long." She paused and adjusted her purse and then started again. "So Christopher was a drug addict; that was his illness. To be fair, addiction is like a cancer, so I don't feel so bad calling it cancer to strangers or nosy people who ask too many questions." She shifted her weight from side to side. "It was a disease that took our boy. I took him to all kinds of specialists, but like any illness, if you don't take the medicine, you don't get better, and Chris refused to be cured. Didn't think he needed to be cured."

"He overdosed?" Veronica blurted, wanting to give Gillian an out so she didn't have to say the words herself. But Gillian shook her head.

"No, no . . . I've thought about it a lot, and I can honestly say I wish he'd overdosed." Gillian shivered as the wind blew again, this time a little harder.

"Oh" was all Veronica could say, unsure of what to expect anymore. She could see Mark watching them from the front seat of the car, and she longed to run there to the safety of that warm seat, his comforting personality, and distance from the scary truth that was slowly unfolding.

"He was eighteen, had been out at a friend's house all night . . . using." She swallowed when she said the term. "He told his friends that he was going home to sleep it off and go to work that night, but on the way home, something happened." Gillian, who had been looking right in Veronica's eyes, was suddenly staring at her feet. The way she swallowed and smacked her lips several times made Veronica know that she was trying not to cry. "He got in a car accident that morning."

"Oh, Gillian, I'm so sorry," Veronica said without a moment's hesitation.

"His dad said it was my fault 'cause I let him have the car and I didn't find the right doctor to help him get better and . . . I still wonder if it was." Now there were actual tears on Gillian's cheeks, leaving wet trails through the face powder.

"Don't listen to Carl. I can tell you from the five minutes I spent getting to know him that he's one of the stupidest people I've ever met. God, to say that to a mourning mother. That's just evil. Accidents happen."

Veronica said the words that well-meaning individuals had said to her after Sophie's death. She'd hated it then, but after her time at Green Oaks, she'd started understanding that it was true—no one planned these things, not even God. Terrible things happened, and sometimes there was nothing you could do about it.

Gillian still didn't look up, even with Veronica's encouragements and kind words. There was so much shame there that she couldn't even lift her own head because of the weight of it. It was easy for Veronica to spot. She still wasn't a great hugger, but knowing how difficult that story was to hold on to, she wrapped her arms around her friend.

Gillian shook her head against Veronica's shoulder. "But it wasn't just Christopher. Other people died. And lots more injured."

Veronica trembled, still holding Gillian, and a whining cry wormed its way out of her body. She stifled it, trying not to let the slowly creeping realization plummet her back into the abyss.

"How many died?" she asked simply.

"Six," Gillian sobbed and leaned in to Veronica's embrace and pushed her wet face into the soft crevice of Veronica's collarbone and shoulder. "Six little babies on their way to school."

Veronica's mouth was dry and her throat so tight she could only whisper, already certain what the answer to her next question would be.

"The bus crash on Route Forty-Two?"

"Yes," Gillian barely got out before silent cries muted any further explanation.

Veronica couldn't breathe. The nausea from the day she got the call returned, and she wanted to vomit. She wanted to shove Gillian away and run as fast as she could till she couldn't remember the sparkles. They flashed behind her eyelids every time she blinked her eyes. The mother of the devil who took her little girl's life was here, in her arms, crying about her druggy son.

It all clicked together. Barb had gotten Lisa's name off a list from the grief counselor at the hospital. It had been an old list, but she'd never used it till her mother's ultimatum. Gillian must've gotten the same list. Veronica had been sitting by this woman in the waiting room for weeks with no idea that her child had taken Veronica's child's life. She'd shared stories of grief when Veronica was lonely enough to open up to the stranger from the waiting room. She'd even called this woman when she was in desperate need and leaned on her for help.

And over time Veronica had watched this woman hold a gun up to a man who had mistreated her and had felt pride at her strength, had learned that humility, time, and determination could bring healing to even the most broken heart. She'd learned from Gillian what it felt like to be accepted and loved without judgment.

Veronica's stiff arms and complete silence must've registered with Gillian, because she raised her head, tears no longer flowing and just a touch of red in her eyes.

"I'm sorry. That was too much, wasn't it?" She sniffed and broke away from Veronica. "It's okay to be freaked out. I get it. I mean, at least you know why I lie, right?"

Yes, it was too much. It was far more than Veronica had expected and probably more than Gillian would've admitted if she knew who Sophie really was and her son's part in her death.

But it also wasn't too much, somehow.

"We all have secrets, right?" Veronica hedged. It helped seeing Gillian's eyes again, to put a human identity to the faceless man behind the wheel she'd been imagining and bring light to the darkness that had been stalking her life and keeping her from healing. Christopher, the drug addict who drove a car into her daughter's bus and sent it flying off the overpass on a slippery morning in November, was loved. He was a person with a mother who loved him and did her best to teach him right from wrong. Christopher wasn't evil. Neither was Gillian.

"Oh God, I gotta go," Gillian said, cleaning her face off with the inside of her cardigan, maybe feeling a little shy from sharing so much of her story with Veronica and getting so little feedback in return. She started to put herself back together, readjusted her bag, and sniffed loudly before checking Veronica's expression one more time. "Can I ask you one more question?"

"Sure," Veronica said after a slight hesitation. A shiver ran through her. She was getting colder the longer she stood in the open air and the farther away Gillian got from her embrace.

"Those kids, those little babies on the bus, do you think their parents can ever forgive me for what my Christopher did?"

It was a hard question, harder than Veronica expected. Forgiveness for taking so much joy and light out of the world? Christopher, no matter how much of a mama's boy he was, would not get blanket forgiveness because of how great of a person his mother was in his life. But Gillian wasn't asking if Veronica could forgive Christopher.

"You know what, Gillian . . ." Veronica glanced down at the empty spot on her left hand and then back up at her friend. "I think they can." She squeezed Gillian's hand with just her fingertips and then let go, but held on with her eyes. "I really think they can."

It may have been from the chill in the air or the whipping wind making her eyes water, but Gillian seemed to flush and blink rapidly, a little hiccup giving away more about her feelings than she'd probably intended. She mouthed the words, "Thank you," and then headed for the heavy glass door that lead to the medical complex.

"Tomorrow at Dave's. Don't forget!" Veronica shouted out, hoping Gillian could hear over the wind.

She waved back. "Tomorrow!"

Veronica headed to the car, where Mark was still patiently waiting, probably with the heat on to warm her up. She jumped in, and it was comfortably warm just like she'd suspected it would be. Mark liked taking care of her, and she was starting to like having someone in her life who wanted to be there for her.

"Where are we headed now?" he asked, hands on the steering wheel like he owned the car. He still made the Prius look like a toy with his long legs and broad shoulders, but she was getting used to him being there.

"Um . . ." She thought about what she wanted, what she really wanted. She wanted her heart to stop hurting every day when she saw something that reminded her of Sophie. She wanted to remember what it was like to be loved in that innocent things-will-never-fall-apart kind of way Nick had loved her before the accident. She wanted . . . Veronica stopped herself, buckled her seat belt with a click, and then tapped on the dashboard. "Home," she said with finality. "I want to go home."

"Your wish is my command," Mark joked, and put the car in reverse.

As they pulled up to a stoplight after driving in a comfortable silence, a yellow glow filled the interior of the Prius. To the right was a school bus, full of kids on their way home from school. The exhaust was pulled in by the vents, filling the car with a smell that used to make her gag. Mark looked at her nervously, like he was waiting for something drastic to happen.

Yeah, it hurt seeing that bus. And she'd learned at Green Oaks that what Nick said was true—it would likely never stop hurting. Buses would always make her think of Sophie's last day on the earth, and sparkly boots would make her think of small, broken bodies in the sterile morgue, but birds made her think of Sophie's laugh, and the sun made her think of Sophie's hair blowing in the wind, and pancakes made her think of Sophie's sticky kisses, and dogs made her think of Sophie's big heart. Remembering would never stop hurting, but it would never stop filling her up either.

The light changed, and the car moved forward, and Mark definitely broke the speed limit as they rushed past the slowly crawling bus.

"Hey, I'm okay," she reassured him, placing her hand on his thigh for a moment.

"I know," he said, like he was not entirely convinced but wanted to be.

She put her hands back in her lap and watched the leaves swirling as they drove through them. Forgiveness was a funny thing—you gave it, but it also gave back to you. She'd said she could forgive Gillian, and she'd meant it. It was an ongoing process, this forgiveness thing, but she was making progress. She'd already forgiven her father for never being there when she was a child and her friends who had slowly dropped off one by one when they didn't know how to deal with her sorrow and Nick for putting Sophie on the bus that November morning and her mother for helping Nick have her committed to Green Oaks. That left one person that she wondered if she could ever truly forgive. And really, that person was the only one who mattered—herself.

# ACKNOWLEDGMENTS

To Counselors Debra Thurston, MA, LCPC, and Elisa Woodruff, LPC, NCC, who shared their expertise and years of experience to make this book accurate and uplifting—thank you for your input, guidance, and inspiration. Thank you as well for your dedication to helping others and shining a bright light in the darkness of so many lives, including my own.

Thank you to my writers' group and beta readers: Joanne Osmond, Mary Rose Lila, Kelli Neilsen, Deborah Brooks, Paulette Swan, Tiffany Blanchard, and Candice Toone. I will never stop being grateful for the day Joanne said, "We should start a writers' group!" I look forward to all the years of growth, encouragement, and creative kismet ahead.

I also have some amazing Lake Union authors that make my creative life so complete. All the Ladies and Lads of the Lake, I love reading your Facebook posts and the comradery you all help me feel in this sometimes lonely profession. Publishing is such a team sport, and I cheer for each and every one of you.

Thank you in particular to my newest LU friends: Camille Di Maio, Rochelle Weinstein, and Heather Burch. I feel like I found kindred spirits when we finally met face-to-face at RWA. You ladies have my heart and my admiration. Never stop texting me about the dangers of Diet Coke, and I'll never stop sending you pictures of me chugging a cold one. I love that we get to share so many wonderful milestones together.

To my fellow author Mallory Crowe—you, lady, are the real deal. You are smart, kind, thoughtful, and creative. I count myself lucky to have met you online in the AQC chat room after googling "how to publish a book." Keep moving forward, my friend. You deserve happiness, success, and the bright future I know you have ahead of you.

Emily Hanson—the best "friend turned assistant" any lady could ask for. You are a hard worker and inspire me with your quick mind and fierce dedication. Though you are far away, I will always feel connected to you. Thank you for being a friend, a colleague, and my guiding light when I needed you most.

Dearest Kelli Swofford Nielsen—I don't think you know how special you truly are. Thanks for your hard work on this story. Your editorial eye and willing hand carried me through writer's block, self-doubt, and impending deadlines. I'm not sure how one person can embody so many impressive qualities. I really hope I can be just like you when I grow up—one day . . .

Thank you to the author team at Lake Union Publishing. Gabe Dumpit—you are such a rock star. Thanks for celebrating your thirtieth with all of us and being the best dang author relations manager the world has ever seen. Ever. I asked. Everyone. In the world. You are the best. Here's to many more books and birthdays through the years. Thank you as well to Dennelle Catlett for your wonderful PR work and to the rest of the team that works tirelessly to put lives on pages of paper and dreams in physical form.

To my developmental editor, Tiffany Yates Martin—thank you over and over again for your patience and hard work. This was a fun one, wasn't it? I'm always so eager and grateful for your insights and guidance. I love seeing a manuscript transform into a novel as we work together through the editing process.

To my newest editor, Chris Werner—it has been a pleasure and adventure working on our first story together. I appreciate your input, support, and gentle, guiding touch. Thanks for sticking with me through ups and downs and seeing this story for what it could be while helping me wrangle it into what it has become. I've learned I can trust your editorial eye *and* your taste in Netflix recommendations. I'm currently watching *The Great British Baking Show*—how about you?

Danielle Marshall—the woman who keeps placing bets on my career, thank you for giving my voice a place to be heard. Whether in person, on the phone, or through email, I've enjoyed getting to know you better and have mad respect for your skillz in this business. Yeah, you read me right—skillz with a *z*.

Thank you to Marlene Stringer, my superagent, for reading the synopsis of this story and calling me immediately, saying, "This! Write this!" Your passion for this project has kept me going full steam ahead. I can never thank you enough for taking a chance on me four years ago and continuing to do so every single day since.

Thank you to my readers. You are such a loyal and thoughtful group. I love getting to know each of you; hearing your stories; connecting with you through email, Facebook, and my blog; and visiting with your book clubs. Please keep reaching out, and I will keep reaching back. I can't wait to hear what you think about Veronica, Gillian, Mark, and Sophie.

Mom and Dad—you've really stepped up and helped me learn how to balance life as a single mom of four kids. Thank you, endlessly, for your love and support. I hope my kids will look at me one day and know that I love them as unconditionally as you love me.

To my siblings—I'm so glad we have each other. There is nothing else in the world like being friends with the people who knew you when you hair sprayed your bangs and snuck down to see the Christmas tree at 3:00 a.m. just to make sure Santa came despite your naughtiness. It's too late—you are stuck with me, and it is a biological imperative that you at least pretend to like me.

My sister, Elizabeth—you get your own thank you. You've given me so much of your time and heart. Thanks for your calls, texts, and amazing advice. I don't know how I would make it through my day, much less my life, without you.

And to my sweet and ingenious kids—you are my biggest inspiration and my favorite fans. Thanks for cheering me on and for your endless patience with the balancing act that is our lives. We are on an awesome journey together, and I love having each of you by my side every step of the way. Onward and upward, my little ones . . .

# ABOUT THE AUTHOR

*Photo © 2018 Organic Headshots*

Emily Bleeker is a former educator who learned to love writing while teaching a writers' workshop. After surviving a battle with a rare form of cancer, she finally found the courage to share her stories, starting with her debut novel, *Wreckage*, and followed by the *Wall Street Journal* bestseller *When I'm Gone* and *Working Fire*. Emily currently lives with her family in suburban Chicago. Connect with her or request a Skype visit with your book club at www.emilybleeker.com.